Bury Your Dog

Eva Silverfine

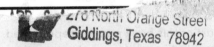

Black Rose Writing | Texas

ISBN: 978-1-68433-821-4
PUBLISHED BY BLACK ROSE WRITING
www.blackrosewriting.com

Printed in the United States of America
Suggested Retail Price (SRP) $18.95

How To Bury Your Dog is printed in Palatino Linotype

*As a planet-friendly publisher, Black Rose Writing does its best to eliminate unnecessary waste to reduce paper usage and energy costs, while never compromising the reading experience. As a result, the final word count vs. page count may not meet common expectations.

To the hemlocks, those past and those that continue to hold their ground

How to
Bury Your Dog

During the initial stage of decomposition,
visible changes are limited.

Burial

"I should have put him down yesterday."

"It's a hard chore."

"I just can't stand seeing him hurt so much," Lizzy said, as she wiped the counter yet again. "Another cup of coffee?" she asked, reaching for the pot.

"No thanks," Sam replied, gently waving his already trembling hands.

Lizzy looked over her neighbor's white-haired head, through the storm door, and out to the gravel driveway. The house's shadow fell across the browned grass, but the tops of the pines glittered in winter's morning light.

The sound of claws scraping against wood turned Lizzy's attention toward the hallway. Happy walked into the kitchen slowly, stepping gingerly to avoid putting weight on his hind legs. He set himself down in stages, front first, at Lizzy's feet. She squatted down and gently stroked his head.

"It's going to be all right, Happy," she spoke this untruth soothingly. "It will be all right.

"He's been with me the longest. Well, except for Alice. We found him when he was just a pup. Imagine, dumping a full-breed basset hound."

Sam shook his head. "He may have been the first, but I think word got out about you taking in hard-luck cases."

A lopsided smile appeared on Lizzy's face. She stood up. "Some more coffee?"

"No thanks," Sam declined again with a gracious smile that showed the full depth of the creases in his face. "It shouldn't take Nancy long to get here. I've heard they may widen Due West Road all the way out here."

"If they widen Due West all the way out here it won't be worth living 'out here' anymore. This place will be carved into hundreds of one-acre lots—or less. It's getting bad as it is."

"It's going to happen, Lizzy. Can't really stop it," Sam said as he ran a finger along the rim of the crock pot he had come to return that morning.

"It's all those damn greedy developers."

"It's all those people who want their own home with their own yard—just like you have."

"Yeah, well there's damn too many of them too."

Sam laughed. "Well, there's only going to be more."

"I know. That's why we're doomed. Too many damn people on the planet." Lizzy wiped the counter. "I was thinking on that little rise out back, near the crape myrtle. He likes to lie there in the summertime. The myrtle casts some shade, and he can keep watch of the backyard as well as the road from there."

"That sounds like a nice spot, Lizzy," Sam said in his comforting made-for-radio voice.

"Do you think the ground is frozen?"

"Lizzy," Sam said, shaking his head, "we haven't even had a light frost yet." He stood up and pushed in his chair. "Why don't I go and get things ready?"

Lizzy sighed. "That's a good idea. Thank you, Sam. It's very kind of you. There's a spade in the shed."

"Thank you, Lizzy, for bringing over the soup," he replied, nodding toward the crock pot. "You've taken good care of us since Leona got the news."

When Sam headed for the door, Happy raised onto his forelegs, indicating his intention to go outside. Sam pushed open the storm door and held it. Alice, who had been waiting outside, rudely ignored, entered and continued on a path that brought her nose to nose with Happy. He had just managed to get up on all fours and let out a deep-pitched growl.

"Now, now, Happy, Alice just wants to see how you're feeling," Lizzy admonished. But Alice was actually reasserting that she was queen of the household, even if everyone was paying way too much attention to Happy. Happy walked past Alice and stood at the threshold, considering. Lizzy, watching, went over to the door, gently scooped him up, and carried him outside. He was so much lighter than he used to be. Happy trundled after Sam, who was headed for the shed.

"Well how are you, Miss Alice?" Lizzy asked as she bent over to pet the fat, fluffy orange ball. Alice rubbed against her hand. "And where's CB?" Lizzy asked. "I haven't seen her all morning."

CB, Child-Baby, was in the shed where she had a mouse cornered. But Alice wasn't about to divulge CB's whereabouts; there was no reason to call any more mouths to the table.

Just then Lizzy heard Nancy's car pulling into the driveway. She stroked Alice on the head once more and headed outside.

"Hey Nancy," Lizzy called as she headed toward the car. Pete and Clem were already frenetically jumping and yapping around the car door. Nancy was bending over the front seat to gather her belongings while keeping the dogs at bay with one leg. She straightened up with her hands full. Wisps of her frizzy blond hair had escaped her hasty pony tail.

"Here, give me some of that," Lizzy said as she reached the driveway. Reflexively, Lizzy tucked some loose strands of Nancy's hair behind her old friend's ear. In exchange, Nancy handed Lizzy a bag of donuts and a book she had borrowed months before. When Lizzy turned to go back to the house, her eyes fixed on Happy, whose tail was wagging as he watched Sam dig the hole.

Nancy called, "Hey there, Mr. Tutwiler. I brought some donuts." Sam stopped to wave but returned to his task.

When Lizzy and Nancy reached the kitchen door, Pete and Clem were there waiting. Everyone wants to be fed, thought Lizzy, so totally oblivious to their friend's impending departure.

"How about some coffee?" Lizzy asked as she began to collect the various feeding dishes and pushed away her impatient charges.

"Sure," replied Nancy, helping herself to a cup. She then grabbed a plate, put it in the center of the table, and emptied the bag of donuts onto it.

Once Lizzy had finished feeding Pete, Clem, and Alice, she joined Nancy at the table and quietly nibbled a donut and sipped her now-cold coffee.

"You know, Lizzy, I can do this alone. You don't need to be there."

"No, of course I want to be. Whenever Sam is ready."

"Okay." Nancy pulled another donut in half.

Lizzy watched. Nancy could still eat anything and not gain weight.

"How about coming over for dinner tonight?" Nancy asked.

"Thanks, but I want to catch up on things around here."

Nancy looked around. "Like what? Polishing the silver?"

"Just stuff," Lizzy defended. "I've been at work all week. I want to stay home."

"You've become such a hermit," Nancy chided, knowing already any admonitions were useless.

Lizzy ignored her and looked out the window. Sam had laid down the spade and was talking to Happy. She slowly stood up, and when she did Nancy reached into her pocketbook and removed a small, black case.

At the door Lizzy blocked Pete and Clem from escaping. "Happy doesn't need these two idiots jumping all over him." But Alice slipped right past her legs.

"I think this will do," said Sam, nodding toward the hole when Lizzy and Nancy arrived.

4

"How are you, Happy?" Nancy asked in the tone one uses when one already knows the answer is not good. She knelt down beside him.

He had worn himself out and was lying on his side, his breathing labored; he wagged his tail limply.

"I know it hurts, baby," she said, stroking him, "yes, I know it does." Still squatting and stroking Happy, Nancy looked up at Lizzy and said, "Whenever you're ready. First I'll give him a sedative."

Lizzy squatted beside Happy, and as she stroked his head and told him what a good boy he was, Nancy injected the sedative. Happy lay calmly; his breathing slowed. Then Nancy gave him the second injection, which worked quickly. After a few shallow breaths, he stopped breathing.

"Wait," said Lizzy. She ran to the house to fetch Happy's braided rug and hurried back outside with it. She laid the rug next to Happy, and Sam and Nancy lifted him onto it and folded the edges over him. Then they lowered Happy into the hole.

"Liz?" Sam asked. She nodded, and he filled the spade with soil. As the first shovel-full of the reddish-brown bits of earth landed on the rug, Lizzy felt the donut, the coffee, and an earlier slice of toast defying gravity and peristalsis. She hurried away from the grave and looked out to the road while Sam finished.

"It's done," Nancy said, placing her hand on Lizzy's shoulder. Lizzy turned around and looked toward the crape myrtle. CB, the young, scrawny calico, had appeared and was sitting atop the freshly turned soil.

●　　　　●　　　　●

Once Sam and Nancy had left, Lizzy mindlessly cleared the table of coffee cups, put the donuts back in their bag, and poured the last bit of coffee down the drain. As she washed the dishes in the sink, she looked out the window. The backyard swept gently downhill toward the woods that bordered Narrow Passage Creek. Her eyes traveled from browned lawn to dried brown stalks of sunflowers and thistle intertwined with brambles of leafless blackberries to the fissured gray trunk of a sweetgum. Her gaze lifted upward to the tree's leafless branches splayed against the clear sky. Just a few days earlier, scarlet leaves still clung here and there to the branches but since had been scattered by the wind. Her gaze rested among the bare limbs but eventually wandered back groundward and toward the crape myrtle, where she saw Pete and Clem digging in the softened dirt while both Alice and CB looked on.

"Get off there, you dumb asses!" Lizzy shouted as she flew out the door. The dogs looked at her, hesitated, and then bounded across the backyard and around the far side of the house.

Lizzy went to the shed, hunted down some old wood boards, and carried them to the myrtle. She then went back to the shed to fetch a rake, and when she returned Alice was daintily sniffing the soft ground. Lizzy smoothed the soil and laid the boards over Happy's grave. From behind the well house she ferried over several bricks from a stack bought for a planned-but-never-started project and placed them on the boards.

Regarding the now less-than-aesthetic brick and board gravesite, Lizzy heard a vehicle slow on the road. She looked up to see Beryl pulling over to deliver the mail. She waved but deliberately circled behind the house. After penning up Clem and Pete, she retrieved her mail, grabbed the newspaper from the front path, and returned to the kitchen door, where CB was waiting. Inside, Lizzy dumped the wad of papers on the counter, washed her hands, and fed CB. Then picking up the mail and paper, she headed for the living room. CB followed her, jumped up on the couch, and purred loudly as Lizzy stroked her skinny neck.

Lizzy glanced over the headlines—a speech by President Reagan on the Soviet Union, a local businessman indicted for falsifying loan documents—nothing she wanted to read. Instead, she started sorting through the mail. Junk, Christmas card, junk, bill, Christmas card, catalogue, bill, junk. Well, maybe junk. Local junk. Lizzy opened the folded flyer.

Save Bartons Mill Pond!

Did you know that Bartons Mill Pond is slated to be part of a major residential development?

Plans to build 200 houses on acreage bordered by Due West
Road and Bartons Mill Road are underway.
Join your neighbors Wednesday night, 7 pm, at Centreville
Library to discuss this development before it is too late.
Protect Our Community and Our Heritage!
Protect Bartons Mill Pond!
Contact Donna and Doug (353-6733) or Mike (353-8419)
for more information.

Damn. More houses. More damn houses. And at Bartons Mill Pond. No doubt across the creek too. Call Donna, Doug, or Mike. No surprise there. As if they could stop it from happening. Lizzy refolded the flyer and added it to the stack of bills and Christmas cards—things to look at later. She placed the catalogue on a pile of magazines already on the coffee table and neatly rearranged the pile to be carried to her desk. She wasn't ready to deal with any of these things. Bills, Christmas cards, and flyer in hand, she crossed the living room and pushed open the door to the office.

The room was dark, but Lizzy didn't part the heavy curtains. She liked the insulated feel of the room, so she turned on the lamp instead. She placed the bills and cards on the large, old oak desk that dominated the room. She smelled the damp, earthy scent that emanated up from the root cellar below. Sure enough, the small door to the cellar had worked itself ajar again, as if some underground gust had pushed it open. She went over and closed the door to that dark, subterranean space firmly.

Lizzy looked over the office crowded with its accumulated treasures, books, saved magazines, unsorted photos, and unfinished projects. She had told herself many times that she should sort through the books and magazines, clean out the drawers, throw away the old birds' nests and found bones, but she never seemed ready to start. The desktop held the things that needed timely attention, although even there were papers untouched for months on end. She turned off the lamp and left the door open so the room would warm up, and air out, a bit.

In contrast to the office, the living room was uncluttered. The curtains were open, and the room was furnished somewhat sparingly, giving it an appearance of spaciousness and lightness. The couch and two armchairs were upholstered in large, muted floral prints. On each side of the fireplace was an old crock filled with dried flowers, thistle heads, cattails, and grasses she had found on walks over the years; on the small mantle above the fireplace were a few framed photos and some decorative pottery. Lizzy grabbed a rag and wiped off the end tables and coffee table; she folded the afghans neatly over the back of the couch.

Upstairs, Lizzy pulled the sheets off her bed, gathered all the towels from the bathroom, and carried the laundry basket downstairs. After starting the wash, she returned upstairs and remade the bed while CB skittered across the mattress. She turned to straightening up her room, her mind humming blankly. This was the catharsis of cleaning, the purging of conscious thought or at least the temporary respite. The focus was on clothes to be put away, floors to be cleaned, trash to be gathered. She dusted the tops of the bureaus, lifting each jewelry box, dish of shells, and vase of dried wildflowers on one and the found antlers, turtle shells, and miscellaneous skulls on the other. She straightened up the night stands and put away some hair clips and jewelry left about on the small dressing table. Her eyes ran over her lair; everything was neatly in place.

Picking up the trash, Lizzy headed downstairs again. She put the wash in the dryer and then let Alice in and CB out. Alice went straight to her bowl, waiting to be fed.

"You'll get fat, Alice," she told the cat as she fetched her food.

Alice really didn't care. There was nothing better than napping on a full belly.

Lizzy filled a glass with water and drank it, trying to satiate herself with water instead of food. She wandered through the hallway and into the living room and plopped down on the couch. She was losing her enthusiasm for cleaning. What was the point of it, anyway? She leaned forward and reworked the coffee table—magazines in one stack, catalogues in another, junk mail and newspapers in a bin beside the couch.

Lizzy returned to the kitchen and poured herself another glass of water, but drinking water didn't obviate the need for food. She was starved. She made herself a late lunch and then added water to the kettle for a cup of tea. Waiting for the water to boil, she stood at the sink, listening to the rhythmic rotation of the dryer, looking out the window. She should go to Nancy's for dinner, but it was so much easier not to. She preferred to do her mourning alone.

The sky had become overcast with low-lying clouds that scattered the light. The dried vegetation along the border of the woods now showed itself to be a complex palette of light browns to dark browns, cinnamon, chocolate, burnt orange, copper. Leafless vines on tree trunks, barren stems of bushes, dead wood in the leaf litter were all sharply defined. Lizzy was absorbed in this tableau when a movement caught her attention. CB was coming out of the shed with a mouse hanging from her mouth. Lizzy closed her eyes.

Carrying her tea to the office, Lizzy planned to start writing her Christmas cards. She had barely set her cup down when the phone startled her.

"Hello."

"Hello Lizzy, this is Agatha Prickett."

As if there were another Agatha, thought Lizzy. They had been neighbors for only a dozen years or so—and Agatha's confectionary drawl was unmistakable.

"Good afternoon, Agatha. How are you?"

"I'm doing well, dear, thank you for asking. By the way, before I forget to mention it, I saw that Meyers boy wandering around your yard yesterday."

Jesus! thought Lizzy. Is that what she's calling about? Or is this going someplace else? "Jonas was probably on his way to the creek. He has my permission...." Lizzy replied, subduing any trace of annoyance. She had decided long ago to keep her conversations with Agatha minimal and superficial.

"Oh. That is kind of you. And how are you doing this afternoon?"

"Well, I was just about to start my Christmas cards."

"Oh my!" Agatha said. "That's always a task, but you better get on it. Christmas is right around the corner."

"Well I plan to tackle it today."

"It is a good afternoon for staying in a warm house—it seems to be cooling off suddenly. Speaking of letters, did you get that flyer about George Roper's property?"

Lizzy's mind shot to the flyer she had read earlier. That was what this phone call was about.

"The one that claimed he's threatening to destroy Bartons Mill Pond by putting in some houses," Agatha reminded Lizzy when she didn't respond immediately.

"Oh, yes. I did see that."

"Well, you know, those people on the flyer don't even live out here. They're town folk—you can tell by the phone exchange."

"Really?" Lizzy responded, as if she didn't know this but, more importantly, not wanting to divulge that she actually knew *those people*. "I haven't given the flyer much thought."

"Well, personally, I can't see how it's any of their business what Mr. Roper does with his property."

"Well I can't say I'm happy about his plans. I don't want to see this area become a suburb of Centreville. And Bartons Mill Pond is such a special place—I'd hate to see it ringed by a bunch of houses."

"Oh, I've talked to my brother-in-law about it. He's one of the county commissioners, you know."

How could I not know, thought Lizzy, rolling her eyes.

"Mr. Roper will take good care of the pond—he has a plan to make a park along it, for the development. Those people who sent the flyer are just trying to cause trouble—they think it's their business to tell other people what they should do."

Lizzy smiled to herself at the irony of such a statement coming from Agatha. "I think they're just worried about protecting the pond and the land around it."

"Well, you can't hold on to valuable property just because other people want to see pretty scenes when they drive by. If you owned more land, Lizzy, you'd understand that."

And if you had had your way, thought Lizzy, I wouldn't even have this place. Sam told me what you did.

"Maybe he should sell the land near the pond to the county or state—for a nature preserve," Lizzy said, hoping to get under Agatha's skin just a little bit.

"Shoot!" Agatha declared. "They wouldn't pay him anything near what the land is worth."

"I doubt Mr. Roper is in any dire need of money. I don't know him personally, but I know he owns property all over the county—for that matter, surrounding counties as well."

"Well, I do know George Roper—not personally—but his people are from up around Stumptown, which is where my people are from. The good Lord blessed that man with good sense. He invested in land when it was going for nothing, and now it is worth much, much more."

Lizzy wanted off the phone. The conversation had nowhere to go. "I think people are just worried about preserving the pond and the bluff." As soon as she said it, Lizzy realized her mistake. The bluff was on Agatha's property, the piece that adjoined Lizzy's.

"Well, it's not their pond—or their bluff—to concern themselves with now, is it? You know, someday I may decide to sell my acreage."

"Well, we'll see what happens," was the best Lizzy could manage. "You'll have to excuse me, Agatha, but I have a pie in the oven."

"Oh, I'm sorry dear, you should have told me."

"That's all right. The timer just went off. It should be fine. Enjoy your evening. Goodbye."

Lizzy was hanging up as Agatha was saying "Goodbye, dear."

Lizzy went into the kitchen, subconsciously going through the pretense of checking the pie in her oven. Instead she looked out the window. Already the light was fading. Winter days could be so brief, the sun in such a hurry to set.

•　　•　　•

The house felt empty that night. With Happy gone, it was now just her and Alice. The others were too young; they belonged to a different chapter. Alice, the prima donna, lay on the desk as Lizzy addressed her Christmas cards. Periodically, Lizzy would stop writing and pet Alice.

"I miss him too," she said as she gazed into the space before her, stroking Alice from head to tail.

Even if Lizzy didn't notice, Alice was staying close, allowing herself to be petted like a dog.

Quiescence

Jonas stuffed two leftover dinner rolls, an apple, and a handful of cookies into the bottom pockets of his jacket and quietly closed the door behind him. He walked stealthily away from his house and to the road.

The sun was barely up this Sunday morning on Prickett Farm Road, and the air was frosty and still. In the middle of the night a north wind had swept in and dropped a thin blanket of snow that would doubtless be gone by late morning. Jonas knew that no one except him and crepuscular animals were out in the world yet. Well, possibly Timmy Donohue. He looked out onto the road—no footprints, no bike trail. It was him and cold, white silence—an intimacy in the world transformed.

Jonas walked the short distance to Narrow Passage Road and stood amid the pines that lined his side of the road. The covering of snow seemed to mute all sound. He pulled out one of the rolls and ate it as he surveyed the Tutwiler field. He then walked along the border of pines, inhaling their chilled fragrance, until his yard met Mrs. Prickett's property line. He crossed the road on a diagonal and then continued along the edge of the Tutwilers' field. As he approached the narrow band of pines bordering Ms. Lizzy's driveway, he scared up two does, a mother and daughter, and they took off along the edge of the field and toward the creekside forest. Once they were out of sight,

Jonas proceeded down Ms. Lizzy's driveway and across her backyard, pausing briefly where the snow covered what looked to be a pile of boards and bricks; he then headed into the woods.

Jonas felt some remorse at invading the perfectness of the morning—leaving his footprints, bumping branches where the gap between them was too narrow for his large form. A layer of finely deposited snow balanced on every branch, down to the slimmest. He saw himself, a clumsy being, destroying the perfect crystalline edifices. But the creek called to him, and he soon stood on its bank, beside the leafless, smooth branches of a spicebush that still held a few of its fruit. He squeezed a red fruit between his thumb and forefinger and released its aroma into the dense air.

The snow ended just short of the creek, where the ground was a bit too warm for the thin blanket to remain. Jonas watched the water make its path around the larger rocks that emerged above the creek and held a dusting of snow. Eating his apple, Jonas walked along the streambank. When he squatted down to study what he believed to be the tracks of a skunk, Carolina wrens chattered their concern from the bushes. He regarded his own tracks, which appeared as those of a heavy-footed beast wandering without destination. But he did have a destination and continued on.

About a quarter mile upstream from Ms. Lizzy's house, Narrow Passage Creek fanned into the rivulets that fed it from Bartons Mill Pond. The ground here was often muddy, except when it occasionally froze in winter or hardened during a particularly dry summer. This time of year the ground was mostly a trampled brown mat of last summer's growth of sedges, rushes, and ferns. Jonas took wide steps over the soggy, matted ground, trying to avoid becoming mired in the mud.

He could have avoided the mud altogether; he could have walked farther along the road and cut through the woods near the bluff. However, whereas Ms. Lizzy and the Tutwilers didn't mind where he wandered, Mrs. Prickett seemed uncannily quick to appear whenever he happened to be on her land. Even on a cold morning like this, she would pop out her front door if she saw him. It seemed she stood constant sentry at her front window. In her eyes, he was beholden to her if he crossed her property—the last time a leaves-raking worth of beholden. Apparently, she thought she needed to instill moral fiber in him, so he avoided her. Anyway, walking the streambank was more interesting.

Approaching the pond slowly Jonas stopped at a red maple and balanced on its roots. He searched the lower branches of a tall tulip poplar on the northern edge of the pond and was not disappointed. The hawk was perched above the pond on a lower branch of the poplar. Lifting his binoculars, Jonas watched the hawk, which was grasping something furry in its talons. The hawk held its prey against the branch and was tearing at its catch with its beak. The bird's preoccupation allowed Jonas the longest look he had yet had; now he was sure it was a male.

Jonas lowered his binoculars and smoothly pulled pieces of broken cookies from his pocket. He thought about the flyer in yesterday's mail. Someone planned to build houses on the north side of the pond. Two hundred houses. Homes for families certainly must be more valuable than a perch for an itinerant hawk; or a breeding ground for some frogs, salamanders, and turtles; or a fishing hole for a few local kids; or a place for an odd loner to find quietude.

Jonas watched the hawk. It was a solitary sort too, flying outside its species' normal winter range and passing the season at an isolated pond. Perhaps it had missed a cue, taken a turn on some errant current. The pond was just a small deviation off its course. Like himself, the hawk found refuge here.

Jonas took another piece of crumbled cookie from his pocket as he regarded the hawk. *We are solitary sorts, accumulations of traveling molecules. Our mass moves through space on self-perpetuated trajectories.* He lowered his gaze and looked over the pond. *Sometimes my molecular integrity seems to isolate me though. I travel through space, a solitary thought, contained energy in motion.*

• • •

Lizzy rolled over under her thick quilt. Alice sat sphinxlike on the other pillow, staring at Lizzy's face, willing her awake. At this first sign of Lizzy's stirring, Alice meowed. CB, who was sleeping with Pete and Clem in the dog dorm, heard Alice and came to the bedroom door. She sat on the threshold looking up at the bed wild-eyed—one yellow eye in a black patch, the other in an orange patch. She didn't dare enter the bedroom when Alice was there.

Lizzy was awake. She knew the cats were waiting. She pretended to be asleep, though. It was Sunday. The wind last night had made the old house creak and kept her awake half the night. She was supposed to sleep late. She had been up with Happy before dawn yesterday, and she would have to get up early tomorrow. She was awake though. She opened her eyes. Alice meowed more insistently.

"What do you want?" Lizzy asked. Then, looking toward the doorway she said, "Come on, CB, don't let her bully you." Lizzy patted the bed. Instead, CB took off running, sliding when she hit the rug on the smooth wooden floor, crashing into the wall, and continuing in a falling run down the steps.

Lizzy got out of bed. "It's chilly in here, isn't it?" She pulled on a pair of sweatpants under her nightgown and then quickly switched her nightgown for a turtleneck and sweater. "Come on, Alice." They headed for the stairs.

Pete and Clem ran halfway up the steps to greet Lizzy, but Alice puffed up to remind them to keep a respectable distance, even in their jubilance. They tumbled back down the stairs. Only Happy had stood up to Alice, or she had deferred to him.

Lizzy greeted the dogs at the bottom of the steps. Clem, as was customary, had the kitchen towel in his mouth; Lizzy pulled it away and hit him over the head with it. The dogs were anxious to go out. It wasn't until she unlocked the kitchen door that Lizzy noticed the thin blanket of white. The sky was a brilliant blue. She tried to inhale the scene before releasing the dogs into the stillness. When she opened the storm door, Pete and Clem bolted outside. She thought of Happy, who had regarded the infrequent snow with distrust.

Lizzy started a pot of coffee, looked out the front window to the road, and saw that Timmy had already delivered the paper. She returned to the long hallway, the original back porch that now joined the old farm house and its modern indoor-plumbing addition. The hallway, although wide, was too narrow to be used for much of anything; besides housing a hall tree, it served as the dog dorm. Lizzy slipped on a pair of oversized, old work boots that were tucked under the bench and went out the front door. It was cold, but she figured the snow would be gone by noon. She walked to the edge of her porch to fetch the Sunday paper. She could see the trail left by Timmy's bike; he had stopped halfway up the path to toss her paper onto the porch. As her eyes followed his track crossing the road, she noticed a hawk flying over Mrs. Prickett's field.

Pete and Clem were making their round of the yard, periodically stopping to taste the snow while on their daily mission to sniff each bush, mark each tree trunk. Lizzy wondered if they were lingering, confused by the scent but absence of Happy.

Back inside Lizzy returned to her slippers, fed the cats, poured herself a cup of coffee, and glanced over the headlines on the front page: more fighting in Lebanon, more discussion of aid to the Nicaraguan Contras. Looking up, she saw Pete and Clem dashing back and forth outside. Cup in hand, she walked to the storm door and watched the dogs in the winter scene. Pete, the huskier-bodied of the two with some black lab obviously in his mix, chased Clem back behind the house. When they reemerged, Clem, who showed some classic features of a Brittany spaniel, was chasing Pete. They were going back and forth this way until all of a sudden they both dashed off toward the woods. When they reappeared, Lizzy saw they were encircling Jonas, who was trying to make his way across her yard. Lizzy opened the door and called to the dogs, who broke their tight circle but wouldn't abandon Jonas.

"It's okay," Jonas assured her when she called to them again.

"You're up and out early. You look kind of wet. Why don't you come in and have something warm to drink."

"Uhm, okay."

"Good morning, Jonas," she said when he reached the doorway and started to step inside, all five foot eight inches and two hundred plus pounds of him. "Whoa! Stay right there," she added. Jonas stopped on the mat, but Pete and Clem slid right past him and slipped into the hallway to check for breakfast. Lizzy pulled a chair from the table to the door.

Jonas sat down and began to untie his wet and muddy boots. At sixteen years old, he still had a softness about him that Lizzy attributed to his ample baby fat. There were no well-defined lines in his round face, as if he were not yet fully formed. Slightly curly light brown hair and soft brown eyes added to his prepubescent visage.

"Would you like some coffee? Or would you prefer hot chocolate or tea?"

"Hot chocolate."

"What are you up to so early this morning?" Lizzy asked as she put the kettle on the stove.

"Just walking."

Walking seemed to be Jonas's favorite pastime from what Lizzy could gather. Happy often had been his walking companion, which Lizzy thought was good because Jonas seemed to spend much of his time alone. It was uncanny how Happy seemed to recognize Jonas's footfall from afar, heading to the door before Jonas even reached the driveway.

Jonas slowly removed his boots, deliberately loosening the lace at each eyelet. He never appeared to be in a hurry, a quality that all Lizzy's charges seemed to appreciate about him. When he finally finished taking off his boots he looked around the kitchen. "Where's Happy?" he asked.

"I had to put him down yesterday."

Jonas was quiet for a moment and then said, "I'm sorry."

"It was time. He's near the crape myrtle out back. Where the boards are."

As if they understood they were on Lizzy's mind, Clem and Pete began to dance around the counter to remind Lizzy they had not been fed.

"Do they realize he's gone?"

"Hard to tell." Lizzy filled Pete and Clem's bowls and carried them into the hallway. When she returned, she saw that Jonas was peering into yesterday's bag of donuts. She nodded an invitation for him to take one.

"Would you like some breakfast?" asked Lizzy, one side of her mouth pulled up in her characteristic smile.

Jonas hesitated—not because Ms. Lizzy looked a bit deranged with her lopsided smile, uncombed hair, and tattered and oversized sweater—but because he had never been invited to breakfast at someone else's home before.

"What are you having?"

"Oh, I don't know," she replied, amused by Jonas's lack of social grace. "Would French toast suit you?"

"Sure," Jonas answered as he bit into a donut topped with shredded coconut.

Lizzy pulled a skillet from the cabinet and started to prepare French toast. She glanced over at Jonas and saw he was stroking Alice, who had settled on his lap. Alice didn't grace many people with such affection. CB sat on the floor next to them as if absorbing the strokes, purring with her eyes closed.

"So, what have you been up to?" asked Lizzy.

"School."

"Anything more exciting?"

"Walking. Reading."

Lizzy took some plates from the cabinet and placed them on the counter. "What are you reading?"

"School stuff . . . and field guides . . . and some science fiction."

"I've never read much science fiction," Lizzy said as she searched the refrigerator for jam and syrup. "How is your mother doing? I haven't seen her for a while." Lizzy knew Jonas's mother, Sylvia, from the hospital, where Lizzy worked and Sylvia sometimes came to investigate insurance claims for a law firm. They chatted when they saw one another there, but that was the extent of their relationship.

"Okay. Working a lot," replied Jonas. "And worrying about me, as usual," he added.

Lizzy looked at Jonas as she placed the jam and syrup on the table. "Oh? I suspect she's just concerned about your well-being in the big bad world out there."

"I got out of the house before she got up."

Lizzy let out a short laugh and went to fetch the plates and silverware. "Go wash your hands," she said with a feigned roughness.

Jonas gently placed Alice on the floor and headed for the bathroom.

The floor creaked as he walked down the hall to the bathroom. Jonas liked Ms. Lizzy's house, although he had never gone beyond peering into the living room. It was old, unlike his. It had character without having to try to build it in. He opened the door to the bathroom, which really was just a continuation of the hall—except that a claw-footed tub, a sink, and a commode lined one wall.

When Jonas returned to the kitchen, he observed that Alice and CB were sitting across from one another below his chair. Alice was trying to stare CB into moving out of her path, but CB wouldn't budge. So instead Alice walked past CB as if she hadn't even noticed her in the first place.

"She is a bit of a prima donna, isn't she?" Lizzy said as she carried the plate of French toast to the table. They both sat down. "I pampered her when I took her in, thinking she would blossom with a sense of security—didn't work quite right, did it? She's so spoiled. The strategy worked better with Happy. He became a gentle guardian, although he never ceased needing reassurances."

"How about CB?"

"CB is a good balance. She's very independent, cautious but not afraid. As to those two," she motioned toward Pete and Clem, "the jury is still out. When I took in Pete, he was obviously a neglected dog. He was afraid of coming close and needed to be close at the same time. He's not as smart as Happy or Clem, but he's had a few years to watch and learn from Happy. I've tried to instill some sense of pride in him."

Jonas smiled at this comment, thinking of his own mother's efforts.

"Of course, Clem has caused Pete to regress some. Since Clem arrived Pete has been living the childhood he never had. I guess Pete is accustomed to being the subordinate male, so Clem may take more of a lead now than I would like. Happy didn't recognize his pivotal role around here."

"I think he did," said Jonas. "I'll miss him."

20

"So will I," replied Lizzy, looking down at her plate. They continued to eat in silence.

When his plate was empty, Jonas picked it up and carried it to the sink. He sat in the chair by the door and tied up his boots halfway. "Thank you for breakfast. I better get home."

"Tell your parents I said hello," said Lizzy, standing up to clear the table.

Rinsing the dishes, Lizzy looked out to see Jonas standing by Happy's grave. Already, beyond the shadow of the house, the snow was melting; only small patches were left out in the yard. Alice had followed Jonas out and was standing next to him. She stretched to smell the edge of the closest board and then walked the perimeter, sniffing the edge of each board carefully. Jonas continued to stand there, looking down at the grave. Eventually he squatted down next to Alice, petted her, and touched the board closest to his hand. Then he was off, headed toward the road, toward his home. Lizzy realized she was glad for his company that morning.

• • •

"Where have you been?" Sylvia asked, her annoyance apparent, when Jonas returned home.

"On a walk."

"You could have left a note as to where you were going."

Jonas looked at her. Where did she think he could have possibly gone?

"You must have left very early," Sylvia observed.

"Yeah."

"Well, there are some pancakes in the oven."

"I'm not hungry."

Sylvia looked at him, surprised. "Do you have homework for tomorrow?"

"Some."

"When are you going to do it?"

"Later."

"I'd like you to clean up your room today."

"Okay."

"When are you going to do that?"

"Later."

"What are you going to do now?"

"I don't know," he shrugged. "Take a shower?" And with that he started up the stairs. He intended to hide from his mother for as long as he could.

Sylvia watched him as he went up the stairs and then turned sharply and returned to the kitchen.

Phil looked up from the newspaper and regarded his trim, dark-haired wife. "So, the wanderer has returned?"

"Phil, I can't help but worry," she said as she started putting away the breakfast she had been keeping warm. "When is that boy going to wake up? College is just around the corner, and he is so casual about school, so completely unmotivated. He never thinks about his future."

"Well, I think we've learned that we can't instill motivation in him. We've been there, and we ended up being involved in things that he — and we — had absolutely no interest in. Remember how it felt to force him to go to t-ball practice, just because we thought it would be good for him?"

"The games were even worse," Sylvia added. She bit her lip. "All those teachers and school counselors telling us year after year we should encourage him to participate in extracurricular activities with his peers so that he would develop his social skills. He's just as resistant now to participating in anything as he was when he was six."

"He does have a hobby," offered Phil; "he loves to wander the countryside. And look at the books he brings home — field guides to every critter and plant."

"I just don't understand him — he's so different from the way I was as an adolescent."

Phil grinned. "It's hard to understand how he is the son of two nerds who were involved in every club in high school?"

"As much as I may have been nerdy," said Sylvia, "I wasn't a loner. I can accept that we can't change his disposition, but I worry. Kids ostracize loners."

Phil sighed. "Yes, but the more we let Jonas know we are worried about him, the more we give him a sense that there is something to be worried about."

Sylvia nodded in resignation. "Well, I guess moving out here was a good decision. What would he have done if we had remained in town?"

Standing on Narrow Passage Road, Jonas heard the bus before it came into view. It slowed and then came to a stop, its red lights flashing. He nodded a good morning to the bus driver and slid down in his self-assigned seat. Mornings on the bus were better than afternoons—he was almost the last stop on the way to school; unfortunately that also meant he was almost the last stop on the way home. Another advantage of his morning ride was everyone was asleep; he could slide into the school day unnoticed. Over the years he had earned a reputation of being "weird," so he had willed himself invisible and had been largely successful: most of his classmates ignored him. Once in a while some pumped-up-on-testosterone smaller guy wanting to impress a friend would try to provoke him. It was a safe bet that Jonas would walk away without saying a word.

The bus continued west down Narrow Passage before turning onto Stumptown Road. It then headed back east to town, picking up a few more kids along Due West. Arriving at school, Jonas entered the arena, also known as the cafeteria, where students sorted themselves as they arrived. Each group had some proprietary claim to a portion of this common area. Jonas, being unaffiliated with any of these groups, made a direct path across the cafeteria to the library, where he could claim a table, or part of one, and read until classes started.

When the bell rang, he went to World History. The text, most of which he had already read, was interesting, but the class itself was often tedious. A majority of his classmates were disinterested, and the teacher taught the class with them in mind. From World History he went to Geometry and then on to English—a hodgepodge of disjointed fifty-minute sessions with five minutes of mayhem in between. Why did his parents think that once he was finished with high school he would want to spend four more years of his life sitting in a classroom? He didn't need college to learn about the things that interested him.

"Okay, settle down now," Mr. Farquhar said, herding the stragglers to their seats as the late bell sounded. "Today we're starting the Renaissance. Who can tell me what this word means and why this era is so named?"

"It means re-birth in French," Robert quickly answered. "It was called that because ancient Greek and Roman writings were rediscovered, and they inspired a re-birth of intellectual activity in the late Middle Ages."

"Excellent." Mr. Farquhar appreciated this nearly quoted textbook response. "And where is the period known as the Renaissance thought to have first emerged?"

"Italy," Rosalie responded.

"Yes, northern Italy," said Mr. Farquhar. "And why was that so?"

As Robert began to parrot one answer after another, across from Jonas, Cole was displaying the product of his artistic endeavor to his friends behind him. It featured Mr. Farquhar and Robert.

Jonas wasn't sure if he found Cole or Robert more annoying.

Mr. Farquhar chose to ignore the giggles Cole had generated and continued to lead the class through an ordered discussion of the Renaissance that closely tracked the textbook. Jonas began to think about this re-birth. It was a re-birth, or a return, of ideas long dormant, as a seed remains vital but quiescent over the winter. Some seeds, such as those of the persimmon, could remain dormant for years. Like seeds, the ideas of antiquity remained vital and germinated centuries later, when Man's perceptions of the world became fertile for a sense that he could use his own abilities to direct his path and accomplishments. For seeds and humans, climates change—sometimes gradually, sometimes abruptly, as in the form of a genius who could catapult human knowledge forward. Each plant species has particular conditions that support its germination—the germ awaits conditions that are right for its emergence. The seeds of what will come are already planted. The concepts of the Renaissance didn't sprout de novo; rather they evolved from the time, the framework, the conception in which they arose—the passing, the Middle Ages, fertilized the new.

"Jonas!"

"Yes," Jonas responded upon hearing his name.

"Jonas, if it's not too much of an imposition, please pay attention."

The class tittered, and Mr. Farquhar grimaced. "Rosalie, an important invention of the period?"

The bus dropped Jonas at home a good hour and a half before either of his parents would be there. He had some chores and homework, but there was only so much light in a winter's day. He dropped his pack just inside the front door, went to the kitchen to grab an apple and a granola bar, and headed out. He walked up the road toward Ms. Lizzy's but was drawn beyond her house by a flattened mass of fur in the road. From about one hundred feet he could tell it was a cat, a tabby. Not Alice or CB. He didn't risk getting closer as he might come into Mrs. Prickett's unwavering view.

Jonas walked back the way he had come. Ms. Lizzy wasn't home, but he walked to the fenced pen and talked to Clem and Pete, who were thrilled to have company, especially company who shared a granola bar with them. Jonas then walked around the back of the house to Happy's grave and kept Happy company for a while. Eventually he took off for the creek, walked along it briefly as daylight was rapidly dwindling, and then cut across the Tutwiler field and headed home.

Phil was already home when Jonas returned, which was uncharacteristically early. Jonas headed to the kitchen, where he expected to find his father, but the kitchen was empty. He proceeded through the house until he found his father in his room, changing out of his dressier work clothes. Phil was a graphic artist who ran a small printing business that catered mostly to businesses in and around Centreville.

Jonas watched his father for a minute. He had inherited his father's hair and eye color but not his long, lean stature or his graceful movements.

"Hi," Jonas said, not knowing whether his father was aware that he stood in the doorway. Phil seemed totally absorbed elsewhere.

"Hey Jonas," replied Phil as he turned around.

"You're early."

"I was delivering drafts to a new client out on Due West, so I decided to come straight home afterward. Where have you been?"

"Walking."

Phil looked down at his clothes on the bed and went to the closet for a hanger. "A bit chilly, don't you think?"

"Not really."

Phil nodded. "Yeah, I was impervious to the cold when I was your age. It was nothing to spend a few hours outside with my friends on a winter day . . . or to go for a long walk when my parents were bugging me." Phil hung up his dress pants. "So, how was your day?"

"Okay."

Phil began to say something but stopped. Then he asked, "Learn anything interesting?"

A faint smile showed on Jonas's lips. "That Gutenberg's printing press changed the face of the world."

Phil smiled. He had just been privy to a fleeting glimpse of his son's humor.

Sainthood

Timmy debated whether he would want to be Pope. Pope or president. Being the Pope, he would be God's right-hand man throughout the world. But the president was a pretty important person worldwide too. Of course, here the president was more important than the Pope—he was in charge of the country and was on TV and in the newspaper far more than the Pope. But then presidents from countries all over the world went to see the Pope in the Vatican. The Pope was like the king of all kings.

That was the real reason Timmy wasn't sure he would want to be Pope. The Pope was so close to God that God probably watched his every move. Timmy was sure God watched the president too, but at least the president had the Pope between him and God. And surely the president had more fun—he went horseback riding, went to fancy parties with famous people, had his own jet, and got to invite anyone he wanted over to the White House. The problem was that Timmy might be stuck with someone like Ryan being Pope. That would be the worst.

Ryan definitely wanted to be the Pope. He sat with his hands folded on his closed notebook, his clean, neatly trimmed fingers interlocked and wrapped over the backs of his smooth, soft hands and his head, his hair perfectly combed, held straightforward, looking at the blackboard. Ryan wanted Sister Gertrude to see he was the first one done with his math problems. His uniform was perfectly neat—not one unintentional crease in it even after recess. Ryan would never be chosen for Pope, though; even if he could finish his math problems faster, Timmy was the one who got the highest grades in religion. And Timmy always won their Hail Mary contests—he could say his Hail Marys faster than anyone else at school.

"Timmy!"

He heard his name with the simultaneous slap of Sister Gertrude's ruler on his desk.

"Are you finished?"

"No, Sister."

"What are you doing then?"

"Thinking."

"No. You're daydreaming. If you were thinking, you would be looking at your paper. Get back to work."

Timmy didn't have to look. He knew that Ryan was smiling. Timmy went back to work on his math problems.

Sister Gertrude put down the dusty eraser with a look of displeasure on her face, a small deviation from her usual countenance. As she brushed the dust from her hands, she looked over her class. "Well class, this afternoon we're going to learn about Saint Augustine. First, though, I've selected this week's composition to be read to the class. It is Timmy Donohue's composition entitled, 'Why Dogs Can't Go to Heaven,' and it seems particularly appropriate to a lesson on Saint Augustine. Timmy, please come to the front of the room and read loudly and clearly."

Timmy took his paper from Sister Gertrude and faced the class. He caught Ryan squinting at him, his lips pursed. Timmy smiled; he was up by two compositions now. Ryan quickly looked down at his desk. Timmy began to read.

Why Dogs Can't Go to Heaven

You have probably wondered at some moment in your life where your beloved pet, or your neighbor's, would go once it departed from this life on earth. This pet, say his name is Happy, may have been your best friend. His faithfulness and loyalty have been complete. He has been perfectly obedient. Because he has been a true friend, because his behavior has been so virtuous, you want to imagine that he will be rewarded as you would if you were as true in heart to your Master.

But dogs cannot go to heaven!

"And why not?!" you ask.

Because even though your pet has been faithful, loyal, and obedient, he is an animal with only instincts to hunt, to fetch, to protect, to please, but he cannot choose between right and wrong! But we were given souls to see right from wrong and to follow the path of right and goodness so we can dwell with our Lord, Jesus Christ. We must choose to do God's will, and as smart as you may think your dog is, he cannot choose to know and love God.

Your dog, even if he is your best friend, is a beast of the earth. Your dog is one of God's perfect creations, but God made him for us, to help us in our lives here on earth, to help us behave virtuously.

You may ask, "But where does my dog go?"

God returns your dog to his ashes, to be made part of the earth again. God gave us an immortal soul to know and love Him, but dogs do not have an immortal soul.

This fact may trouble you—the vision of your beloved friend becoming no more than the mud of the ground, not being rewarded for his good behavior. But remember, God's reward is the life He gave your dog, the chance He gave him to be your companion, to help you, protect you, guide you, and live in your memory forever. It is your responsibility to reward your dog's good behavior by treating him well. Your dog may not

reach heaven, but he is never threatened by losing his
step and falling into Hell. He has had a dog's life.

Timmy looked up in time to see a slim hint of a smile on Sister
Gertrude's lips as he finished reading his composition. He returned to
his seat, quite pleased with himself.

Sister Gertrude launched into her lesson on Saint Augustine.
"Saint Augustine was born in northern Africa in the fourth century.
He is an example of someone who certainly didn't start out living a
saintly life, but he came to be not only a saint but a Doctor of the
Church."

Timmy listened to Saint Augustine's story. He knew that the
Sisters wanted them to aspire to saintliness, to look past worldly
comforts and live a virtuous life. Each week they learned about
another saint who lived for the glory of God, who might have given
his—or her—own life so true was his faith. The Sisters wanted them
to follow the examples set by the saints, but most of the kids in the
class didn't truly understand what saintliness required. They thought
to be saints they should be wusses. But Timmy saw that saints took
risks, that they accepted challenges to show their true allegiance to
God.

Timmy's attention returned to Sister Gertrude upon the word
"vandals," although it turned out she was talking about a tribe from
Germany that had destroyed Rome and gone on to northern Africa.
Saint Augustine lay dying during the siege of his walled city by the
Vandals. This information reaffirmed Timmy's own belief that at the
heart of most saints was a warrior, even if they didn't bear weapons.

School was almost over. Timmy was ready to blast out of his seat.
There would still be a couple of hours of light once he got home if he
could slip out before his mom—

"Timmy and Ryan," Sister Gertrude's voice pierced his
imaginings, "please take the erasers outside and clean them."

"Yes, Sister." They jumped up, grabbed the erasers, and headed
outside.

The air was cold and chilled the inside of their nostrils. They could see their breath, and Timmy blew out air in audible puffs. The mid-afternoon sun heralded the fading of another winter day.

Ryan held his erasers as far from himself as his arms would allow and gingerly tapped the white and yellow chalk from them. Timmy slapped his together as hard as he could, raising a cloud of dust around him. Ryan stepped farther away from Timmy and dramatically brushed off his jacket sleeves. "Some of us prefer not to be filthy," he said.

Ryan is a prime example of a saint–wus, thought Timmy. He has no backbone. His saintly actions would come from only cowardice. Timmy threw one of the erasers high into the air. "See how high you can throw yours," he challenged Ryan.

Ryan ignored him, so Timmy threw his eraser even more forcefully. It arced and landed on the ledge above the entryway.

With narrow-eyed glee Ryan informed Timmy, "You're going to be in so much trouble with Sister Gertrude!" and ran back inside.

Timmy hesitated, looking up to where the eraser had landed, and then took off after Ryan. He entered the room as Ryan was slipping into his seat, betraying a hint of gloating. Timmy put his remaining eraser on the blackboard ledge.

Sister Gertrude didn't miss a beat.

"Timmy, where is the other eraser?"

"Uh, I dropped it."

"And . . . you didn't pick it up?"

"No, Sister."

"Why not?"

"Well, it was a bit hard to reach."

"Where did you drop it?"

"Uhm, on that little roof over the doors."

"You dropped it on the roof? Everyone is dismissed except Timmy."

So much for going anywhere after school today. His mother would be so mad at him. Hopefully Sister Gertrude would at least let him do his homework.

When the classroom emptied, Sister Gertrude told Timmy to sit with his hands folded on his desk. Well, at least she didn't have him writing sentences. After fifteen minutes or so had passed, she looked up from her desk and asked, "Why did you throw the eraser on the roof?"

"I didn't mean to. I just want Ryan to understand that saints have to take risks."

"Saints first must learn to be obedient," said Sister Gertrude and returned to her grading.

Ryan is a prime example of a saint was thought Timmy. He has no backbone. His saintly actions could come from only cowardice. Timmy threw one of the erasers high into the air, "See how high you

On her way home from work Lizzy stopped at the grocery. She pushed her cart around the store as one Christmas song followed another. Displays proffering holiday gifts and treats were trimmed in green, red, and silver tinsel; patrons stopped to consider items they normally would do without. "Isn't this cute?" a woman remarked to no one in particular as she held up a cookie tin featuring kittens wearing holiday scarves and booties. The holiday hype in the store was almost too much to bear—the music, the decorations, the mass market sentiments—and Lizzy picked up speed as she went along. She selected fresh fruits and vegetables to keep herself on her diet and stocked up on cat and dog food. As she made her way to the check out, she succumbed to one final display of candy wrapped in brightly colored foil and picked up a box to bring to the lab. She and her coworkers did this to one another—corrupted each other's better sense with unhealthy indulgences of sweetness. "It's beginning to feel a lot like Christmas," chimed the clerk as she handed Lizzy her receipt.

Although the quickest route home from the grocery store was via the bypass, Lizzy stuck to her personal boycott of this five-year-old addition to town. She drove south on old Route 11 toward Main.

Main Street was still a two-lane road with diagonal parking. The businesses there had been marginalized by the sprouting of strip malls that offered ample parking. As she headed west toward home, Lizzy passed the few blocks of vendors—restaurants, bars, and gift shops lit up with Christmas lights; a struggling boutique; the florist, book store, and music shop; Phil Meyers's print shop. Students and faculty from the state college in South Fork Crossing, Lizzy's college, still made their way to this well-worn part of Centreville, and the businesses along Main did what they could to capitalize on their "old-town" appeal to tourists from North Fork Crossing.

At one time Centreville had been the largest of the three towns strung close together along Route 11; the railroad had determined Centreville's stature as the center of what was once a largely agricultural economy. And because it was the largest town, the hospital where Lizzy worked had been built there. But more recent decades had seen Centreville lose its status. South Fork had the growing state college, and North Fork had the fortune, or not, of bordering the interstate highway. As those towns grew, Centreville became a quieter, less expensive commuter town for its northern and southern neighbors. North Fork had long since built its own hospital, and there was talk of South Fork doing the same.

On the western side of the bypass, Main Street became Due West Road, which had been widened to four lanes when the bypass was built, purportedly to improve safety and traffic flow. From Lizzy's perspective, all the road widening had done was sprout subdivisions: Deer Meadow, Forest Glen, Whispering Oaks, Lost Pines—well that was truth in advertising. Five miles on, Due West returned to its former rural, two-lane self, and it was there that Lizzy relaxed. The road descended into a small stream drainage, Possum Creek, and this slight relief always gave her the sense of returning home. The western vista opened up here in a patchwork of fields and forest borders, as yet sparsely cluttered with human habitations although the landscape had been altered generations ago. It was a vista that existed on borrowed time. As she flipped down her visor to block the sinking sun, Lizzy noticed a few vultures gliding effortlessly on the air currents.

Ten miles from town she turned onto Bartons Mill Road and passed the cemetery. Gray, leafless grapevines twisted around the black, wrought-iron pickets of the fence; curled brown leaves were piled up against its base. Just inside the fence well-spaced elms towered upward, and evergreen shrubs were interspersed among the stones of gray. Lizzy's eyes began to run up the gentle slope, but she quickly refocused her attention to the road before her.

On Narrow Passage, just beyond Agatha Prickett's house, she noticed a vulture inspecting something on the road. The vulture reluctantly hopped back from the carcass as Lizzy's car approached, as if expecting competition. Poor kitty, thought Lizzy as she stopped to pay her respects to the young tabby, didn't look both ways.

Everyone was waiting for Lizzy when she pulled up. She let out Pete and Clem from their fenced enclosure, and after greeting her excitedly, they took off for their yard inspection. Lizzy unlocked the kitchen door; CB sat alert on the table, and Alice stood by her bowl. Lizzy shooed CB off the table, dumped her things on the counter, turned up the heat a bit, and fed the cats. She filled the dogs' bowls and then opened the storm door to call them in. Instead she watched them as they sniffed around the edges of the planks that overlay Happy's grave. Without forethought, she headed out the kitchen door, Alice and CB following, and they all walked over to Happy's grave. It was so quiet, so still, that Lizzy could hear the creek. "Hey Happy," she called softly.

The sky was on the verge of twilight. It was chilly, but Lizzy rearranged some of the bricks so the appearance of the grave was not so crude. Alice and CB walked over the boards, sniffing them, and then CB began scampering across them, poking her paws through the cracks, pretending she had something live pinned. Alice knew better and just stared; she would not be party to such pretense.

Lizzy looked eastward from the small rise, past the bird feeder, to the overgrown patch that used to be her garden. The dogs had trampled several paths through the tall, dried weeds; tree saplings were beginning to emerge above the herbaceous growth. Her garden was transforming into a forest. Remembering the dogs, Lizzy realized they had taken off. She whistled for them, waited, and then whistled again. They came bounding out of the woods; Clem's legs were wet.

Lizzy let Pete in the house, but she put Clem's bowl of food outside the door. After she had finished carrying in the groceries from the car and putting them away, she poured herself a glass of wine and went to the living room with the newspaper.

Clem's yapping startled her. There was a soft rapping at the back door. Lizzy went to the kitchen and saw it was Timmy Donohue. She had forgotten. He hadn't come by on Saturday.

"I've come to collect for the paper, Ms. Lizzy," he called upon seeing her through the storm door.

"Come on in, Timmy," she responded as she turned on the outside light.

He opened the door and tried to enter without letting Clem in, but Clem knocked the slim boy out of his way and flew past.

"Don't worry—it's time for him to come in anyway," Lizzy said. "You look cold. Want some hot chocolate?"

"Oh yes, that would be great. Thank you, ma'am."

Lizzy winced at this address. It made her feel old and distant.

"You didn't stop to collect Saturday."

"I came by early and saw you . . ."

It took Lizzy a second before she understood. "I had to put Happy down."

"I'm sorry about Happy."

"Yep. Me too. But he's not in pain anymore."

"Are you going to get another dog?" asked Timmy.

Lizzy cocked her head. "Hadn't thought of that. No. I think I already have enough freeloaders to take care of, don't you?"

"Yeah, I guess so. The kitchen just seems a bit empty without Happy."

"That's the way it feels when someone dies," Lizzy said matter-of-factly and busied herself at the stove.

Timmy considered this. Despite what he had written, he couldn't reconcile the thought of Happy being returned to the dust so abruptly. Happy was a sweet dog who loved Ms. Lizzy. And she loved him. How could they love one another if Happy didn't have a soul?

Lizzy glanced at Timmy. His short, light hair was askew, but his green eyes were intent on whatever he was thinking.

"Ms. Lizzy, what do you think happens to dogs when they die?"

"They abide in one's memory," she responded without hesitation. Wanting to end this conversation before it went any further, she asked him, "How's school?" She placed the cup of hot chocolate down on the counter.

"Okay," Timmy responded as he climbed up onto one of the tall stools and started blowing on the hot chocolate.

"When does Christmas vacation start?"

"Next Friday. And we have only a half day then," he said, pleased.

"Are you putting on a Christmas program?"

"Unfortunately."

"You don't like to?"

"I hate them."

"Why?"

"I hate dressing up like an idiot." Timmy hesitated, then added, "I got in big trouble when I said that at school. Sister Gertrude said I was insulting my classmates, but it's not like I called anyone an idiot."

Lizzy failed at suppressing her half-suppressed smile. "Well, what are you going to be?" she asked him.

"Luckily I've only got to be one of the town people."

"That's not too bad."

"I guess not. I wish I didn't have to be in it at all."

"I didn't particularly like to be in plays either. I don't sing well, and there were always songs. When I was older, though, I liked to make the scenery and costumes."

"I don't think I'd be any good at that," Timmy replied. He gulped down the hot chocolate now that it had cooled slightly. Lizzy went and retrieved money from her purse and handed it to Timmy.

"Thanks a lot, Ms. Lizzy." She always tipped him.

"Tell your mom and dad I said hello." About all her communication with Helen and Tim Donohue was through Timmy.

Timmy slipped off the stool, out the back door, onto his bike, and into the winter evening. As he approached Prickett Farm Road, he saw the unmistakable outline of Jonas standing in the middle of Narrow Passage. He and Jonas often crossed paths, but they usually didn't say more than hello—or rather just nodded at one another. Jonas was already in high school, and Timmy figured Jonas wasn't particularly interested in talking to an elementary school kid. At least Jonas hadn't said much the couple of times Timmy tried talking to him.

"What are you looking at?" asked Timmy as he stopped next to Jonas.

Without breaking his skyward gaze, Jonas replied, "The moon. And Venus."

"I like when the moon is just a sliver, when you can barely see it but you know the whole moon is there. You can sort of see the dark part of the moon tonight. Venus is really bright."

"More of its surface is illuminated than usual—from our perspective, that is."

"Like the moon then."

Jonas looked down at Timmy. "Yes. Except it's orbiting around the sun, like we are."

"Do you know what those stars are, over there?" Timmy directed Jonas's attention higher in the sky. "The ones in a sort of triangle?"

"That's called the winter triangle."

Timmy grinned at the name. "Is it a constellation?"

"No," said Jonas. "Those are the three brightest stars in three different constellations. The brightest one is Sirius. I forget the names of the constellations."

"They usually have complicated names from Greek myths. I can remember only a few, like Pegasus and Andromeda."

"The ancient Greeks used to think Venus was two different stars— a morning star and an evening star."

"I wish I could take pictures when it's dark," said Timmy, shivering. He put his foot back on the pedal. "I better get home. I'm already in trouble," he said and took off on his bike.

Jonas watched him leave. That was the most extended conversation he had ever had with his young neighbor.

•   •   •

"Don't bang the door," was the greeting Timmy received from his mother, Helen, followed closely by "I told you not to dally after getting started so late. Go wash your hands for dinner."

"Dad isn't home yet?"

"He'll be here in five minutes. Make sure Chris washes his hands too."

There were six Donohues. At ten, Timmy was the oldest child. Eileen was not quite two years younger than he, and Katie was six. Christopher was three.

Timmy knew his second punishment of the day was imminent. Somehow he had to get to his father before his mother did—without interrupting. If he could tell his father about his composition being selected two weeks in a row, that might lighten the punishment. Since his father was late, they probably would sit down to dinner as soon as he got home—Timmy would have to act fast.

As the Donohues were assembling at the table, Timmy took his best chance. "May I say grace tonight?" he asked his father as he glanced at his mother furtively. She didn't miss the glance, but she didn't say anything.

A bit surprised, his father responded, "Certainly, Timothy."

With all his heart Timmy said, "Bless us, oh Lord, in these thy gifts which we are about to receive from thy bounty through Christ our Lord. And I want to give thanks today for Sister Gertrude, who is helping me learn obedience and who encourages me by considering my compositions worthy to read to the class. Amen."

"Amen."

"Very good, Timmy," said his father. "I was impressed with your composition too—a complex topic."

So far, so good, but he wasn't out of the woods yet. As his mother began to fix a plate for Chris, his father began to tell them about his day at work.

"I had a policy renewal for David Brown returned by the post office today. Remember him, Helen?" he asked and then continued when she nodded. "Anyway, I remembered that the plumbing supply company he worked for had moved up to North Fork early in the year, so I pulled out the North Fork phone book. There were two David Browns and three D. Browns. So before I left work today I started calling—that's why I was a bit late. Anyway, by the third call I got an answer—it wasn't my D. Brown, but we got to talking. This fellow, Doug Brown, knows some Donohues from Reliance and wondered if we are related. By the end of the conversation I had made an appointment with him for tomorrow morning," Tim said, pleased. "I better get out early."

"Did you find the man you were looking for?" asked Timmy. Timmy thought his father, an insurance salesman, knew everyone in town.

"Yes, I did, on the last call. He didn't realize his request to have his mail forwarded had expired, so he appreciated my tracking him down. How was your day?" he asked, looking at Helen.

Timmy's mother and Chris had been at the St. Xavier's preschool program, where she worked a few mornings a week. "After preschool, Chris and I did a little holiday shopping, mostly window shopping, while we waited—"

"We looked at toys," corrected Chris.

"Yes, we did. Window shopping is an expression—it means we didn't buy anything. Anyway, when we went—"

"But we did buy—"

"Remember, it's a secret!" hushed his mother.

Timmy still expected his mother to say, "and after school we went to the library because Timmy had detention—again," but she didn't. Either she forgot or gave up, thanks to Chris. Among the older children there was a code of silence regarding troubles at school, broken only when immediate retribution was sweeter than the benefits of reciprocal silence. Penance was made at school: there was no need to pay twice. Actually, Chris was the biggest risk for the rest of the evening: he might still bring up the trip to the library.

That night when Timmy said his prayers before bed, he wondered if he should give thanks for his mother's silence. Did she forget or did she just feel that his detention was not that important? She usually told his father. Was her not telling a lie? They had been taught about the lie of omission. He wouldn't want his mother to lie for him. Perhaps she was testing him. She was waiting for him to tell his father. He should tell him—but then, might his father be upset with his mother for not saying anything? And if he were mad, wasn't it Timmy's fault for not confessing in the first place? Living a virtuous life wasn't simple or easy. Perhaps being Pope was not such a good idea.

Following initial decay, chemical processes break down the main components of the body.

Groundwork

Even before Lizzy opened the kitchen door, everyone in the house knew it. Alice, CB, Clem, and Pete were all waiting there, lined up and looking at her expectantly. When Lizzy opened the door, they all rushed outside—well, except Alice. She wouldn't stoop to rushing. Lizzy inhaled deeply—a trace of early spring, a light, sweet warmth, an earthy perfume, was in the air.

Over the last few days high notes from the creekside forest sang the change to anyone who was listening. Spring was encroaching upon winter; winter was yielding to spring. There was still a nip to the air, but the angle of the sun revealed the tipping of the balance.

With her first cup of morning coffee, in her robe and slippers, Lizzy went out the kitchen door too. As she walked around to the front of the house her clan joined her. Pete and Clem were slightly ahead, sniffing each bush. Clem rushed from one spot to the next, looping back to coax Pete into advancing, but Pete took his time for a more thorough examination. CB was threading around Lizzy's legs while Alice followed indifferently behind with her tail up in the air. Along the front pathway Lizzy sought and found the stiff blades of crocuses pushing through curled brown leaves. Years ago she had dug up the crocuses, hyacinths, and irises, broken apart the clumps of bulbs, and replanted them. Long before she had moved here, the yard had been planted to have something in bloom much of the year. All Lizzy had done was resuscitate the garden after several years of renters' neglect, although now she saw she was guilty of largely neglecting it herself. She fetched her newspaper and walked back along the side of the house, looking toward the woods.

Even if some of spring's color has been planted, thought Lizzy, nature sure does a hell of a job on its own. A tint of light green, almost chartreuse, revealed the swelling of leaf buds freeing themselves from the stems to which they had been appressed all winter. They had been waiting since fall, dormant, until longer days signaled it was time for the nascent leaves to escape their sheaths and flush full. Soon Lizzy would see the fuchsia blooms of redbud, the yellow clusters of spicebush, the white racemes of serviceberry—the trees and shrubs that bared blossom before leaf and gave full show to what might later be lost in the thick of green. Lizzy put down her paper on the kitchen doorstep, walked past the shed, and rounded the back corner of the house. Yes, something in the air was calling her too.

Lizzy's eyes rested on her overgrown vegetable garden. She walked to its edge and put down her coffee cup. CB peered into the cup; she liked coffee if it had enough milk. Lizzy leaned over and grabbed a handful of tall, dry grass stems and pulled them out of the ground. Then she pulled a few more handfuls and tossed them into a pile. Without knowing when the decision had been made, she realized she intended to plant a vegetable garden. It had been years. If she were going to make progress before work she better get dressed. It would soon be time to put in spinach, lettuce, and peas.

Lizzy had been enamored with growing vegetables since she was a child. She wasn't a farm girl or even a country girl. Growing up she had claimed a corner of her family's small suburban backyard for a garden. Some book she had read had sparked a fantasy of living off the fruits of wild trees, and her first vegetable garden transformed this idyllic image into some sort of attainable reality—even with its paltry crop. She remembered how proud she was to bring her mother her first handful of green beans. But it wasn't only about the harvest, eating the fruit; from her first garden she had been taken with the marvel of seeds—dry and small—giving rise to sprouts that grew and eventually gave rise to plants with fruit that bore new seeds. She found something miraculous about that cycle.

Maybe she just liked the color green. She always had worn her green crayons to a nub. The color spoke to her somehow—as if something instinctive recognized green as the color of vitality itself.

Heading back toward the kitchen, Lizzy paused at the myrtle. She had dreamt of Happy again last night, although in this dream he wasn't muddy from digging in the yard. He sat at the window, looking out wistfully, which was strange only in that he couldn't actually sit and see out of any of the windows. Remembering the dream made her think of Alice, who for weeks had spent hours sniffing the boards and then resting on them. Sometimes she even spotted Alice rolling around on the planks—when Alice thought no one was watching, of course. Now Alice largely ignored the boards; yet if she happened to wander near the myrtle, she seemed to pause, as if listening to something—or was that just Lizzy's imagination?

It was time to take those boards off. Lizzy removed the bricks from an outer plank and flipped it over. A heavy, musty odor rose from the ground. Sow bugs, millipedes, and other assorted multilegged creatures scattered. Lizzy dropped the board back down. Hadn't she been on her way to get dressed? She had better get some gloves too.

She was on her way back to the yard, clothed and fed, when the phone rang.

"Hi Lizzy, it's Russ."

At the sound of his voice her defenses went up.

"Are you busy?" he asked when she didn't respond.

"No. Not really. Just headed out to the garden."

"Lucky you. It's a beautiful morning. Listen," he continued, "do you know about George Roper's plans to build at Bartons Mill Pond?"

"Oh, yes." She relaxed; she should have guessed. "Agatha Prickett keeps bringing it up. You remember her?"

Russ laughed. "Yes, how could I forget old hawk eye—the inquisition revisited. Well, anyway, I've been working with Donna and Doug—a lot of the old crowd—and we're trying to put the brakes on the development. We'd like to get some adjoining property owners involved."

"Do you really think there's any chance of stopping Roper?"

"We're certainly going to try. We've been sorting out whether the pond falls under any sort of protection. And, as I said, we're trying to get directly affected landowners involved. . . . I was hoping I could get you to join us for a meeting tomorrow evening."

"I'm working evenings this week," said Lizzy, happy to have an easy excuse.

"How about Saturday? Are you working Saturday morning?"

"No. Are you meeting twice a week?" Already hesitant to cede any ground, Lizzy found this level of intensity well beyond her comfort zone.

"Well some of us, a smaller group, are getting together at Donna and Doug's to evaluate where we are, what we need to do next. Could you make that?"

"No" was on the tip of her tongue. She didn't want to get sucked into one of Russ's causes. She had lost what little patience she had for groups and meetings. More so, she had lost her belief that she could effect change. And she didn't know if she wanted to work with Russ or Donna or Doug or anyone in "the old crowd." But still, she couldn't bring herself to simply say no—she couldn't just cede to the development. Agatha had brought up the flyer again just the other day, relishing the thought that Roper must have put "those people" in their place. "Well . . ."

"Lizzy, I know you hate the idea of a major subdivision out there."

"Yes, but you also know I've given up fighting the world. It doesn't budge."

"We just want to try to stop some Roper sprawl. As soon as he finishes one subdivision, he's on to the next."

"Have you spoken with Sam Tutwiler yet?"

"No. I was hoping you might."

Lizzy let out a short laugh. "And Agatha Prickett?" she asked.

Now Russ laughed. "That will be next week."

Wouldn't that give Agatha something to fume about, thought Lizzy. "Okay," Lizzy acquiesced. She could at least hear them out. "What time?"

"Ten."

"Do they still live on Crabtree?"

"Yes. Should I call to remind you?"

"No, you don't need to do that."

"Okay. See you then."

"See you."

"Liz."

"What?"

"Enjoy the garden."

"Yeah. Bye." Lizzy hung up the phone. She went to the sink, filled a tall glass with water, and drank half of it. Still standing at the sink, she rubbed hand cream over her hands and looked out the window at the birdfeeder. She watched a mixed flock of titmice and chickadees that had alighted in the Rose of Sharon beside it. They were taking turns making forays to the feeder, and one titmouse was throwing less-desirable seed to the ground as he searched for a sunflower seed. With his reward, he flew back to a branch of the bush and hammered at the seed he held between his toes. Russ had made the birdfeeder for her—well, perhaps more so for Wes—when she and Wes bought the house. Lizzy refilled her glass, remembered the gloves, fetched them from the hall tree, and headed out.

Slipping on the gloves, Lizzy pulled the bricks off the remaining planks. She then carried the boards over to the shed, where she leaned them against the wall to expose their undersides to the sun. The remaining resident fauna fled. The ground where the planks had lay for months was compressed and rather damp. A few pale, spindly sprouts that had sought light at the edges of the boards were matted to the earth. She should cover the bared soil with some flowering groundcover. She would have to keep her eye on Pete and Clem to make sure they didn't start digging there again.

After carrying the bricks back to the well house, Lizzy perused the garden. What a mess. It would take several days. She took another drink of water and then started pulling.

Russ. It had been months since she had talked to him. But Russ had been weaving in and out of her life for years—apparently, she had just made way for him to weave back in.

Russ had arrived in Lizzy's life the first week of college in South Fork. It would have been hard not to notice the tall, dark-haired, dark-eyed, handsome guy who arrived late to class that first morning and slid into the seat next to her. He caught her eye, smiled, and then turned his attention to the professor. When she saw him in her second class of the day, he gave her a bigger smile and introduced himself. There was an hour between the two classes, and the next day their earlier class met, Russ invited Lizzy to go get a cup of coffee during the break. Going for coffee immediately became a morning ritual. Russ amused Lizzy by his delight in this routine, his coffee being the "right" temperature, his preferred muffin being available. During these morning breaks they would talk about what they were studying in class or something in the news. What she quickly came to like most about Russ was how he spoke of his interests and beliefs with passion but not without humor.

Early in their friendship Lizzy began to think that Russ was "interested" in her—it did seem he had sought her out—and she began to envision an evolving relationship. One evening at a party she began flirting with him—an embarrassment she could still readily recall. Later in the evening another new friend of Russ's arrived. Like Russ, Lisa was tall; she was also slim and had long blond hair, sky blue eyes, and a perfectly proportioned face. Even dressed casually she looked elegant. The two of them together looked like they were on their way to a modeling shoot. Lizzy felt so foolish that evening—not quite average height; not such a lean, blatantly feminine body; nondescript brown hair that wasn't quite straight, wasn't quite curly; nondescript brown eyes; a pleasant face but not a beautiful one—what had she been thinking? She had misread his friendship. They were classmates, coffee buddies.

But she and Russ had become close friends, and over the next several years Russ had drawn her into a sequence of student and community groups, the underlying focus of most being protecting the environment. Back then she believed that she, along with others, could make a difference, although even then she saw so much of the groups' efforts dissipate in internal struggles that owed themselves to personality conflicts and competing egos. But Russ's optimism and energy kept convincing her that the new group, the new alliance, the new effort, would be better than the last. Ironically, he never convinced Lisa, or subsequently Amy, of the same. They seemed to appreciate his looks and sociability more than his interests; Lizzy tried to reserve judgment as to what he saw in them.

Midway through college, Amy had arrived. Amy, with black hair and green eyes, was even more striking than Lisa. After college, Russ and Amy had married and remained in South Fork Crossing, where he taught high school biology and she started a catering business. Her cooking skills and flair for appearances—both herself and her food— blended well. The more successful her business became, however, the more financial success meant to her. Eventually, she decided not only had she outgrown South Fork but she had outgrown being the spouse of a high school teacher. She moved on to greater catering opportunities.

Russ and Lizzy remained friends, although after college they spent less and less time together. Russ and Wes got along reasonably well, considering Wes found Russ naïve and Russ found Wes cynical. Eventually, after his break up with Amy, Russ moved to Centreville. And after Lizzy had been on her own for a year or so, Russ began trying to lure her out of the somewhat solitary lifestyle she had chosen for herself. He would drop by, invite her to dinner or a movie or try to get her to go with him to get-togethers with old friends. But she would decline. She couldn't be around Russ very long without thinking about the past. She didn't want to make any mistakes about the nature of their relationship, and she didn't want to feel that she was Russ's second—or third or fourth—choice, or he hers for that matter.

Lizzy realized she was trying to pull out a sumac sapling, and it was resisting mightily. Her garden was on its way to returning to forest. Needing a shovel, she went to the shed where the old spade was leaning exactly where it had been left the last time it was used. That was one advantage of living alone. She carried the spade back to the garden and pushed it down into the earth and under the sumac. She loosened the ground in a circle around the sapling, sank the spade below the sumac, and evicted it from the earth with surprising ease. Leaning over, she pulled up a few remaining roots from the soil and shook them. As she straightened up, she heard a rushing in her ears and was suddenly overtaken by a dizziness that quickly morphed into nausea. Supporting herself with the spade, she lowered herself to the ground. She looked around for her glass of water and saw it was beyond her reach. She took a few deep breaths. She was fine. She must have stood up too quickly. She sat and listened to the titmice and chickadees fussing at one another at the bird feeder. After a few minutes she returned to pulling weeds, and another hour soon went by.

Lizzy fixed her lunch and dinner at the same time, packing away her dinner for work and then eating her lunch. After showering, she dressed in one of her many white lab outfits. Alice was lounging on the bed—cleaning her fur, getting ready for a good sleep. Lizzy picked out some reddish earrings for color and then kissed Alice on the head. "You be lazy for me today, Alice," she said and went downstairs. CB, in the living room, sat next to one of the crocks by the fireplace. She had bent over a thistle stalk so that she could chew its dried head. This was a favorite indoor pastime of hers. Lizzy half-heartedly pushed her away, and CB playfully returned the swat and then continued to chew the dried plant. Lizzy fetched her things and headed out the door with Clem and Pete. She easily corralled them in their fenced yard and headed off to work.

Lizzy entered the hospital through the back entrance to the wing that housed most of the diagnostic services. Passing the histology and cytology labs, she entered the small reception room of the blood lab. A few outpatients waited in the well-worn upholstered seats.

"Good afternoon, Kristen," she said to the young, red-headed woman who sat at the receptionist's window. Kristen looked up from her desk—a layer of foundation, colored lips and cheeks, outlined and shaded eyes below hairdryer-perfected permed hair. Lizzy wondered how early Kristen got up to do her makeup and hair; more so, she wondered how Kristen avoided making giant smudges across her face during the day. "Busy morning?" Lizzy asked.

"No, pretty quiet. Only a few minor emergencies."

"Carolyn in?" Lizzy asked.

"Yes. And Vince. And Sandy hasn't left yet."

Entering the small lounge just beyond Kristen's cubicle, Lizzy hung her pocketbook and jacket in her locker, placed her dinner in the refrigerator, and then headed into the lab. The familiar hum—the refrigeration units, the centrifuges, the fluorescent lights, the computer, and the new automated analyzer, which they all looked upon with suspicion—greeted her.

Lizzy hadn't set out to be a blood tech. She did have an interest in biology but a stronger love of drawing. In college her facility for drawing and interest in biology brought her to an anatomy class—she was looking for a career that would afford her an income and had come up with the idea of becoming a scientific illustrator. Instead, the anatomy class drew her deeper into biology—the architecture of the body—and then a summer job at the hospital as a nurses' aide propelled her in a new direction: helping people with real, immediate crises. At the time this path appealed to her altruistic aspirations while complementing her pragmatic side: she could quickly arrive at a point at which she could pay off her college loans and earn a living. She could always continue to draw.

The blood—perhaps that was an inspiration based on color. Or perhaps it was that by the end of the first summer as an aide she realized the day-to-day contact with patients demanded too much from her—too much being pleasant-on-demand. That had never been one of her talents. Also, the idea of blood just appealed to her. It was primal. All organisms had to get nourishment and gases into their bodies and wastes out. Primitive organisms lived in water and carried out these basic functions through permeable skins. But from there organisms developed increasingly complex ways of accomplishing these tasks—for many animals, blood was the answer, an internalized liquid medium. Nutriment, waste, oxygen, carbon dioxide, and those precious leukocytes coursed through the internal conduit system of the human body via blood. Blood, like water, was the life-sustaining liquid that cycled continuously—bringing what was necessary for life to go on, taking away what was necessary for life to go on.

Of course, this early inspiration was now only a memory. When Lizzy had started her training, blood analysis was less automated. She had spent more time manually conducting analyses and visually examining slides of blood drawn from patients. When she had started, no one had known about AIDS. That had really changed the atmosphere in the lab for a while. Now she was much more removed from the medium, and her gloved hands moved through the daily tasks with routine familiarity. Except for rare cases, she proceeded through samples as if following a familiar but fussy recipe. Still, the job gave her the financial independence that had first attracted her and allowed her to maintain herself, her home, and her menagerie. She was still helping people, no matter how removed.

Carolyn, Sandy, and Vince were gathered around the computer terminal. Carolyn, ten years Lizzy's senior and the lab supervisor, was seated. Her head was tilted slightly backward so she could see through the bottom of her new bifocals.

"Still trying to figure out the new logging system?" asked Lizzy as she joined them.

"No," said Carolyn. "Sandy ran standards on the new automated analyzer this morning. We're just checking the results."

"And how did the monster perform?"

"Looks good so far." Carolyn turned toward Lizzy and smiled. "But let's type our blood the good old-fashioned way, eh?"

• • •

Why had she told Russ she would go to this meeting? She didn't want to leave the comfort of home on her morning off, especially when she had been working the evening shift all week. She didn't want to feel compelled to become involved. She didn't want to see Donna and Doug and who knew who else and have to chat about "where she'd been keeping herself." But she had told him she would go and had no excuse for going back on her word.

As she reached the bottom of the staircase, she heard a faint rapping at the kitchen door. Clem and Pete were yapping a welcome;

it must be Timmy collecting for the paper. She hung her lab clothes on the hall tree.

"Good morning, Timmy. Come on in."

"You sure look nice today, Ms. Lizzy."

Lizzy almost blushed at Timmy's remark. "So, what are you up to today?"

"So far just delivering the paper—and collecting for it. May I have a glass of water, please?"

"Why certainly, young man." As she fetched him a glass of water she said, "It's a pretty day out, isn't it?"

"Yeah," said Timmy, clearly disgruntled. "I was going to ride around some after I was done collecting on my route. It's been really nice out all week, but I've been at school. Now my mom says I have to get straight home because we're going to visit my grandparents today—what a way to ruin a perfectly good Saturday."

Lizzy smiled as she pushed a bowl of nuts toward him.

"Thank you," Timmy said, taking a few. "We usually go on Sundays, after church, but my grandparents are going somewhere tomorrow."

"Where do your grandparents live?"

"Up in North Fork."

"Well, maybe you can bring your bike with you," suggested Lizzy.

"We're not allowed to leave the block they live on, and there's only so many times you can ride, or walk, around the same block. Their neighborhood is really boring."

"I guess your parents just want to keep you safe in the 'big city.'" Even though North Fork had grown substantially, Lizzy still regarded it as a large town.

"My dad says next year, when I'm bigger, he'll let me take Eileen and Katie to the school playground. It's about five blocks away. Sometimes he takes us, but usually he and mom tell us to go play in the yard, which is totally boring unless some of our cousins are there too. Only Katie and Chris still like the swing set."

Lizzy shook her head. "It's rough—too old for swings, too young for roaming. Want some more water?"

"No thanks. I better get going. I'm 'dawdling' again."

"I guess I'm dawdling too. Let me get my purse."

When Timmy left, Lizzy hurried back upstairs and switched out of the red blouse she was wearing into a plain beige pullover. She headed back downstairs, grabbed her lab clothes, put the dogs out, and left. She planned to stay in town after the meeting and go straight to work. The night before she had called the Meyers and asked Jonas to tend the animals for her. Depending on how long the meeting lasted, she would give Nancy a call and drop by there.

Donna and Doug lived on the east end of town. It had been a while since Lizzy had been out their way, but not much had changed, unlike the north and west sides of town. As she crossed Route 11 headed east on Main, she passed Barefoot Realty, which had recently been bought by a national chain. Next door was Ogletree's pharmacy and across the street was Fairburn's hardware store, which Nancy's husband, Lou, and his brother had inherited. Another block down she passed the train depot, went over the tracks, and passed Fishers' feed and seed. She smiled as she spied the fading but still visible letters on the worn red wooden slats of the now vacant corner shop: Hump's Ham House. She then entered the post–World War II residential section of town, where she turned on Dogwood, drove past the ball fields, turned on Crabtree, and parked with a small bevy of cars outside a brick rambler that looked quite settled in its luscious yard.

"Why Lizzy, it's been ages," Donna greeted her with a tight hug at the door. Lizzy acquiesced. It wasn't that she didn't like Donna, she just wasn't partial to long, meaningful hugs. "Where have you been keeping yourself?" Donna asked as they stepped into the foyer.

"I'm still at the farmhouse," Lizzy responded.

"And the lab?"

"Yes, there too."

"Well, come on in. We can catch up later. We were about to get down to business. Would you like some coffee or tea?" asked Donna as she gestured toward the kitchen.

Lizzy shook her head no and then braced herself before stepping into the arched entranceway to the living room. Russ, sitting across the room, smiled. Donna came up behind her with a mug of coffee and, always the perfect hostess, began to introduce everyone, even though she knew Lizzy knew almost everyone there. Doug, Donna's husband, was seated on the sofa to her right, along with Leslie and Seymour Real, a couple in their early sixties who lived not far from Lizzy. Seated opposite the sofa in armchairs in front of the picture window were Suzanna Phelps, who seemed to be related to or know nearly everyone in the county, and Mike Wheeler, who had been in every group Russ had ever convinced Lizzy to join. Directly across from Lizzy were three chairs that had been carried in from the dining room; seated there were Russ and Greg, the only one present whom Lizzy had never met. He was a fit-looking young man in his mid-twenties. Apparently, he lived out her way on Bartons Mill Road. Donna slipped into a swivel chair to the left of the arch. Russ grinned at Lizzy and patted the open seat between him and Greg. Lizzy crossed the living room and with feigned annoyance brushed aside Russ's hand, which lingered on the seat.

"Well," said Donna, picking up a steno pad and pen, "maybe we should get started by bringing Lizzy up to date."

Mike jumped right in. "When we first learned of Roper's plan, we thought Bartons Mill Pond might be protected by federal wetlands law. We quickly learned it wasn't—the law doesn't pertain to small, isolated areas like Bartons Mill Pond. I could go into greater detail after the meeting if you would like."

Lizzy waved her hand and shook her head no. She didn't need details, and she knew Mike well enough to know the details could take hours.

Mike nodded and continued. "Our only other possibility with federal law is through threatened or endangered species protection, but I'm jumping ahead. We still need to investigate that avenue.

"Anyway, to continue," Mike sped along, "we have been researching state laws too. And again, the avenues open to us are limited because it's a small and isolated wetland. Furthermore, the building site isn't a wetland at all. In fact, only the swampy area on the southwest corner of the pond is technically a wetland—and that area is barely over an acre. We might have a hard time establishing that development on Roper's land will impact it directly."

As soon as she heard a slight pause, Lizzy asked the group, "Aren't there protections for the pond itself? I thought it is the only natural pond around here."

"Well yes, but no," Mike said. "Again it gets rather technical."

Lizzy glanced at Donna, who winked at her.

"A large part of our problem is that the place we want to protect is small enough to fall through the cracks in regulations. There are some state laws that pertain to controlling erosion from a building site, but I'm sure those minimal regulations will be followed."

Doug was leaning so far forward Lizzy thought he was about to stand up, but Mike ignored him.

"And there are laws that affect wastewater—particularly if a drinking water source is involved, which the pond is not. And it's all private property. It will be hard to get any state oversight. Anyway, that's sort of where we are." Mike shook his head and threw up his hands.

Doug took advantage of the opportunity. "Seymour, Leslie, any update on what's going on at the local level?"

"Well, to fill Lizzy in, as she probably already knows," Seymour, in contrast to Mike, proceeded in a slow-paced cadence, "being outside the town limits means the property is almost totally unregulated. Of course, some prefer it that way, but it does have its drawbacks. The county has never passed any zoning laws and hasn't established any rules that regulate development other than some very basic wastewater requirements—you know, regulating septic systems."

After forty years, Leslie still tried to hasten her husband along. "And most of the county commissioners certainly aren't interested in regulating development," she added quickly.

"Except for Claudia Ayers," Suzanna interjected, raising her index finger. "I talked to her about all the new subdivisions at a family get together."

"Well, what about sewage?" asked Doug, steering the group to stay on course.

Seymour took a deep breath. "From what we understand, Roper plans to put in sewer lines."

"What?" a few voices asked in unison.

"We've been talking to a few of our acquaintances along Due West Road—the Pendletons, the Houghs, the—"

Leslie made a small circling gesture to her husband.

Seymour wagged his head at Leslie, then continued. "We've been told that a few people have been offered deals on their property fronting Due West—a good price for a narrow strip. The rumor circulating is that George Roper is behind the offers, although his name is never mentioned. No surprise there. Furthermore, rumors are that he and the town are working on some sort of deal."

Leslie broke in, "There's also a lot of talk about the town planning to incorporate property along Due West, eventually all the way out to Bartons Mill Road."

"How can they do that?" Donna asked.

Russ sighed. Lizzy turned toward him.

"They would do it in stages. They would hopscotch westward— incorporate some close-in properties with frontage on Due West, extend the extrajurisdictional boundary, follow that with annexation, and then extend that boundary again."

"We've also heard talk of widening Due West beyond Possum Creek," said Leslie.

Lizzy found this news almost as crushing as the housing development. Possum Creek was like a bulwark, holding against Centreville's expanding suburbia.

"Is the county pushing back?" asked Lizzy.

Seymour shook his head. "Not that we know of."

"Does anyone go to town—I mean city—council meetings?" Doug asked.

"We better start going," Donna said to him.

"And to county board meetings." Doug replied.

Donna rolled her eyes.

Leslie looked toward Lizzy and Russ. "You know, Agatha Prickett's brother-in-law is a county commissioner."

"That's not in our favor," said Russ. "We need to figure out if the town and county are both in on some annexation–sewer line scheme."

"Suzanna, can you talk to your cousin-in-law Claudia about this?" Doug asked.

Suzanna nodded. "I'm on it."

"I'll start looking into this too," said Mike. "Minutes of the city council and county commissioner meetings are public record."

Russ shook his head. "If any of it *is* on record. . . ."

"Let's have as much as possible on this by our next general meeting," Doug said, running his hand through his hair. "We really need to know who will have jurisdiction over what. How are we doing at the state level?" he asked Greg.

Greg, perhaps feeling out of his league, had sat silently beside Lizzy. He now straightened in his seat and furrowed his brow. "I had a meeting in North Fork with two people from the state's natural resources department. They're familiar with Bartons Mill Pond and said they'd like to see it protected, but they can't conduct an environmental assessment unless their agency receives a formal request through the proper channels. That would start with the county or landowner."

"Well, besides Roper, that would be Agatha Prickett. Her land is on the south side of the pond." said Seymour.

"Doesn't your land extend to the pond, Lizzy?" Doug asked.

"Barely, maybe. Sam Tutwiler says it does. Long ago the Tutwilers and Pricketts agreed that the Tutwilers had access to the pond regardless of any fluctuations in water level. Sam says as current owner I inherited that agreement, but Agatha holds I didn't." Lizzy thought of the time Agatha, in her over-sweetened tone, "granted" Lizzy permission to visit the pond. When Lizzy told Sam this, it was the one time she heard him utter a profanity—"bullshit!"

"The original survey is hard to interpret," Lizzy continued. "It's very old, and some of the landmarks used are gone—but the property boundary lies in the vicinity of the pond. I rather not tangle with Agatha over it. Anyway, we're talking a mere sliver."

"I believe the Bartons still own their acreage between Mill Pond Creek and Trinity Cemetery—the site of the old mill," said Suzanna. "I haven't run across a Barton in years, though," she reflected.

Greg cleared his throat. "The natural resource folk suggested we might try to appeal to an elected official at the state level. Someone with some clout could possibly intercede, push the local jurisdictions to request some sort of environmental assessment from the developer."

Mike was on the edge of his seat. "That is exactly what we should do. We should meet with our state representative, our senator too."

Doug shook his head. "I think that's a bit premature."

"Well, I don't think we can afford to waste time," Mike said. "Some publicity and pressure at the state level might at least slow down Roper's steamrolling of the local boards."

"I doubt anyone at the state level is interested in pushing the county to slow down Roper," responded Doug tersely.

Now things were beginning to sound like old times to Lizzy. She glanced sideways at Russ, whose palms were moving upward to gesture stop.

"Let's consider this a bit," Russ refereed. "Meeting with Frank Daniels and Jeff Earl might apply some public scrutiny to the local boards' actions, but we should have a plan in place."

"I don't think it would hurt to send a small group, a representative one," Donna said in a conciliatory tone, looking at her husband. "Someone who knows the legal aspects, someone who knows the biology, someone who would be directly affected."

Lizzy's jaw tightened. Everyone else seemed to be nodding in assent.

"Who are the other big landowners out there, besides Prickett, someone whose land would border the development if not the pond?" Doug asked Lizzy.

"Sam Tutwiler," she answered, "but I'm not sure how he feels about all this. Farther out Narrow Passage is H. H. House, but I don't know him."

Suzanna let out a snort. "From what I know about Horace Hugh House, he explores every money-making angle he can. I suspect he'd welcome Roper's development—it will make his property, which is really his wife's, more valuable, so I doubt we'd get any support from him."

"Might you talk to Sam Tutwiler?" Doug asked Lizzy.

"Well, I . . ." Here it was—they were casting the net. Yes or no. Was she in? All eyes were on her. How could she say no—she had crossed that line by coming to the meeting. "Yes, I'll talk to him. But even if he's sympathetic, I doubt he'd be willing to get involved."

"What about you, Liz?" suggested Donna.

"I own only five acres."

Russ rescued her. "We might want to find someone to work with us who's done this sort of thing before—that is, who has already met with Daniels or Earl on behalf of a local organization—before we get too far along in any planning."

"Such as?" asked Mike.

"Perhaps Melissa Drummond," suggested Doug. "She's done this sort of representation for other groups. She has a good presence."

"Yeah, and she's pretty overextended," said Mike.

"More coffee, anyone?" asked Donna, recognizing it was time for a break. Most of the group stood up and began filing toward the kitchen.

Russ leaned toward Lizzy. "Not too bad?" he said.

"No. Actually more organized than I expected. And Doug and Mike are keeping their nipping better under control. I see Donna doesn't reflexively side with Doug anymore."

"We've all grown up some," he said, grinning. "And you missed the first meetings—mostly griping, little progress. Having some new people in the mix, Seymour and Leslie, Greg, helps. Still, there have been some flashbacks that have made college days seem like just yesterday."

"It's best to let Mike steer his own course."

"He gets a lot done." Russ smiled. "What time do you go to work?"

"Start at 3:00, but I want to get in a bit early."

"How about lunch when we're done here?"

"I'm going over to Nancy's."

Everyone had returned to the living room.

"Russ," Doug said once they were all reseated, "Do we definitely have someone from the college lined up for our next meeting?"

"Yes. Dr. Clayton from the biology department will be our speaker. I told him we're particularly interested in whether there are any rare or endangered species, but a general overview about the pond and its surroundings would be appropriate for the audience."

"What else is on the agenda?" asked Donna.

Doug sighed. "We still need a lawyer."

"I'm working on it, I really am," Suzanna reassured them.

"I think that's a lot to take care of for now," said Doug. "And don't forget, we want to involve people who come to the next meeting. We need to expand our base—develop a network of people willing to work on preserving green space in both the town and the county. This isn't just about Bartons Mill Pond."

Lizzy flashed a wary look at Russ. What was he trying to drag her into this time?

The group broke into multiple cross-room conversations in which the nuts and bolts of who was doing what was worked out in more detail. Lizzy decided to slide out before her task became more than talking to Sam. She quickly said goodbye to Donna and Doug, telling them she had business to take care of before work. Russ caught up to her at her car. "Will you come to the next meeting?" he asked.

"When?"

"A week from Wednesday."

"Maybe," Lizzy replied, her lips pursed as if disgusted. "But I'm not going to start attending county board meetings."

"There's a lot of other stuff to do, Lizzy. You could bake cupcakes for a fundraiser."

She hit him with her handbag. "See you later," she said with her crooked half smile, got in her car, and drove off.

•   •   •

Lizzy called Nancy from Ogletree's pharmacy. "Hey Nancy. Want to go out for lunch?"

"When?"

"Now."

"I'd love to, but I can't. The kids are home, and Lou is at the store. What are you up to?"

"I'm in town but don't have to be at work until 3:00."

"Why are you in town so early?"

"A meeting."

"A meeting?"

"A group that's opposing a big development out my way—at Bartons Mill Pond. Russ asked me to go."

"Oh yeah? Well why don't you just come over here if you can stand the chaos."

"You sure?" Lizzy hesitated.

"Come on over. I'll call in an order to the pizzeria. The girls will love that. Would you pick it up?"

"Sure."

Nancy was beginning to clear the dining room table when Lizzy arrived. The business bills and books, household bills and checkbook, stamps, stapler, calculator, and assorted accoutrements were on one side of the table and the kids' drawings and schoolbooks had taken over the other; the table was balanced in perfect cluttered harmony.

Nancy's house was always messy. Nancy attributed this to her kids, but Lizzy knew better. Nancy had always lived like this; her critical threshold for mess was set high above Lizzy's own. Nancy's tendency to pile had driven Lizzy a bit crazy over the years—hours spent looking for IDs, car keys, and purses. Lizzy acknowledged that she was a bit compulsively neat, and living alone had only reinforced her tendency toward static organization.

"Those two," Nancy said to Lizzy, "I told them to clean up their schoolwork. They each picked up one thing and disappeared." She called up the stairs, "Abigail, Hannah. Come get your books off the table."

"Right now, mom?" Abigail called back.

"Yes, right now!"

"Aw, mom," Abigail came dragging down the stairs.

"Abigail," said Lizzy when she came into sight, "why are you giving your mother a hard time?"

"She is working us to death," Abigail complained.

"I doubt it."

"She's cruel," Hannah chimed in, running down the steps when she heard Lizzy's voice.

"Your mother is one of the kindest people I know," Lizzy told them.

"Maybe to other adults," Abigail said.

"Send them out to my place, Nancy; I'll show them what work is."

"Oh, can we go mom?" Hannah said excitedly.

"I wouldn't do that to anyone," said Nancy. "Now get that junk off the table so we can sit down and have lunch."

The girls gave in. They wanted to keep Lizzy as an ally.

Lizzy followed Nancy into the kitchen. Nancy finished making a salad while Lizzy collected what dishes and condiments they needed for lunch. They worked together with ease. They had been roommates for years despite their differences in housekeeping standards. They met as assigned roommates in the dorm their freshman year. The day they moved into the dorm they started talking—about their plans, about where they grew up, about their siblings and parents, about their friends at home—and found in each other familiar threads as well as unexplored territory. They were both piecing together paying for college with scholarships, work-study, and loans. Unlike Lizzy, Nancy had grown up in a semi-rural community and was from a large family. Ironically it was Nancy who had planned to go into health care—nursing. Instead, she returned to her rural roots and became more and more interested in nonhuman patients. She ended up studying animal science and had worked as the assistant of a well-liked Centreville veterinarian ever since she had graduated.

"So, what is this group about?" asked Nancy.

"Do you know George Roper?"

"I've heard the name."

"Well, he owns lots of property around the county, including over one hundred acres right near me—across the creek. He's planning to build a bunch of houses there. The group I met with is trying to find a way to prevent the development—particularly because it would be right on Bartons Mill Pond. Donna and Doug Witte are involved, Suzanna Phelps, Mike Wheeler, Russ."

"Well the area is growing, Lizzy—I don't see how anyone is going to stop that."

"Someone has to defend against the march of humanity."

"I thought you gave up trying to save humanity from itself."

"I thought so too. I guess I'm just trying to save my own backyard."

"So, you're going to work with Russ's old crowd?" Nancy asked.

"It's sort of mine too, isn't it?" Lizzy reminded Nancy. "I don't know. They asked me to do a few things. I guess I will."

"Hmm. So, will you be seeing much of Russ?"

"Damn, that's all you want to know," Lizzy pushed Nancy with her hip.

"No. It's just the most interesting part."

"I guess I'll see him some. He invited me to lunch today."

"Why didn't you go?"

"I didn't think we needed to spend that much time together."

"Is he seeing someone?"

"We weren't discussing his private life. We were talking about the development, for goodness sake." Lizzy fell silent, but after a moment, betraying a hint of annoyance, she said, "Listen, I'm not looking for a guy. You know that."

Nancy rested her hand on Lizzy's arm. "Sorry."

They carried the salad and pizza into the dining room and called the girls, who hurried back down the stairs for lunch.

"Can you come with us to the movies later?" Hannah asked Lizzy.

"No, sweetie, I've got to go to work."

"Call in sick."

"That's a chronic condition; I can't afford to take off work all the time."

Lizzy and Nancy lingered at the table after the girls had eaten and left.

"Lizzy, I still don't understand why you push Russ away. You are so compatible, and you obviously care about the same things."

There were several answers to this question, and Lizzy figured Nancy knew all of them by now—it wasn't a new topic between them.

She knew Nancy was trying the rational approach. But the decision—as much as it was a decision—was an emotional one.

"I don't meet the height requirement."

"Lizzy, that's nonsense and you know it. So he's been involved with a couple of tall women. He could see their heads above the crowd. He has always cared for you."

Tall and beautiful, thought Lizzy. "Yes. He's been a friend. It's not that I don't care for him or him for me. But that's different from being in love, isn't it? I think part of me would always be comparing my relationship with him to my relationship with Wes, and his to Lisa, and then Amy, and then to Linda—you never met her—and up to whomever he may be seeing now. That wouldn't be good for either of us. And I've grown comfortable with being on my own."

Nancy crossed her arms and asked, "Andddddd?"

"I'm even-keeled now. It's taken me a while to get here. . . . I'll forfeit the highs to escape the lows."

"Lizzy, that monotone palette is going to wear thin."

Reconnaissance

"Jonas!" Sylvia called sharply from the doorway.

Jonas sat up, his jaw hanging.

"Didn't you hear me calling?"

"Maybe." As he slowly gained consciousness he said, "I was dreaming . . . I was eggs . . . frying in a skillet . . . and it was time for me to get out of the pan."

Sylvia's eyes rolled toward the ceiling.

"But then I realized I was the butter in the skillet, so I didn't have to go anywhere."

"Well that's not the case. You have to get ready for school. Dad has already left, and I have to go in early for a meeting. So please get yourself out of bed and ready for school. Okay? I'll see you later this afternoon." She walked over to his bed and kissed him on the top of his head.

Forty-five minutes later Jonas stood on the road, waiting for the school bus. The day promised to be spectacular—the air was early spring crisp laced with a trace of damp humus. Jonas lifted his nose as he envisioned Pete or Clem lifting his snout. The aroma had been on the air all week, an organic scent accentuated by a certain temperature–humidity combination. Still a dog, he cocked his head to listen to a note of urgency in the air—the incessant chirping of a male cardinal. Luckily he had an early release day; he would be home by one . . . only a half day of school . . . why waste it?

Lizzy donned the appropriate apparel for her walk—boots, a scarf to keep her hair pushed back from her face, and a light jacket with a water bottle in one of its large pockets. She looked at herself in the hall tree's mirror. She looked like she was pretending to be an outdoorswoman. She reached for the smaller of the two pairs of binoculars, Wes's first gift to her, and placed them around her neck. Her costume was complete.

Having the day off, she had decided to go look at the pond before she went to the meeting that night. She wanted to envision houses sprawled along the pond's northern shore and extending as far as she could see. She hadn't spoken to Sam yet, and she wanted to strengthen her own resolve before she tried to convince him of anything. Not that she could sway Sam in any way. His family had been here for generations, and his bond to the land and the community ran deeper than hers or anyone else's around. She knew he saw some of the local changes as improvements—like the county putting hard top on Narrow Passage Road and opening a new fire station on Due West. But he also relished the lifestyle in which he had grown up on his family's farm. He was the one who had chosen to stay. Anymore he just cut hay on much of his acreage—long ago he had gone to work as an electrician because the farm's income was too variable to raise a family. Sam had been talking about retiring a bit early and farming full time, but then Leona was diagnosed with breast cancer.

Lizzy's home had belonged to Sam's uncle, Dolan Tutwiler. Dolan had given up farming and sold most of what remained of his acreage many years earlier. Once their children moved away, he and his wife, Ethel, had moved to town and rented out the old farmhouse, eventually to Lizzy and Wes, who subsequently bought it. Sam had once told Lizzy that when Agatha had gotten wind of the impending sale, she had offered Dolan a better price. But Dolan had made an agreement and wouldn't go back on his word. Dolan and Ethel had both since passed away.

Lizzy debated whether to bring Pete and Clem with her. Hell, she thought, they hadn't been on a real walk together in a long time. She called them, and they all went out the kitchen door.

As they headed up the road, Pete sniffed the ground just ahead of Lizzy, as if making sure the path was clear. Clem raced ahead and then bounced back. Although she could walk along the creek to reach the pond, Lizzy didn't like making her way through the muck just below the pond. She knew that she shouldn't call it muck—it was a wetland. She planned to cut across Agatha's property and come out on the south side of the pond. There was always the possibility of meeting Agatha, who put in long hours at her front windows, but this was Lizzy's favorite route.

Agatha brought up the pond and Roper's plans during every one of their thankfully infrequent exchanges. Lizzy tried to move conversation away from this topic, but Agatha wasn't so easily thwarted. Lizzy figured that by now Agatha had pretty much surmised her opinion. Over the years the number of topics Lizzy avoided with Agatha had grown—church attendance and church socials, dating, adopting abandoned animals, the nebulous religious affiliation, or lack thereof, of the Meyers—and those were just the more personal issues, not larger politics. Essentially, Lizzy found it hard to tolerate Agatha's intolerances, which were always served with plenty of sugar. But they both worked to keep the peace as neighbors.

Agatha's house, a clapboard colonial, stood obliquely across the road, but a relatively small piece of her land was adjacent to Lizzy's— a wedge formed by road, water, and their ambiguous property boundary. The wedge followed a rather unique local feature—an isolated uplifting on the south side of the pond had created a bluff that overlooked the pond and the creeks that flowed from it. Because of its incline this triangular quadrilateral had remained forested, unlike much of the surrounding land, which had been cleared at one time or another for crops or livestock. Mature trees grew here, although close to the road Lizzy passed through a border of young pines and sweetgum. She entered the woods just before the approximate property line; Pete and Clem understood the rules and followed quietly behind her. They had been shooed away by Mrs. Prickett more than once. Under cover, though, they dashed ahead, excited to be going—where did not matter.

Agatha looked out her front window just in time to see Lizzy slip into the woods with her dogs. Lizzy could at least ask permission, Agatha thought to herself. And bringing those mutt dogs on her property . . . bad enough those boys were sneaking around her woods, up to what mischief she could not be sure. Especially that Meyers boy. She never should have sold that parcel to the Meyers. But she needed to turn some land into cash back then, after Woodrow, God rest his soul, had passed. At least Timmy Donohue was typically carrying a fishing pole—she could tell where he was headed. And at least the Donohues attended church, even if they were Catholics. But adults should know better than children. Anymore it was only the likes of Sam Tutwiler and Horace House who knew how to be respectful neighbors. Even George Roper could use a lesson in manners—that she had learned about his plans from a flyer, from strangers. He should have written or called her, told her personally. He should have shown her greater regard. After all, he must know she is from an old Stumptown family of some note.

Well, Lizzy had turned out all right, for a hippie. At least Lizzy was polite and a decent neighbor, risking a fall to come over to check on her during that ice storm this winter when the phone line came down. She didn't understand, though, why Lizzy, still not quite middle age and pleasant looking, hadn't remarried. It wouldn't take much for her to slim down to a nice date weight. Without children, who could Lizzy count on to take care of her in her old age—certainly not neighbors given the way young people weren't being taught basic civic values anymore. She would keep an eye out and try to catch Lizzy when she came out of the woods. She could step out to check her mailbox. She needed to let Lizzy know she was concerned about those dogs getting hit by a car, tell her how broken hearted she would be if she saw one of them dead on the road in front of her house. That was why she had called animal control that time—she was worried about the dogs. And she did tell Lizzy where they were. Of course,

Lizzy claimed that the gate latch must have broken just that day, while she was at work. That seemed quite a convenient excuse. But what she really wanted to know was whether Lizzy had heard any more from those town people who sent the flyer—she suspected Lizzy knew more than she was saying. And maybe she should mention again that her church had a singles' mixer once a month.

As Lizzy walked away from the road, the pines and sweetgum quickly yielded to mature oaks and hickories. The forest floor was covered in a rustling layer of browned leaves; the oak leaves still held a rich leathery shine. Pete and Clem plowed narrow paths through the leaves with their snouts, smelling their way through the woods. Lizzy put some attention to the forest floor too, but she was using her eyes.

Pete stayed with Lizzy as she walked to the bluff, taking over Happy's role of security detail, whereas Clem disappeared. As she made her way up the incline, the now familiar changes in vegetation greeted her. Slender-trunked sourwoods appeared; she knew these small trees from their summertime racemes of white flowers. As the ridge crested, she spied the leathered-leaved mountain laurels that would soon explode in showy pink flower clusters. Appearing just beyond the mountain laurels was the prize: the hemlock trees, some of which year after year remained precariously perched on the edge of the bluff. Approaching the bluff's edge, she stepped gently on the carpet of moss. She felt the barely perceptible coolness to the air. In the summer the temperature difference was more dramatic. Lizzy never tired of this spot. In its magic she found she transcended boundaries of time and place—she felt connected to the life that coursed through everything around her. She could close her eyes and smell the first time she had ever come here, with Wes.

From the bluff one had a full view of the pond below. Narrow Passage wasn't the only creek that left the pond. Mill Pond Creek flowed into the pond at its northeastern edge, between Roper's property and the cemetery, and exited the pond on a southeastern course, passing under Narrow Passage Road. From the eastern corner of the bluff one could see remnants of a small dam and the stone work that had housed the water wheel of the old Barton grist mill. Some of the mill's foundation remained on the property, but the mill had burned down long ago. Through the leafless trees one also could see the cemetery from this eastern corner, but Lizzy wasn't headed in that direction.

From the high point at its eastern corner, the bluff sloped gently downhill until it graded into the bottomland forest that adjoined the sparsely wooded, often muddy, lowland—the wetland—which was laced with small rivulets that coalesced to form Narrow Passage Creek. Narrow Passage was somewhat of an anomaly, flowing almost due west once it left the pond, as if pushed in that direction by the bluff. Although it was a small creek, Sam said neither he nor his parents remembered it ever having dried during a drought. Lizzy wondered if this would change with Roper's development. Perhaps that was how to draw Sam in, if he were concerned about the creek that ran through his land.

Lizzy looked to the northern bank of the pond, George Roper's land. A few mature tulip poplars stood out among the oaks and hickories. Beyond the wooded boundary of thirty feet or so the land had been cleared for agriculture for generations. Lizzy noticed a big bird—a hawk—sitting in one of the tall tulip poplars. Its attention appeared to be focused on something—a large, dark shape amid the bramble of vines at the edge of the forest. It was Jonas.

Walking downhill along the edge of the bluff, Lizzy reached an old path worn down by likely centuries of visitors. It led from the bluff to the creek. Clem reappeared and raced ahead of her on the path. She now had not only Jonas's attention but the hawk's.

Jonas remained where he was as she made her way slowly toward him. The ground was wet and covered with the uncurling furry fronds of emerging ferns. She tried to stay off the soft ground as much as possible by using the roots of the occasional red maples as stepping stones. Clem and Pete had made a direct path to Jonas and were already there, sitting next to him with their tails wagging, as if proudly displaying their find.

"And why aren't you in school today?" she asked as she approached.

"Half day."

"You're going in this afternoon?" she asked, a bit confused.

69

"No," Jonas said. Realizing this wasn't a sufficient answer, he added, "Going to school for just a few hours seemed a waste of a nice day."

Lizzy gave him her crooked smile. She wondered if his parents had a clue as to where he was this morning. "So, are you hiding out here?"

"No. Just watching the hawk."

"Is it a broad wing?" asked Lizzy, knowing the names of a few of the commonly occurring hawks better than she knew how to tell them apart.

"Oh no," said Jonas. "He's a rough-legged hawk—he has feathers on his legs. It's rare for one to come this far south. He's been here all winter."

"Is that what it is?" Lizzy picked up her binoculars and took a better look. "It's a he?"

"I think so—my binos aren't very good. The coloring on their front is a bit different between the sexes."

"Try these," Lizzy said as she handed her binoculars to Jonas. "I'm not much of a birder. I've never had the patience."

They both watched the hawk, perhaps disturbed by their presence, take off over the pond and then turn northward. Jonas followed the bird with the binoculars until it was out of sight.

"Did you know that a man is planning to build about two hundred houses across the pond—and the creek?" Lizzy said as Jonas handed the binoculars back to her.

"Yeah, I know."

"Even if he leaves that border of woods, it will never be the same. It certainly won't be as peaceful as it is now." Lizzy sighed and shook her head. "I don't know what will become of the pond."

"Depends on whether Mrs. Prickett comes stand guard." Jonas flashed Lizzy a rare smile. "These ferns—well, all the plants that grow here—won't survive much foot traffic. I don't think the turtles, frogs, and salamanders will fare very well either."

"How do your parents feel about the development?"

"They don't want it to happen, but they feel awkward, like they're being hypocrites. We moved out here not long ago ourselves. Mrs.

Prickett reminded them of that when those flyers first came. Of course, she feels like she owns our place because she sold us the land."

Lizzy frowned and shook her head.

"I'm supposed to go to a meeting tonight about the development," she said. Then, without forethought, she added, "Do you want to go?"

Jonas shrugged his shoulders. He didn't know what a meeting would entail—it might be pretty weird.

Lizzy gathered Jonas shared her distress about the development. "A biologist from the university is supposed to talk about the pond. It might be pretty interesting."

Jonas considered the invitation. Ms. Lizzy seemed to want him to go. His mother might even be pleased. He would be showing some initiative. He actually would be doing something that involved other people. That would make her happy. "Okay."

"I'll pick you up then," Lizzy said, glad she had asked. "Around six thirty. Well, I've got to get home. Are you staying?"

"At least until one. You don't have to mention to my parents that you saw me here today."

Lizzy smirked. "Did you bring lunch?"

Jonas shook his head no.

"Come along then." Lizzy turned to head back the way she had come.

"Don't you like walking along the stream?"

"I don't like the mud."

"It's not that bad," Jonas said earnestly.

Lizzy looked at his sneakers, which were filthy. She shook her head and looked down at her rubber boots. "Lead the way." Pete and Clem jumped up the moment Jonas prepared to stand.

Jonas led the way, trying to step widely and gingerly to avoid crushing the spring's new growth. As they made their way from the soggy substrate to the streamside forest, Jonas was Lizzy's guide: he pointed out the green and maroon sheaths of some Jack-in-the-pulpits already in bloom and the thick, lobed leaves of hepatica; he identified the call of a chestnut-sided warbler and then a Carolina wren. In a way Jonas reminded her of Wes, who could name every flower, tree, and bird in the forest. Lizzy had never bothered to remember names; she hadn't thought she would ever need to. The recognition without a name had been enough for her; still, hearing the names again was sweet.

As soon as Narrow Passage Creek became a well-defined channel, Clem took off right down the center of it.

●   ●   ●

After lunch at Lizzy's house, Jonas returned to the creek and headed westward along it. The creek didn't meander much; along much of its length it was a few feet wide and half a foot deep. In a few spots it did widen and deepen, and alongside one of these pools Jonas located a patch of the upright mottled leaves of trout lilies; he had come across them last spring. Many of the lilies were graced with nodding yellow flowers at the ends of tall stalks. Jonas squatted to look at them. He had read that they could grow in colonies that were hundreds of years old, perhaps not a second in geological time but impressive for an herbaceous plant nonetheless.

"You're lucky there aren't cougars here anymore." Sam Tutwiler's sonorous voice startled Jonas. "I had the drop on you a long way off."

A small smile appeared on Jonas's face. Sam had caught him off guard.

"No school today?" asked Sam.

"Half day."

"There are a few more patches of those trout lilies as you walk west—at least as far as my property goes," Sam's gestured westward with his head. "Don't know what House has done along the creek. Growing up I used to walk the creek almost every day, all the way to Stumptown Road. That was before my Uncle Albert sold his farm to Mrs. House's family. I trapped—mink, muskrat, raccoons—brought me some real money when I was a teen."

"I've never seen a mink," said Jonas. "Are they still around?"

"I suspect so. They were the hardest to trap." Sam nodded at the memory. "They have a good sense of smell, and you can't really bait them in. You have to figure out their path—exactly where they might step—and hide a trap there. Anymore, though, I rather see them left

72

alone, even the raccoons, unless they become a nuisance, that is. It used to seem there was no end to the muskrats around here either, but not anymore."

"How far west have you followed the creek?"

"Miles. Do you know where it ends?"

"No," said Jonas, a bit surprised at himself for never having wondered about this.

"It empties into the North Fork. Most creeks round here empty into the South Fork. I guess it was named Narrow Passage because it follows a narrow path."

"That's interesting," said Jonas. A subtle topography must send the creek northward. Now thinking about it, he realized its gentle bend northward started soon after the creek formed. Not only were the pond and the hemlocks anomalies, so was the creek.

"Well, I better get to work. Came home early. It's past time to get the ground ready for planting," said Sam. "Just couldn't help coming down here to rile you. Keep your eyes open for snakes. They could be out already in the sunny spots."

"I should head home," said Jonas, figuring it must be after two and wanting to erase the evidence of his day's activities before his mother got home. He accompanied Sam back to his tractor and then continued on toward home.

Jonas was retrieving his backpack from under a pine along Narrow Passage Road when the Donohues drove by. He knew Mrs. Donohue was giving him a long stare, wondering what he was doing. He stood up and waved to dispel any suspicion. As he crossed his yard, he saw Timmy was headed toward him, across Prickett Farm Road, so he waited. Timmy had begun to make a point of talking to him whenever their paths crossed.

"Hi," said Timmy as he reached Jonas.

"Hi," replied Jonas, noting that Timmy had taken in the mud on his pants and shoes. "I had a half day of school today."

"Lucky."

"You're home early."

"We get out a bit early on Wednesdays—some kids come to our school for religion classes. So on Wednesdays Sister Gertrude gives us a ton of homework. Plus I have to write sentences." Timmy grimaced.

"Sentences?"

"Well, one sentence twenty-five times: 'I will not speak in class unless Sister Gertrude has given me permission.' A long one. I'm lucky it's not fifty."

●

"We've got to get the city moving on this annexation," George Roper said to John Turnbull, his full-time, full-service lawyer. "Every property along Due West I can sell as commercial will make that sewer line more profitable. I'm going to have Sally arrange a lunch next week with the mayor. We need to figure out if any councilmen are going to be a problem. I want you to be there."

"No problem."

"How's it going with House?"

"He's in, no question. It's just a bit delicate. The property belonged to his wife's parents. He doesn't want to push too hard on the selling. She has a bit of an attachment to it."

"Understood. Some of these old families, you can't pry them off the land even if they're broke, which the Houses are not."

"Like the last of the Tutwilers?"

"Yep," Roper said, grinning, "like that fossil. Not that he's much older than me. He's just hanging on to another century."

"Well, once you convince the county to widen Due West and the state to extend Stumptown to the interstate, those troglodytes will wake up to the twentieth century."

●

It was getting late in the afternoon, and Lizzy no longer heard Sam's tractor. She didn't want to put off talking to him until another day, not when she had prepared herself to do it today. She walked over to the Tutwilers' house and knocked on the front door.

"Well hello, Lizzy," Sam said opening the door. "Come on in."

"Enjoying the beautiful weather today?" Lizzy asked as she stepped in.

"Sure am, although it means work. It's time to get planting."

"I've actually put in some spinach and peas."

"You've got a leg up on me. We're supposed to be getting some rain before the weekend."

"That would be about perfect timing. As long as we don't get any cold snaps."

"Nah, we're past that."

Whereas Lizzy lived in Sam's grandparents' house, Sam and Leona lived in his parents' house, which meant theirs was a bit more modern in design but still rather modest. Leona was seated in an armchair beside the unlit stone fireplace; the end table next to her littered with her necessities—water, pills, tissues, glasses, and magazines.

Lizzy bent over the chair to give Leona a gentle hug. "How are you doing?" she asked.

"I'm fine. I'm just worn out by this time of day—tired but not sleepy."

"Well I won't stay long," said Lizzy.

"Oh no, sweetie. It's so nice to see you. How have you been?"

"Oh, just fine," said Lizzy. "How are the kids?' she asked, which led to fifteen minutes or so of catching up that allowed Lizzy to warm up to her real topic of conversation.

"Sam, Leona, I've been talking to those folks who sent out the flyer months ago about George Roper planting houses on his property. They'd like those of us with land adjacent to his to meet with them."

"Agatha has been chewing my ear off nonstop about all this business," Sam answered, shaking his head with a smile. "Lizzy, I think you already know I'm not going to tell Roper what he can and can't do on his property. He owns it now, and no matter what my preference, I have no say so. If I believe it's my business to tell him what he should do with his land, then I better believe it would be okay for people to be telling me what to do with mine."

"I understand, Sam," Lizzy said, nodding. "But what Roper wants to do with his land won't end at his property line. We'll have a mini-city just across the creek. Maybe a mini-mart too. What he plans to do with his land will change our lives."

Sam smiled at her. "I remember when Uncle Dolan sold his share of the family homestead, excepting the house of course, to Roper. I was darn mad, but I held my tongue. I didn't have the money to buy it, so it wasn't my business. And then Uncle Dolan moved to town and started renting out the old place. I was steamed about that too. For a while we had one set of hippies living there after another. But soon you and Wes came along, and except for a few loud parties, I saw you were good neighbors, people who appreciated what this place has to offer."

He took a deep breath and exhaled slowly. "I'd rather it all stay like it is, but I think the change is inevitable. Our piece of the Garden is shrinking. I'm sorry to see it, but it's true. I was telling Jonas just today about my childhood, and it led me to thinking about how different the world will be for my grandchildren. Nature's bounty seemed to be without limit when I was a boy. But the world as I've known it is fading. I think the best we can do is hold onto our little piece of green oasis."

"You're probably right, Sam, that it's inevitable. But that's a self-fulfilling prophecy, isn't it?"

"I'll think about it, Lizzy. I'm pulled both ways." Sam's soft blue eyes went from Lizzy's to Leona's. "Who's to say what our kids will do with this land when we're gone? I hope that they'll want to hold onto it. This place has always anchored me; I'd be lost without it. I guess there are far too many people nowadays for everyone to have his own little piece of the earth." He sighed deeply. "Heck, the thought scares me." He looked down at his hands. "I'm a relict, Lizzy, just like those hemlocks at the pond."

Jonas looked at himself in the bathroom mirror. He had showered and put on clean clothes, which he had done largely to disguise the fact that he had been at the pond all morning. Besides a shower and clean clothes, though, he wasn't sure what else he could do to prepare for the evening. He wanted to look more grown up. At least that's what he thought he wanted. He wasn't sure. Most of his classmates seemed to obsess over this preoccupation, their appearance, and Jonas had thought their attention to this aspect of themselves somewhat inane. Now, however, he realized he had no idea how to improve upon his appearance even if he wanted to do so. He looked like an oversized kid. Not even a teenager. He combed his hair, brushed his teeth, shrugged at himself in the mirror, and headed back to his room.

"Maybe I should go too," Sylvia called to him from the bottom of the stairs.

Jonas stopped mid-step. "Why?"

"Well, I care about what's going on too."

Jonas walked to the top of the stairs. "I can tell you about it."

"You can, but will you?"

"Yes. I promise." He'd promise anything to keep her from going with him.

Sylvia looked up at him and after a moment said, "I'm very happy you're getting involved in this."

Jonas shrugged.

"It's good to have extracurricular activities on your college apps," she said.

"I have to finish a reading assignment for school," Jonas told her and walked back to his room. Jonas lay back on his bed and picked up the book he had been reading, one of a science fiction series he had read years ago. He already had read his assignment. He just wanted to escape his mother's nervous energy, her talk about college. Unlike his parents, he just didn't see why college had to be the central focus of his life. Why were they more concerned about his future than he was? He saw enough years ahead of him of working all the time like they did—why would he want to start now?

Lizzy pulled into the Meyers's driveway shortly before six thirty. She hoped Jonas would just appear at the door, ready to go. No such luck though. She would have to go knock on the door and have a polite chat with Sylvia, Phil, or both. She had already had enough conversation for the day, and the day wasn't over. She had even managed to talk about the weather, imagine that. Her younger self thought talking about the weather was something adults did when they had nothing to say, but then she hadn't appreciated that the weather was an experience people shared whether they wanted to or not.

Sylvia opened the door. Her neat and trim appearance was a stark contrast to Jonas's. Her dark hair, sporting a few gray strands, was pulled back into a tidy twist, and her dark brown eyes were alert. Reading glasses hung from a beaded chain necklace. She was in her work attire—a mid-calf maroon skirt and a rich fuchsia blouse.

"Lizzy, hello. Come on in. How are you? It was so nice of you to invite Jonas to the meeting tonight. Do you think they'll really want a teenager there? We weren't planning to go ourselves—not that we don't agree with the effort. I guess we don't have any good excuse, do we? We just feel awkward because we feel a bit like outsiders. But I guess that's silly, isn't it?"

"I'm sure Jonas will be welcome," Lizzy selected the easiest question to answer. The last thing she wanted to do was escort the entire Meyers family to this meeting.

"Well, let us know what's going on—maybe we'll go to the next one. Well, at least one of us will go. It seems like one of us is always working late."

Lizzy forced a smile and nodded. "Where's Jonas?" she asked. "We should get going."

"In his room, as usual. Jonas!" Sylvia called up the stairs. "Jonas! Ms. Lizzy is here."

Jonas came lumbering down the stairs. Lizzy winked at him.

"We won't be late," Lizzy told Sylvia, and she and Jonas headed out the door.

The meeting was being held in the community room of Centreville's public library. When Lizzy and Jonas arrived, there were a few dozen people in the room, some seated, some milling around, chatting. Lizzy looked around the room for Russ but didn't see him. The rest of Saturday's group was there. Doug was standing at the front of the room and within moments projected his voice above the murmur of conversation, "Good evening, everyone. Let's get started please."

Folding chairs had been arranged in several short rows. Lizzy headed toward one of the back rows, and Jonas followed her.

"We have a lot of business to cover tonight before the library closes," said Doug. "First, I'd like to welcome our guest and any newcomers to this meeting of the Greenspace Alliance of Ware County."

Lizzy shifted in her seat. The group had a name.

Doug made some announcements and then said, "I'd like to introduce our special guest, Dr. Clayton, from the biology department of South Fork State University."

Dr. Clayton stood up to polite applause. He was a slim man in his mid-thirties with unruly sandy blond hair and wire-rimmed glasses. His dress was casual—a plaid shirt with the sleeves rolled up and drab olive pants.

"Dr. Clayton, please," Doug motioned him toward the small podium. "Dr. Clayton is here to speak to us about Bartons Mill Pond and the surrounding area."

"Please, call me Dave," said Dr. Clayton as he approached the podium. Once he was situated behind it, he transformed into a professor. "Well, as I'm sure you all feel, Bartons Mill Pond is quite a unique treasure to this part of the Piedmont. Underlain by an outcrop of granitic rock that has created one of the few natural year-round lentic, that is, standing water, environments in this area, the pond most likely has persisted here at least since the Pleistocene, that is, the Ice Age."

A scraping sound drew everyone's attention to the doorway, and the woman who had dragged the chair waved an apology to the group.

Dave continued. "The granitic rock apparently extends deeply and extensively underground, and in doing such has a great stabilizing effect on the temperature of the pond's waters as well as the immediate vicinity. This temperature effect adds to the site's species composition and diversity. What makes the pond and its adjacent terrestrial environment *extra*-ordinary is its spatial heterogeneity—by that I mean in this small area we see some very different microhabitats."

Dave motioned to Doug to turn on the slide projector, and a map of the pond and its surroundings appeared on the screen behind him. "The northern shore of the pond, essentially north of Narrow Passage Creek and west of Mill Pond Creek, the land to be developed, that is, hosts an assemblage of plants typical to our area." He turned sideways and used a yardstick to point out the area he had just identified. "Along the pond's southern shore, however, is the bluff, created by the granite outcrop, and it houses a plant community typically found in cooler climates west and north of here. The southwestern corner of the pond," he pointed with the ruler, "is relatively shallow, most likely again owing to the underlying granite."

Dave turned back toward the audience and held the yardstick over his shoulder. "It is the southwestern shore area that can be considered a wetland, or marsh. It's an excellent habitat for amphibians—frogs and salamanders. You see here some typical wetland vegetation—ferns and rushes and the like. From this southwestern edge Narrow Passage Creek runs westward through a remnant of a rather typical bottomland forest. But again, it is the great diversity of community types within such a small area that isn't typical. And because the pond is still largely forested along its banks—and its water level doesn't fluctuate very much with season—it is an oasis for terrestrial wildlife as well."

Lizzy glanced over at Jonas. He seemed to be listening intently. She was glad he had decided to come, that she had thought of asking him.

"As you probably know, Mill Pond Creek enters the pond at its northeast corner and exits it at its southeast corner." Dave turned and pointed to the creek's path with the yardstick and then continued to point out areas of the pond as he spoke of them. "The eastern section of the pond is relatively deep. Along the southern shore the pond grades fairly gently between the two extremes. The depth along the northern shore appears to be pretty uniform. I doubt, though, that anything close to a bathymetric map—like an underwater topographic map—exists for the pond. At least I haven't been able to locate one."

Dave then shared a dozen or so slides of plants, indicating where they would be found in relation to the pond. When he finished, he looked around the room. "Are there any questions?" he asked, leaning the yardstick against the podium.

There was some rustling and throat clearing. The audience seemed to need a moment to collect itself.

"I gather what you are saying," said a man sitting a few rows in front of Lizzy and Jonas, "is that because the land north of the pond is not a wetland it can't be protected as part of the wetland."

"I'm not an expert on wetland delineation, but I am pretty sure it would not be considered part of the wetland in terms of any sort of protection," Dave said shaking his head.

Mike sprang up. "We've been investigating wetlands' protection and have already determined that the existing regulations are not a viable means for combating this project."

Seymour raised his hand and Dave nodded at him. "Do you feel, given what you know about the pond and its surroundings, that we could make a case that the area should be preserved based on any rare or threatened or endangered species that occurs there?"

"Well, as I said, some of the vegetation is uncommon for the area, but it isn't for the state. There are some rather uncommon plants that have been collected around the pond in the past—they are in the university's herbarium—and in the recent past I've collected a salamander species not common in this area." Dave moved away from the podium and closer to the assembled audience. "It is possible that with closer examination one might find some threatened or endangered species—likely a plant species if so, maybe an insect. That wouldn't guarantee protection, though. There are certain criteria the population would have to meet—for one, that a viable population, as opposed to a few individuals, is present."

"Can you say the proposed housing development will cause the pond and the wetland to deteriorate?" asked the woman who earlier had dragged the chair. Lizzy vaguely recognized her but wasn't sure from where—the hospital, perhaps, or some group from college days?

"I would think that the integrity of the entire area likely would be compromised, although that isn't a quantitative assessment," Dave

81

said. "I don't know what the development plans look like exactly, but general habitat deterioration may be pretty pervasive. Any harm to the pond, the creeks, the bottomland may not be immediate or dramatic. The changes, the losses, would be gradual—fewer salamanders, fewer frogs, turtles lost to cars; maybe loss of an aquatic insect species or two that are particularly sensitive to changes in water quality; maybe loss of some less common herbaceous species as foot traffic increases around the pond—and so on."

Lizzy thought back to Jonas saying just that earlier in the day.

Dave had paused but then continued. "Deterioration of habitat is often marked by a loss of species diversity. At first it's noticeable only to those paying attention. But I haven't seen the actual plan for the development," he reiterated, "and that would be needed for a more accurate assessment of the development's impact."

"We've been trying to get the plat from the county office," said Doug, stepping toward the podium. "Legally we should have access to it. We've been told the final plat is not yet available. Our suspicion is that the plans have been drawn, and Roper is waiting for the right moment to move his plans through the process as quickly as possible so that we won't have much time to act."

"We need to apply pressure on the county to bring this out into the open," called a wiry older man, his voice shaking. Murmurings arose from the audience.

Doug raised his hand to regain the floor. "Dr. Clayton, Dr. Dave, we will continue to work on getting the plat. From what we understand, the state's department of natural resources can't go ahead with any sort of site assessment unless its requested by the county or landowners. Can we, as a citizens' group, push forward on our own assessment? I'm afraid plans to develop will move faster than any effort to protect the property. We would like to make a case for preserving this area."

"Well, you could document the diversity—make an inventory of species present in the different habitat types in and around the pond. I suggest you get specialists to verify identifications, particularly of any species that might be considered rare."

"Might you be willing to help us get started on that?" asked Doug.

"I figured I was being recruited when I agreed to come tonight," he said, grinning. "I think a lot can be done quickly. I probably can enlist a few of my colleagues and some of our students to do the inventory—"

"I'd like to help," Mike called out.

"Well sure," said Dave. "A few people who know the site well would be helpful."

Lizzy nudged Jonas. "You certainly do," she whispered. "Maybe you can help out."

Jonas shrugged.

"There is the problem of access though," Dave continued. "We used to park along Due West and walk the old dirt road that crosses the property, Roper's property. No one was ever out there. But now a gate has gone up on that road, so I'm hesitant about gaining access that way—and with a larger group, especially given our purpose, crossing Roper's land may not be a wise choice."

"Lizzy," Doug said, "could they walk in from your place? You're close."

Lizzy felt every pair of eyes in the room turn toward her. Put on the spot, Lizzy uttered, "Uhm, sure." Now she was in even deeper. It felt as if she were allowing her world to be invaded instead of protected.

The meeting continued with a variety of updates, most of which Lizzy had already heard. The discussion regarding wastewater issues really got some members of the audience riled.

As the meeting broke up, Russ joined Lizzy and Jonas.

"Well hello Jonas," said Russ, extending his hand. "Glad to see you here."

Lizzy realized it should have occurred to her that Russ knew Jonas.

"Hello, Mr. Henderson," Jonas responded, looking down as he awkwardly shook Russ's hand.

"Are you escorting Ms. Lizzy this evening?"

Lizzy flashed a warning at Russ; she knew he was teasing her, but Jonas might not realize that. "And when did you get here?' she asked Russ with a note of reprimand in her voice.

"I've been here; I just stood in back. Got here a bit late. I had to give Melissa Drummond a ride—her battery was dead. You know Melissa," he said to Lizzy just as Melissa, with her wavy auburn hair and hazel eyes, slid beside Russ, so close her arm grazed his. Russ shifted his weight slightly to more neutral territory.

God, thought Lizzy, is he seeing Melissa now?

"Well hello Lizzy. Didn't know you'd be here."

"Life is full of surprises, isn't it?" Lizzy responded. "You know, Jonas knows Bartons Mill Pond pretty well," she said, looking at Russ. "I think he'd be a big help to the university group. He seems to know every plant and bird out there."

"Oh no, not at all," said Jonas.

"Well, you spend a lot of time at the pond, and you probably see things other people don't notice if they're there just for the day."

"I think that's a great idea," said Russ. "I'm planning on helping too." He smiled at Lizzy, knowing that she might be less than thrilled about being pulled into the group's plans even more. "Let's go get this all worked out with Dr. Dave."

•   •   •

Lizzy got up early on Saturday to make muffins. She put out coffee cups, poured a pot of coffee into a carafe, and made a second pot. When Jonas arrived, she asked him to pen up Clem and Pete. Everyone else seemed to arrive at once. There was Dave, two of his colleagues, Barbara and Michael, and half a dozen students that came with them. Mike came out with Russ. The biologists had brought clip boards, field guides, string, measuring tapes, wading boots, nets, and plastic bottles.

They all walked along the creek to avoid the attention of Agatha Prickett. Unknown to them, however, Agatha was already on patrol and had taken note of the unfamiliar cars passing her house and pulling into Lizzy's driveway. She knew something was up. She'd have to give Lizzy a call.

It was a clear morning, and the green seemed particularly vibrant after Friday's gentle rain. The group moved slowly along the creek as someone or other stopped to examine every plant along the way. Jonas kept his distance but paid close attention to the conversations.

When they reached the end of the clearly defined channel that was Narrow Passage Creek, Dave suggested that they divide into three approximately equal groups. Barbara, who studied the microscopic plants and animals that lived in freshwater, gathered the waders, nets, and plastic bottles and headed for the pond itself with Russ, Mike, and two students. Lizzy joined Dave and two students and headed to the base of the bluff. Dave explained to her that they would divide the bluff into three or four zones, starting with the narrow strip of ground along the base of the bluff, moving up its vertical face, and ending with the vegetation on top of the bluff. They would create an inventory, or list, of plants within each zone. The widest zone would be the face of the bluff that was out of their reach; lichens and mosses in a variety of shades of green to gray and yellow grew here. Lizzy felt she was of little assistance beyond helping to set the strings that marked the zones and writing down information they called to her—often names they had to spell out. Beyond recognizing a fern from a moss and these from lichens, she hadn't a clue.

Jonas chose to work with Michael's group. They were making an inventory of vegetation along transects—corridors they created by stretching string between stakes. They started at the ambiguous boundary between the bottomland forest and wetland, where trees and bushes thinned and graded into sporadic red maples and clumps of dried stems and blades, and stretched the strings to the edge of the pond and head of the creek. Jonas saw that the ferns that had been curled earlier in the week were already splayed fronds.

Spring's green was emerging amid last year's matted growth. Because it was early in the season, Jonas didn't recognize many of the young plants. Michael and his students, however, were astutely identifying plants from the earliest leaves sprouting from the ground, and Jonas was eagerly learning from them. He forgot himself, and soon he was moving with the group from one plant to the next, learning from Michael and his students where else these plants occurred and what other plants they resembled, learning pieces of each species' life history. He began offering his own observations about plants he had seen around the pond and creek.

"Looks like some wood anemone," Jonas said, pointing out a small plant and squatting down. "Maybe—the leaves are usually more deeply notched, though, not so evenly serrated. I'm not sure," he said as he regarded the leaf that rested gently on his finger. He looked up at Sara, who had been recording a plant on a clip board, and she was smiling at him.

She squatted down. "I believe it's dwarf ginseng," she said, flipping through her field guide, then showing him the picture. "Good spot. So," she said after adding the ginseng to her clip board, "are you going to be a botanist?"

A smile spread across Jonas's face, and he became aware of an unfamiliar feeling—it wasn't just that he was enjoying himself, but he was enjoying himself with other people, and they seemed to be interested in what he had to say.

The groups began to converge around noon.

"The bluff face is covered in mosses and lichens," Dave said. "I do reasonably well with ferns and even some mosses after years of chasing herps, but I am far from an expert. And I know next to nothing about lichens."

"We'll be in trouble if the fate of this area rests on a lichen," Michael said. "People get rankled over endangered birds. I would like to come back soon to explore the bottomland forest, though," he added, looking at Lizzy. She nodded her assent. "It appears pretty typical for the area, actually pretty healthy and diverse, but I'd like to take a closer look." Michael looked to Jonas. "Would you like to help me with that?"

"Definitely," Jonas replied without hesitation.

"Short of a more intensive effort," said Barbara, "I think it's safe to assume the pond has a typical bass and sunfish community with some catfish—at least that's what we've seen. We need to check whether Bob has collected out here. He's an entomologist," she explained to those in the group who didn't know him. "Insects."

"What about birds and mammals?" asked Jonas.

"Given their mobility, I doubt we need to include them in the inventory—whatever occurs here would occur in the wider area," explained Dave. "Although that's not to say this isn't a highly utilized feature in their environment."

"I think the pond also attracts migrants," Jonas said. "There was a rough-legged hawk here all winter. And early last spring I saw a marsh wren."

Russ looked at his typically reticent student with surprise. "Perhaps you could put together a list of what you've seen here, Jonas," Russ suggested.

Jonas nodded in response, and with that they all started to head back to Lizzy's. Jonas walked with the group of students, listening to their conversation but largely remaining silent. He had retracted from his expansive moment but was still savoring the experience.

The biologists, Russ, and Mike walked in a group and discussed how best to compile the information, including data Dave had already collected. They also talked about additional trips to the pond.

Lizzy took up the rear of the group. She had always loved the delicate beauty of ferns and mosses; now, after looking at them closely, she appreciated them even more. The morning had passed quickly and pleasantly; she didn't regret having the group assemble at her home or going out with them.

Russ dropped back after a while to join her. "I'm glad you've involved Jonas in doing this. He was my student last year, and I never got much out of him. It would have been easy to think there was nothing going on there—except that he aced his exams. But I couldn't get a word out of him in class unless I called on him."

"I guess Jonas doesn't try to impress anyone, not even his teachers."

"No, I'd say he goes too far in the other direction."

· · ·

Phil was out digging in the middle of their front yard when Jonas returned. "How did things go?"

Jonas had been turning over his full and satisfying morning in his mind. "Fine," he replied. Then he efforted to say more. "I'm going out with the botanists again next weekend."

"Oh yeah? That sounds great."

"I haven't had any lunch," Jonas said and headed to the house. Phil followed him.

"How many of you were there?" asked Phil as he got a drink.

"Um, about a dozen," said Jonas as he looked in the refrigerator. "One of my science teachers came."

"Any other teenagers?"

"No. College students, though."

Phil nodded. "Were they friendly?"

"Yeah."

"Did you learn anything?

"Yeah. Lots."

Jonas felt Phil watching him as he pulled out the makings for a sandwich. He knew his father wanted to know more, but he wasn't sure he wanted to share more. To say more would encourage his father to ask more, and Jonas preferred to keep his thoughts to himself—at least that's what was comfortable.

Phil finally tapped the counter with his hand. "Well, when you're done eating, how about helping me outside? I told your mother we'd get that flower bed prepared for her today."

"Sure," Jonas said.

That night in his room Jonas picked up the book he had been reading but soon put it down. He found himself thinking about the hawk that spent the winter at the pond. He didn't liken himself to a hawk, but he thought about how he tended to remain on his own perch, not interacting with his classmates. He understood how it had come to be like this—not knowing what to say to other people and consequently not speaking to the point that most people thought he had nothing to say—but he couldn't see how to undo it. Where would he begin, what would he share? How could he tell kids at school that when he touched a leaf or watched a deer or listened to a cardinal or smelled the fruit of a spicebush that he felt connected to the world, whereas when he was at school, he just felt isolated. That would just convince them he was weird, and maybe he was.

He got up from the bed, sat on the floor, and then reached under the bed. He pulled out the box in which he kept his notebooks. In one he recorded general observations and in others he kept lists of species he had seen and when and where. He opened up his plant notebook and started to record the plants he had seen that morning. But then he put down the notebook, got up, and went to the child's desk he had outgrown long ago. He found an old spiral notebook still full of blank sheets, picked up his pencil from the floor, sat back on his bed, and began to write.

Looking at the pond, no one could guess its depth or tell what dwelt below its surface.

Challenges

Going to school was daily torture. Every morning the sweet air bid Timmy to set off on an exploration rather than to go sit in a classroom. His mother seemed to know this and had clamped down hard to keep him focused on school. Not that she needed to—Sister Gertrude held fast against any springy impulses.

At least the end of the school year was in sight. Timmy was in countdown mode to the day that he would be released. He couldn't wait. He was itching for it. He had rewrapped the tape on his bike's handlebars. He had cleaned out his tackle box and rearranged his rubber worms, spinner baits, and hooks again and again. He had changed the line on his reel. He had stocked up on pellets for his pellet gun, and he had bought a few rolls of film for the small plastic camera he always carried with him on his adventures. Last Saturday he had lain on his belly on the bluff, searching for the shadows of large bass in the pond below.

But this morning he was on his way to school. His father loaded him and his sisters into the car and dropped them off at St. Xavier's on his way to work. They were early, as were many other kids, and milled around the school yard until Sister Catherine opened the doors and sharply clapped her hands.

Sister Gertrude was in a particularly sour mood. She picked on Mary Wilson until she made Mary cry. Knowing he could be a lightning rod on days like today, Timmy was determined to lie low. He didn't want to do anything that would risk being held after school. He locked his jaws together so no utterance beyond his control would escape him, would work its way through his lips. NO. Not today, a Friday. He was going to stay out of trouble. If his mother had to wait for him after school, she would ground him for the weekend. He couldn't risk that, not for anyone or anything.

If he could make it through the morning—keep his head down and his attention on his work, not look out the window, not talk to another kid, not blurt out any smart answers, he would make it to lunch. The afternoon should be easier. Sister Gertrude hadn't returned their compositions yet this week, which probably meant she would return them after lunch. Then she would probably tell them about another saint—he usually had no problems during these lessons; he listened or at least could pretend to while he daydreamed.

Timmy had written a heartfelt composition on a topic that troubled him deeply. His compositions were the only thing that saved him from Sister Gertrude's wrath. Not that he was a bad student. He just had a hard time controlling those urges that made him do or say things— like last week when he chalked a cross on Ryan's seat. He sort of knew what would happen, but he just wanted Ryan to understand that perfection wasn't always having the cleanest, neatest uniform. But then Ryan was called to the board to work on a math problem, and everyone saw the chalk cross on Ryan's behind and started giggling. Sister Gertrude had called his parents in for a conference; he had to sit there while they agreed that he did not exhibit the appropriate degree of self-control for his age. Now he had to work on his promise to exhibit greater mastery of self.

Timmy made it through the morning, and that afternoon Sister Gertrude, to Timmy's disappointment, called on Ryan to read his composition to the class.

Ryan got up from his desk, neatly pushed his chair in, and walked to the front of the room. Retrieving his paper from Sister Gertrude with a slight bow, he turned toward the class, straightened his tie, and smiled at everyone as he announced his title, "Cleanliness IS Next to

Godliness." Ryan's looked directly at Timmy before he started reading.

"What does the saying 'cleanliness is next to Godliness' really mean? Does it mean you should wash behind your ears? In a way it does. . . ."

Timmy stopped listening to Ryan. He had to pretend to listen, but he thought about what he would do after school, imagined exploring an unknown wilderness, and waited for Ryan to stop droning on and on.

When Ryan finished reading his composition, Sister Gertrude returned everyone else's paper. Timmy's eyes ran over his, although he almost knew it by heart.

Challenges to Faith

There are times when things happen to you in your life, or to the people around you, that may cause you to wonder whether Jesus is really there, whether He really loves you. It may be something small, like losing all the money you just got paid for your paper route, or it may be something very serious, like someone young dying.

When things like this happen, you may question if Jesus, if He really loves you and if you've been virtuous and have shown Him that you love Him, is really there. You may wonder why God would let bad things happen. You may become full of doubt. You may think you have cause to. But letting your faith waiver is dangerous!

Faith is a gift that God has given us. The only true work we must do is to believe in Him. With this faith we can please God, showing Him that we put all our trust in Him. It is through our faith in Him that we can see His works. If we don't believe in Him, we don't see that He brings us the spring's flowers, the food that we eat, the parents who take care of us. And if we don't see that He brings us all these things—and more—we take them for granted. If we don't have faith in Him, we won't see His works around us, and our soul would despair. For what purpose can there be in anything if Jesus is not there? It is through faith in Jesus that we know everlasting life.

Faith would not be faith if we are always given proof that Jesus is with us. Faith means belief in Jesus even when it seems He is not there. We can be thankful that Jesus is always ready to accept us into His arms, to forgive us our sins, and let us receive His grace.

But why do we have times when we are full of doubt? Why do they happen? Does Jesus cause them to test us, to test our faith?

And what if we fail? What if we don't have true faith in Jesus, His words, and His works? What happens to those who do not accept Him? Do they live in a world without wonders? Do they live in a world without meaning? Do they live in a world without salvation? Do they lose any chance of God's grace?

Beneath Timmy's composition, Sister Gertrude had written, "'For it is by grace you have been saved, through faith—and this not from yourselves, it is the gift of God—not by works, so that no one can boast' (Ephesians 2:8–9). The only way to heaven is through Jesus; those who do not see this truth cannot dwell with the Lord. Do not doubt this."

Sister Gertrude had started talking about Saint Jerome, the patron saint of translators, librarians, and encyclopedists as well as Bible scholars, schoolchildren, and students. Timmy sighed. Saint Jerome had to be boring in capital letters. He had had a vision as a young man that caused him to devote his life to God and the study of the Bible. Most of the saints had visions, thought Timmy. He wondered if he would have a vision, if Jesus or a saint or an angel would talk to him. Many of the saints had to wait until they were older until they had a vision. Timmy wished he could have his now. His ears picked up the word "lion," so he returned to listening about how St. Jerome had removed a thorn from a lion's paw. Then Sister Gertrude went on to talk about how St. Jerome's most important contribution to Christianity was his translation of the Bible, the Old Testament, from its original Hebrew. Like Timmy thought from the outset, St. Jerome didn't lead a very exciting life.

When Timmy got home, he quickly changed out of his uniform, grabbed his field bag—an old army bag his grandfather had given him—and slipped out of the house before his mother could insist he take Chris with him. He knew he might get in trouble for sneaking out, but he would never get to where he was headed if he had to take Chris—it was a long walk.

Timmy ran up Prickett Farm Road, which was more of a shared driveway with the Meyers than a road. Timmy had always wondered if Mrs. Prickett had paid to have the road named after her. At the corner he crossed Narrow Passage and walked west along the edge of the Tutwilers' field. He was headed for the old wagon road that ran through a band of forest between fields. He walked with his eyes scouring the ground for treasures, but it was covered by a thick carpet of small red and purple wildflowers. He took his camera out of his satchel, lay on his stomach, and took a photograph. Then he resumed his hunt for some collectible treasure—a shed antler, turtle shell, skull, bone, tooth, or even a feather to add to his collection of miscellaneous animal parts.

Leaving the roadside just short of the wagon road, Timmy roamed along the border of field and forest, looking for deer trails and antler sheds he might have missed on earlier walks. Timmy could see the deer had been browsing on young shoots along the forest's edge. He stopped to study a patch of ground that looked like it had been scratched clear, probably by turkeys, and then he continued his journey. Eventually he followed a deer trail through the thick undergrowth that bordered the field. He stepped carefully to avoid some emerging poison ivy but didn't escape the blackberry vines that scratched his hands and bare forearms.

Once he was beyond the border of brambles, the woods became more hospitable. The narrow band of forest on both sides of the overgrown wagon road had been left intact, so mature oaks and hickories made for an easy passage. Timmy often came here to explore; the old road and large trees allowed him to imagine earlier days, when wagons had used the road, and before then even, before the land was settled and the forests cut for farming. He picked up a stout fallen branch, broke off its thinner end, and proceeded with his half sword, half walking stick. With the spring flush of leaves, the ground was dappled with light. Spring wildflowers, pink and white, grew in patches, and Timmy stopped to take some pictures of these. The small white flower had delicate leaves that reminded him of mittens. As the summer progressed the canopy of leaves would close and shade the woods and road, making this sliver of forest a cool retreat from the fields that surrounded it.

Toward the end of the road was a tall, old windowless barn that belonged to either Mr. Tutwiler or Mr. House. Timmy wasn't sure. He had never seen anyone there. It was apparent the barn hadn't been used in years: it was an old tobacco-drying barn, and he knew Mr. Tutwiler didn't grow tobacco. The wood was a well-weathered gray, and what had once been a red metal roof was now rust colored.

The barn stood not twenty yards from the edge of the woods. Timmy had never been inside, but today the door was open, and the barn seemed to call to him. He walked up to the door and peered inside. Before his eyes could adjust to the darkness, he felt something moving toward him and jumped back reflexively.

A dark-haired, blue-eyed boy, several inches taller and at least a year or two older, stepped out of the barn.

Timmy recognized the boy. He had seen him riding his bike on the road once but didn't know him. "Hi," Timmy greeted him. "You live here?"

The boy smirked. "Nah, I live in a house."

Timmy flushed. "I meant is this barn yours?"

"No. It belongs to Mr. House." The boy cocked his head. "I've seen you before, on the road. But you're never on the school bus."

"My parents drive me to school. I go to St. Xavier's."

"Oh, there."

"What do you mean?" asked Timmy defensively, sizing up the older boy.

"Nothing," the boy replied matter-of-factly. "Just, well, it's a religious school. I don't think I'd want to go to a religious school. Where do you live?"

"Prickett Farm Road," Timmy said coolly.

"Oh, where that big kid gets off the bus. Is he weird or what?"

"He's not weird," Timmy defended Jonas. "He's just kind of quiet."

"Yeah, he never talks to anyone. So, what are you doing here anyway?" the boy asked.

Although some of what the boy had said seemed unfriendly to Timmy, his tone wasn't. "I was just looking around. Where do you live?" Timmy asked.

"Down Narrow Passage, almost at Stumptown Road. We just moved there at the beginning of the year."

"Oh, I don't usually ride all the way down there—my paper route goes the other way, down Bartons Mill Road."

"I tried to get a paper route, but this other kid already has the one on Stumptown and my end of Narrow Passage. What's your name?"

"Timmy. Yours?"

"Matt."

They both looked down and toed the ground a bit.

"You fish?" Matt broke the silence.

"Yeah, sure."

"I have permission to fish in Mr. Horace's—Mr. House's—pond whenever I want. He's my mother's cousin or something."

"Oh yeah?" said Timmy with envy. He had never fished in the pond on Mr. House's property. Well, he had never even seen it.

"Yeah. You want to come over some time and go fishing?" Matt offered.

"Sure," Timmy said, trying but unable to hide his enthusiasm. "How about tomorrow?"

"Can't. Have to go see my grandparents."

Timmy nodded in sympathy.

"How about Sunday morning?" suggested Matt.

"Can't. Have to go to church."

"Yeah, my parents make me go sometimes. We're Methodists, though." Matt furrowed his brow. "Do you really believe all that stuff they teach you?"

"What do you mean?"

"Like a priest can forgive your sins and they go away."

"They don't just go away. You say a prayer for forgiveness, and you have to be truly sorry."

"Same difference."

"No, it's not," Timmy held. "You also have to do penance, whatever the priest tells you."

"Whatever," said Matt, dismissing the issue. "Can you go fishing after church?"

It was late Saturday afternoon before Timmy was able to go collect payment on his paper route. As usual, he left Ms. Lizzy's house for last because she always invited him in and offered him something to drink and often some sort of snack. When he turned in at her driveway, he saw Jonas disappearing into the woods behind her house. Instead of going to the kitchen door, Timmy dropped his bike and followed Jonas. He found him sitting on the bank of the creek.

"Hey Jonas," Timmy said, putting his satchel on the ground. Jonas nodded a greeting, and Timmy began to hunt around for a stick. He then poked the stick into the stream and began to disassemble a wad of leaves that had accumulated between a dead branch and some rocks.

"Don't do that," Jonas said gently.

Timmy stopped. "Why not?"

"Lots of insects live in there." Jonas reached into the stream and lifted a small stack of leaves from the jam. "Some use the leaves for food, which helps break the leaves down." He carefully lifted one leaf at a time. A few leaves in he pointed to some tiny worm-like creatures.

"What are those things?" asked Timmy.

"They're larvae. I think they're midges—a kind of small fly."

"They are small. Have you ever seen some of those hellgrammites? I've collected them for fishing. They can get really big. They turn into those giant dobsonflies."

"Yeah, dobsonflies, dragonflies, mayflies—several different kinds of insects live in streams while they're developing." Jonas reached into the cool waters of the creek, pulled out a relatively flat rock, and turned it over. Several broad, flattened, dark insects with long, delicate tails scattered.

"I think they're mayfly nymphs," said Jonas, and gently replaced the rock. He then picked up another rock, and for a while he and Timmy examined the undersides of rocks.

Clouds had begun to gather and block the sun. With wet hands and sleeves, Timmy began to get cold. "I better go. I still have to finish collecting for my paper route." As he picked up his army bag, his camera fell out and hit the ground. Timmy snatched it up.

"Dag!"

"Is it broken?"

Timmy looked it over. "No," he replied, relieved. "I think I have some really good pictures on this roll."

"Of what?"

"Well, there's a bass I caught. There are also some flowers—and some deer that were holding still. It's hard to get good animal shots."

"Do the fish hold still?"

Timmy grinned. "Not always. But I have taken some really good ones. You want to see them sometime?"

Jonas shrugged. "Yeah. Sure."

"Anytime you want," Timmy said, pleased. He put the camera back into to his bag. "See you round," he added and then left.

Timmy hurried through the woods to Ms. Lizzy's kitchen door and knocked. Clem and Pete arrived at the door first.

"Ah, the disappearing boy," Lizzy said as she opened the storm door, letting Pete and Clem out, Timmy in. "I saw your bike in the driveway."

"I was down at the creek—Jonas is there and was showing me some bugs."

"That Jonas is a regular wildlife encyclopedia. School's out soon, I suppose."

"Five more weeks."

"That's early"

"Not early enough for me."

"We used to go until the end of June."

Timmy didn't say anything. He had heard the same from his parents.

"Have any plans for the summer?" Lizzy asked.

"Not really."

"So, it might get pretty boring?"

"No way!"

Lizzy smiled. "How about something to drink?" she offered.

"Would hot chocolate be too much trouble?" Timmy asked. "I'm a bit cold . . . I got kind of wet."

"No problem at all."

"Thank you, ma'am."

"Timmy, you don't need to call me ma'am," Lizzy told him as she set some water to heat. "Being called ma'am makes me feel so old."

"Yes, m—Ms. Lizzy."

While the water was heating, Lizzy put some nuts in a bowl and placed them and his money on the counter. Timmy climbed up onto a stool.

Sitting at the counter, Timmy alternated between blowing on his hot chocolate and eating nuts. Below, CB was sniffing his sneakers and pant legs. Timmy was debating whether to ask Ms. Lizzy a question that had been on his mind since the other day. There was no other adult he could think of to ask—certainly not his parents or Sister Gertrude.

"Ms. Lizzy," Timmy ventured, "I know you don't go to church and all, but do you believe in the story of the Garden of Eden?"

Shit, thought Lizzy. Why did Timmy always ask her questions like these? Last week it was the "why God lets bad things happen to good people" conversation. That was painful. Well, she had a good idea why Timmy asked her. Still, she wondered whether it was healthy for these types of questions to occupy the mind of a ten-year-old to the extent they occupied Timmy's. She couldn't be insincere in her answer, though—she did believe in honesty.

"Well Timmy," she replied cautiously, "I'm not sure what you're asking."

Timmy struggled to say what he meant. "Well, in the Garden all was perfect—God and Adam and Eve lived in harmony, and all Adam and Eve had to do was trust Him. But then they disobeyed God and that mistake changed everything. Now we all carry that sin."

"Well Timmy, I have problems with that original sin idea. I just have a hard time believing God would give us only one chance to get things right—it seems pretty harsh. Why should we be punished throughout our history?"

"Because we're all children of Adam and Eve, and when they ate from the Tree of Knowledge, they changed what Mankind would be forever. They brought sin and death and corruption into the world."

Lizzy looked into Timmy's penetrating green eyes and considered how to answer. "We do seem to succumb to the same failings generation after generation. . . . But in the end, Timmy, I believe we just have to be concerned with what we ourselves do in the world." She hesitated, questioning if she should say anything more, if she were stepping over some line.

Timmy peered into his nearly empty cup of hot chocolate, the issue unresolved. "We're supposed to obey—our parents, the Sisters, God's will. But we're also supposed to use our freedom to make good choices, to accept God's grace. Sometimes it just feels like there are so many people I'm supposed to listen to that there's no room to make choices—not to mention we already have the biggest strike against us."

What a weight this boy carries, thought Lizzy.

As if he suddenly remembered something, Timmy picked up his money and slipped off the stool. "I better go. I have chores to do—and I guess I've already been gone a long time. Thanks for the hot chocolate, m—Ms. Lizzy," he added as he closed the door behind him.

As Timmy mounted his bike, he glanced back toward the creek. The sun had shifted into its late afternoon position, on its way to the end of the day. White puffy clouds were floating smoothly across the firmament. Above, the clouds were a shining white; below they had a pink–gray hue. Between the clouds, rays of light were streaming to the ground, and a beam of light illuminated the crape myrtle and the flowers Ms. Lizzy had planted over Happy's grave. From the ground, the light appeared to be radiating back upward, as if a reflection on the surface of water. The image seemed almost miraculous in its perfection.

Timmy fumbled in his sack and pulled out his camera. He quickly raised it to frame the image in the view finder, but before he could press the button to take the picture, the clouds had moved and the beam of light had disappeared.

Inside Lizzy was holding CB and stroking her head. Her eyes were on Timmy. Original sin, thought Lizzy. "What do you know about sin?" she asked CB. "You can't even imagine sin, and in that you are graced."

•   •   •

"Timothy James Donohue!" his mother's voice welcomed him when he walked in.

"Yes, mom?" He was clearly in trouble for being late—she had called him by his full name.

"I thought you told me you had no idea where my manicure set had gone to."

Timmy looked at the floor. Even worse.

"How come the nail clippers were in your tackle box, the tweezers stuck in a mound of glue on your desk, and the rest of the kit back in the bathroom?"

"I didn't know where it was when you asked," he offered.

"Don't add another lie to your list."

"Yes mom. I'm sorry. I'll put everything back."

"I already have. Go to your room until it's time for dinner."

Timmy went to the room he shared with Chris. He hadn't known where the kit was the other day when she had asked about it. Then he found it between the couch cushions. He realized he could use the tweezers to glue some teeth into a raccoon skull he had found so they wouldn't fall out, and he had just borrowed the finger nail clippers for his tackle box until he could buy his own the next time he got to go shopping in town. He intended to return the clippers after fishing with Matt Sunday afternoon. Saying sorry to his mom wasn't enough; meaning well didn't guarantee her forgiveness.

He sat on the edge of his bed, his legs extended, bouncing his heels on the floor. Sometimes it seemed so hard to do the right thing. In his own eyes, his choices didn't seem wrong, but his parents, and Sister Gertrude, seemed to have a whole different view. He wondered if it was the same for adults—whether they saw their own behavior differently from how God saw theirs. A lot of growing up seemed to be about learning what was expected of you. But Timmy wondered whether God really wanted obedience or whether adults just thought God wanted what they wanted. What was the point of having choice if there was only one right choice?

As decomposition advances, fluids will be leached into the surrounding environment, and an island of altered soil chemistry will be created around the remains. This stage may initially have an inhibitory effect on nearby vegetation, but later a surge of nutrients may lead to increased soil fertility for plants. A succession of fungal communities also can be observed in conjunction with changes to soil chemistry.

Earthworms

Lizzy looked out her kitchen window. Bumblebees were visiting the large, deep pink flowers that covered the Rose of Sharon. The sky had been a bit hazy, so when the wind picked up Lizzy thought a thunderstorm was on its way. But now the wind had settled down, at least taking with it some of the summer day's heat.

Lizzy headed out to the garden with a basket. She wanted to collect some zucchini, while it was still young and tender, to bring to the lab in the morning.

The garden was lush, at its zenith. Once again, her garden had delighted her by showing that seeds and hands, with soil, water, and sun, could yield a bounty. All her meals now included vegetables from her garden: sliced tomatoes drizzled with olive oil and topped with fresh basil; cucumbers in yogurt sprinkled with fresh dill; green beans and red pepper sautéed with garlic. She had been sending home bags of vegetables with Jonas and Timmy, taking grocery bags to the lab.

Evening was her favorite time to be in the garden. Not only was the day's heat past, but the long light of the summer evening connected her to a childhood sensation, long gone now, of unending possibilities. As a child, the long summer days that graded into nights full of stars inspired her to contemplate infinity.

The bumblebees were moving slowly but deliberately through the garden, systematically checking each blossom one last time before the day grew too late. Their movements were so less frenetic than the honeybees, whose buzzing made the air around the crape myrtle hum. Alice joined Lizzy to look under the broad, scratchy zucchini leaves in search of the dark green fruit. Lizzy also was looking for the flat-backed squash bugs that pierced the stems; squashing them had become a regular summer pastime. Alice studied the underside of leaves along with Lizzy as if there were something there for her too. Once finished with the zucchini plants, Lizzy moved over to check the cucumbers.

It seemed in just two days she had grown a new crop of weeds among the cucumber vines. She started pulling up weeds and shaking the soil, earthworms, and various soil dwellers free of the roots before tossing the weeds into a pile beside the garden. She brushed the disturbed soil smooth with her hand.

After picking a few cucumbers and tomatoes, Lizzy headed back toward the house with her basket. She saw that the haze had muted the setting sunlight, softening the landscape around her. She stopped to examine the pansies she had planted on Happy's grave. On her way to the garden she had noticed that they weren't doing well. The leaves had the dark green, flaccid appearance of overwatered plants. Now she noticed a few mushrooms growing among them. How peculiar; it was as if the ground here was damper than the rest of the yard. She would have to find something else to plant.

In the kitchen, Lizzy set the basket beside the sink and washed her hands and arms. She fetched a glass of iced tea but set it down after one sip and eyed it suspiciously. She went over to her shopping list and jotted down "<u>new</u> tea." Turning back toward the sink, she regarded the basket of vegetables sitting there.

Instead of returning to the sink, Lizzy headed across the living room and opened the door of the office. A hot, stale wall stopped her. Goodness did the room need some fresh air! She went to the double window that faced the road, tied back the heavy curtains, pulled up the blinds, and then, leaning over the bookcase, she tugged and coaxed the old windows until she overcame their resistance. She had a bit of an easier time with the window on the east side of the house, which was shaded by a large white oak. A slight breeze came through the window and lifted papers unaccustomed to movement from their resting place on the desk. But the breeze was light and the papers resettled quickly, some on the floor. Lizzy picked these up on her way to the chest of drawers beside the root cellar door, which had worked itself open again. She pulled a large spiraled pad from the top drawer of the chest and then rummaged for an ancient leather pencil case. She took them both and headed outside.

Setting the pad and case down on the back step, she went to the shed and fetched an old, and filthy, wire mesh chair and its matching small table. She returned to the kitchen for a towel and while there refilled her iced tea, to which she added a good amount of fresh lemon. She wiped down the small table and chair, fetched her pad and pencil case from the back step, and finally settled herself and her accoutrements. Lizzy opened up the pad—randomly toward the back—and then unzipped the case. Searching out the right pencil, she began to sketch the crape myrtle, the slight rise beside it, the downhill slope toward the woods behind them, the corner of the shed in the left foreground, the corner of the well house beyond it. She probably had made fifty sketches of this same spot over the years, through the seasons, at different times of day. Lizzy dug through the case repeatedly for the right shade of green—as with her childhood crayons, her greens were worn to nubs.

The colors of the scene changed before Lizzy in the fading light, and eventually she yielded to the growing darkness. Standing up she whistled for Pete and Clem, only to realize they were lying down right behind her chair. She carried the pad and pencils inside and set them on the table.

Lizzy washed the zucchini and left it in the drainer to dry; she put the cucumbers and tomatoes in the refrigerator. Locking the door, she was headed upstairs for a tick check and a shower. At the bottom of the steps she paused at the doorway to the office. Turning on the light, she saw papers had been blown to the floor again. The curtains hung heavily, though, and the coziness she had attributed to the room in the winter now seemed a weightiness—in the curtains, in the piles of papers and books, in the static arrangements of birds' nests and dried wildflowers, rocks and bones. She had let things lay now for years, untouched. Not tonight, not tomorrow, but soon, she would sort through these things and see what she was ready to let go.

• • •

Lizzy was up early, headed to work the morning shift. Gary White, who leased a good portion of Agatha Prickett's acreage, was already out with his tractor, a windrow of hay left to dry in his wake. Several compact, rectangular bales from an earlier cutting were lined up along the narrow dirt road that led to the barn, which sat behind the house and beyond the well-manicured lawn. Other than her and Gary, though, it seemed like the world was asleep.

Lizzy's thoughts drifted to the afternoon—after work she was headed to Donna and Doug's for another meeting. They were preparing for the trip to the state capitol; the prevailing sense that they had to pursue all options held sway among the group. In the end, Lizzy had agreed to go as the representative property owner. Perhaps it was those wheedling calls from Agatha, perhaps it was the serenity of her garden. At first she had resisted—resisted disrupting her pared-down lifestyle, resisted becoming even more involved—but now she was committed; they were counting on her.

Several pickup trucks pulled over on the shoulder of Due West Road brought Lizzy's attention back to the present. The rest of the world wasn't asleep.

Lizzy grabbed her sack of zucchini and headed for the lab. She greeted Kristen, set the bag of zucchini on the table in the break room, put her things in her locker, and headed into the lab.

Sheryl, one of the phlebotomists, was adding some samples to an already substantial line-up on the counter as Lizzy entered.

"What's up?" Lizzy asked.

"A nasty car accident on the bypass," said Sheryl.

Carolyn was already processing a sample. "I've got the most critical," she said looking up at Lizzy briefly. "But do a screen on those two samples from the accident, just in case. Sandy is on her way—she had a flat tire. I can tell it's going to be a wonderful day."

Lizzy gloved her hands, picked up the first blood sample, and went to her work station. She held up the vial of blood and checked that it had not clotted, entered the label information onto the computer, and transferred the same information to a compatibility card. Flowing through the familiar movements, she placed the sample in the centrifuge and set up the requisite empty vials in a test tube rack. Taking the sample out of the centrifuge with one hand, she lifted a disposable pipette with the other, and deftly pipetted the plasma from the top of the blood sample. She released the plasma into the first empty test tube in the back row. Drop of blood into each of four test tubes in the front row, drop of correct antigen, and, upon examination, the blood was typed: A negative. She then prepared the back row to reverse type the sample. Confirming the type, she then set up an antibody screen: a mixture of blood cells, plasma, and appropriate reagents added to each vial before placing them into the centrifuge. She looked up to see Carolyn headed out with donor bags. Lizzy retrieved her samples from the centrifuge and examined each vial. Antibodies were not present, so finding a donor if required would be easy.

She retrieved the next sample. After she typed the sample, it showed itself to be the kind that challenged her or frustrated her, depending on her mood and the circumstances. Today it was an irritation because the lab was busy. Sandy still wasn't in, and they were getting backed up quickly. The antibody screen showed positive reactions in the two reference lines, each reaction under a different enhancement regime. Lizzy set up a full panel to decipher which antibodies were present. Years of experience guided her through a series of stages—centrifuging, incubating, and adding enhancements—to tease out two antibodies that were present. Once she completed the screening and reviewed the units in storage, as she predicted, she had to call the Red Cross to line up a match in case they needed it. Sandy was in, and all the samples from the accident had been processed. Lizzy decided it was time for a quick coffee break.

Carolyn was in the break room pouring a cup of coffee. Lizzy peered into her bag as she passed the table and saw almost half of the zucchini was already gone. She walked up beside Carolyn with her mug in hand, and Carolyn filled it.

"Of all days to start off tired . . ." said Carolyn, yawning.

"Too much partying last night?" asked Lizzy.

"Yeah, right. No, couldn't sleep. Too much on my mind." They both sat at the table.

"Are you still agitating over work schedules? I hope not. Besides Monday, I'm totally flexible," said Lizzy.

"No, I've got them done through next month. Summer is always difficult, juggling everyone's vacation. I'll post the schedule when we go back in the lab. Remind me if I forget."

"So, what's keeping you awake?" asked Lizzy.

"Oh, my mother's old place."

"Where is it again?"

Carolyn yawned. "Down Possum Hollow."

Lizzy knew exactly where Possum Hollow Road ran into Due West—just beyond the edge of all the development, where she felt her lungs expand and her body relax as she headed out of town.

"We thought the property would sell in no time." Carolyn drummed her fingers on the table.

"So it hasn't?"

"No. It's an older house. It needs repairs. There's some acreage with the property; it's what's left of my grandparents' farm. Not many people are looking for a small farm these days."

"I'm sure the right person would love it," Lizzy said.

"I know. But we can't wait much longer for the right person. We're thinking most people nowadays want a house and a yard. In other words, we're thinking maybe we should subdivide the land—leave a few acres with the old house and divide the rest into couple-acre lots."

"That's a shame," said Lizzy, "to cut it up that way."

Carolyn shrugged. "I know, but we don't have much choice. We need to pay off mom's new place, and we can't do it without selling the old one."

"Possum Hollow is a beautiful road—I remember when it was a dirt road."

"Me too," said Carolyn, "but I'm glad it's paved now. We'd have an even harder sell on dirt."

• • •

Lizzy worked beyond the end of her shift to help the next shift catch up. She was the last to arrive at Donna and Doug's. The contingent that was going to the capitol already had been decided — Dr. Dave would be their scientific expert, Lizzy was their resident property owner, and a Ms. Hager was the lawyer that Suzanna had indeed located. Melissa Drummond had backed out last minute, so Donna was going in her stead, particularly because she had made it her business to start attending city council and county commissioner meetings. And Mike was going because he had decided he was when the idea first came up. The group didn't seem so small anymore.

When Lizzy walked in Mike was advocating that they submit an exposé to the paper, particularly because attendance at their monthly general meetings was dwindling. Doug argued that they needed to wait until they could base such an article on what Roper intended to do, not all the possible options he might pursue. Roper's plans still had not come up at the city or county meetings.

"Well," said Russ, trying to veer Mike and Doug off their collision course, "we can be pretty sure the delay is intentional — I'm sure Roper's plans are not idle."

"A friend of ours called the other night," Seymour told them. "He lives in that subdivision, Lost Pines, a mile or so outside the city limits. It's not an old subdivision, maybe five years?"

Leslie began circling her hand, her speed-it-up cue.

"He told us that he and some neighbors have had visits from two men in nice suits saying they represent a consortium of local businesses. They then proceeded to lay out the advantages of annexation by the city."

"No doubt Roper's men," Leslie added.

Lizzy envisioned two men who looked like they had stepped out of some crime drama. Perhaps Roper looked like some scarred-face mob boss.

"I've been looking up property records along Due West," Mike said. "A New Horizons Corporation owns several large properties, many of them close to town. I haven't had the time to track down its ownership yet, but I suspect it's a new corporation of Roper's."

"I'm sure those properties will look a lot more attractive to businesses if they're on city water and sewer lines," Donna said.

"So, he stands to gain a lot, not just at Bartons Mill, if the city starts pushing out its boundary," Russ said.

"Perhaps he has even bigger plans," Leslie suggested as she placed her mug on the coffee table. "Don't forget, someone—most likely Roper—is buying up road frontage along Due West."

Lizzy recalled Suzanna's comment about House and wondered if he might have already sold his property—his wife's property—to Roper. If he had, the development might eventually be much larger than two hundred homes.

Donna cocked her head. "I wonder what would cost more in the long run, building an on-site sewage treatment facility or financing miles of sewage lines to tie into the city's?"

"For all we know, Roper has a deal with the city to purchase his sewage line as it extends its boundaries," said Russ.

"The option of an on-site facility might give us more leverage," Mike suggested, "more support in fighting the development."

"We can't build opposition based on a supposition," said Doug, shaking his head.

Lizzy sighed. She wished Doug didn't feel compelled to counter everything Mike said. Yes, Mike was always ready to leap in a new direction, but if Doug didn't react, these meetings would be so much shorter.

Russ interceded. "This sewage issue may be affording us some time by delaying the project, but it's really putting us in the position of not knowing what we're up against."

"Do you think we should consider postponing the visit to Daniels and Earl?" asked Donna.

"No," said Mike. "We need to get their attention to the matter sooner rather than later. Perhaps we can put some brakes on the development before the city and county come to any resolution."

"That's optimistic," Lizzy muttered to herself.

Going ahead was the general consensus, so Dave went over a summary of the inventory they had put together. The site was biologically very diverse, and some of the species they had observed were rare to the Piedmont and were even species of concern, but there was no one species they could point to that didn't have more substantial populations elsewhere. There was a state program identifying biologically significant natural sites, but the program couldn't regulate development.

"If only we could get the department of natural resources to designate that the site is biologically significant," said Leslie, "perhaps we could convince the state to work out some sort of trade or conservation agreement with Roper and the other landowners."

"When hell freezes over," said Lizzy. "Agatha Prickett wouldn't agree to anything like that on principal. And Roper would have to see lots of green, I suspect."

"Well, what time should we meet Monday?" asked Donna.

●   ●   ●

Lizzy was looking forward to getting home. As she passed the familiar landmarks, she thought about how she had become so accustomed to her quiet life that a day full of people wore her out—not to mention work. Still, she was becoming caught up in the anticipation of the planned trip. She had tried to suppress expectations when they cropped up—she didn't want to let herself get carried away with false hopes of success. As doubtful as she was about their making real headway with their state representatives, though, she was intent on preserving her little piece of earth, the small piece of ground that was her responsibility to protect.

Her mind was focused on how the group might go forward when a great gap appeared to her left. She should have known those trucks were up to no good. Over the course of her day in town several acres of land had been cleared and graded. Alone, about fifty feet from the road, stood a large willow—in a field through which Possum Creek meandered southward. As Lizzy drove by she read a large sign:

Coming Soon! Creekside Square. What an oxymoron, thought Lizzy. Build it and they will come—be it more retail strips, more homes, or another car dealership. Creekside Square, Piney Woods, Deer Meadow—vanquished realities. History to be forgotten in one generation. Would that be the fate of the hemlocks on the bluff?

She was so distracted by this latest sign of "progress" that she drove right past Possum Hollow Road. But its beckoning entry caught the corner of her eye, and she made a U-turn. The dark, narrow turnoff was framed in amethyst chicory. The road rapidly descended into a thick strip of forested darkness that was the conduit of Possum Creek, and for a fleeting moment she was transported into a lush green corridor of jewelweed and cardinal flower that promised precious, hidden sanctuaries—and chiggers. As the road came back up out of the protective moat, it curved around a massive sycamore before reemerging into a series of small farms.

Lizzy told herself she was taking a look at Carolyn's mother's house, but she knew that was an excuse. She was indulging a sudden urge to take a drive into her past. The road ambled past old houses, sheds, and barns, periodically dipping down toward the creek, which was shaded by sycamores and ash.

She pulled over when she saw a "for sale" sign near the road and looked at the old wood house with its broad front porch and large shade trees. She assumed it was Carolyn's mother's place. Hydrangea bushes laden with blossoms framed the wide front steps. The low summer sun glinted off the bright new white paint and curtained windows. A sagging barn that had been spruced up with a coat of brick red paint stood picturesque in a field that lay fallow. They couldn't have painted the scene any more country, thought Lizzy. She pulled away and continued down the road.

Lizzy was on her way to where Wes used to take her, years ago, to go exploring. As she came around a bend the familiar sight of a dirt road that briefly ran along the creek appeared. She pulled onto the dirt road and, getting out of her car, smelled the scent of the creek—a musty smell, a smell of wet decay that signaled the water was full of life. With her eyes closed, she took in a deep breath. She had spent the day indoors, her mind occupied with business. Breathing deeply, she tried to purge her concerns, to bathe herself in the scents of water, forest, corn, soybean, and a still summer evening.

When she and Wes had first met, before they lived out on Narrow Passage Road, Wes liked to come here to go bird watching. Unlike her, Wes had grown up in the country, and he had learned firsthand a lot of what she, and Russ, had studied in books. He wanted to share his enthusiasm for birding with her, and his first gift to her was a pair of binoculars. She recognized the binoculars as a sign of his true affection, so she worked to learn the various feathered creatures by name, and she did learn, and remember, some of the more common ones. But often she wandered the dirt road or the forest, looking at wildflowers and collecting dried inflorescences and seed pods. Sometimes she even brought her sketchbook and made no pretense of birding.

Lizzy looked down the familiar road, which ended in the middle of a corn field. To the right of the road the land was left uncultivated until the creek and road diverged sufficiently to allow a tractor to turn around. Her eyes ran along the line of trees that curved away from the road and followed the creek, which was winding its way to its final destination. The sight gave sensory form to memory. Lizzy lingered only a moment and then returned to her car; she did not want to indulge in nostalgia for a life gone by.

It was late by time Lizzy reached home. She let Pete and Clem out of their pen, and they followed her inside. Everyone wanted to be fed, including her. She took a drink of iced tea, grabbed a couple of crackers, and then fed her charges. Alice seemed particularly annoyed at the delay and meowed insistently.

Lizzy threw together a salad for herself, topped it generously with feta cheese, poured a glass of wine, and headed out to her front porch. She rarely sat there—even though the road was quiet, she found the front porch too public. But it had a small table and chairs, and she wanted to be outside.

The front yard was relatively narrow; it had been a bit wider when the road was essentially a dirt lane. A hedge had been planted to delineate the yard as the road widened, and when Lizzy and Wes had moved to Narrow Passage, she cut the hedge to half its size because it had been allowed to grow into a green blockade. Likewise she had pruned back the azaleas, roses, and hydrangeas that had grown lanky through neglect. She had dug up bulbs and loosened the soil along the walkway; now a mixed bed of sweet William, sweet alyssum, and ageratum reemerged every summer. As she ate her salad, she saw that she had fallen way behind in tending the walkway bed. But she didn't want to sit here and create a list of chores. She wanted to sit here to enjoy the evening. The light was growing dim. The colors of the yard were becoming distinguishable as only dark and light, the boundaries between leaves fading—the contrast apparent in light was dissipating.

Suddenly Lizzy realized she was hearing the sounds of the night—the frogs, the katydids, the whip-poor-will. Insects—moths, lacewings, mayflies—began to fly at her living room windows and settle there. She had finished her dinner and was examining her window when a voice came from the darkness.

"Hi." It was Jonas.

"Jonas, you saved me a phone call."

Jonas walked up to the porch.

"I was wondering if you could feed Alice and the rest of the varmints on Monday afternoon or evening. That's the day I'm headed to the capitol, and I'm really not sure when we'll be getting home."

"Sure, no problem."

"What are you up to?"

"Walking. Finally cooled off some."

"Yes. It's actually pretty pleasant now."

"Did I tell you I got a job?"

"No! Where?"

"At the library, re-shelving books mostly. Three days a week. My parents are really happy about it. They're already showing me sample resumes."

The corner of Lizzy's mouth went up.

"Oh look." Jonas was pointing at the tremendous winged creature that had just landed next to her window. "A dobsonfly."

Lizzy wasn't afraid of insects, but these primitive-looking beasts gave her pause. They were big—this one was at least four inches long.

"Look at the size of those pinchers," Lizzy said.

"He can't pinch with them, his mandibles—he can't even bring them together. He uses them to hold the female during mating. The female, though, her mandibles could still pinch you—if you bothered her."

"No chance of that," said Lizzy. "He's pretty incredible, isn't he? Look at all that patterning in his wings. And those antennae are so long. Goodness, look at his eyes. The larvae live in the stream, don't they?"

"Yes, for a couple of years. But once they emerge as adults, they don't live long after they mate."

Lizzy straightened up. She suddenly felt exhausted. "I guess I should clean up my mess," she said, picking up her plate and glass. "Good night, Jonas."

"Bye," he said and ambled off the porch, disappearing back into the darkness.

Lizzy rinsed her dishes and left them in the sink. She sent Clem and Pete out and quickly called them back in. She locked her doors, poured herself a glass of water, and went up to bed. She fell asleep immediately.

Lizzy found herself walking a dirt road, perhaps Narrow Passage or Possum Hollow before either had been paved. Happy was out ahead, Alice not far behind him, and Pete, Clem, and CB trailed behind Alice. Happy led them to his grave; he was both alive and dead. As they all regarded his grave, water bubbled up to the surface, spread out over a moss and mushroom mat, and then disappeared back into the ground. Lizzy looked up and regarded her garden, which was as large as Sam's field. She walked over to the garden and stood on rich, fertile soil so full of fat earthworms that it seemed alive. Watching the earthworms, she realized that the soil was like the blood of the earth, the unifying medium that was recycled continuously.

The vegetation in the garden was lush, appearing akin to a tropical jungle. She looked up at a large leaf that arched over her head. On its underside were two neat, tight rows of creamy yellow eggs the size of peaches. The eggs began to swell, and she was sure they were about to hatch. One by one, the eggs opened, and from each egg a baby dobsonfly—not a wormy larva but a miniature adult—fell to the ground. But upon the ground each baby dobsonfly lived only a moment and then died. It melted into the soil, immediately absorbed into the humus. Soon there was only one egg left, and as she watched it hatch, Lizzy overcame her own aversion, her own fear, and when the baby dobsonfly fell, she caught it in her arms. For a moment, she gently cradled this new life as one would a baby. Then she gently turned it right side up. As she looked into its eyes and stroked its wings, it reached out with its small mandibles and pinched her nose.

Lizzy popped awake and looked around. Alice slept soundly at the foot of the bed. The house was quiet. But she felt uneasy—not just because the young life she had just rescued nipped her in the nose but because her dreams of late had her turning the soil, and she wasn't sure if she was planting something or digging something up. She petted Alice, readjusted her pillow, and tried to quell her uneasiness.

Conversation

Alice was waiting at the kitchen door when Jonas arrived. As he opened the door, she walked directly to her bowl and looked up at him impatiently. He saw a can of cat food on the counter along with a spoon. He scooped a generous portion of kitty stew into Alice's dish, and she set upon it as if she had been starved for days.

CB didn't seem to be around, so Jonas decided to put the rest of the can in the refrigerator. Top and center was a pitcher of iced tea, which Jonas took out and put on the counter. He found a glass, filled it with ice, and poured himself a drink. He drank the tea quickly—the walk over had left him hot and thirsty. The tea left an unusual aftertaste—perhaps Ms. Lizzy had changed brands.

He fetched Pete and Clem's dishes from the dog dorm and filled them from a basin of dog food that was in the pantry. When he carried the dishes around the back side of the house to the pen, Pete and Clem jumped up from the shade of the oak, happy to see him. He used the garden hose to top off their water basin and patted both of them when they finished eating. He called for CB, but still seeing no sign of her, he returned to the house.

Jonas poured himself another glass of tea and with it wandered along the hallway. He stopped to regard the hall tree; it was adorned with a few hats, two pairs of binoculars, and, below the small bench seat, several pairs of shoes, including a pair of large, untied work boots. He then stepped into the living room and meandered through it, looking absently over each piece of furniture. At the mantel he examined the few framed photographs—a black and white photograph of a young couple and one of the same couple, a bit older, with two little girls, perhaps one of them Ms. Lizzy, and a boy; there was a photo of a younger Ms. Lizzy with a curly-haired man, and one of the same man, looking tan and fit, holding a fishing pole and a large bass.

Jonas was on his way to look out the front windows when he noticed the open door on the other side of the staircase. The door was usually closed. He set his glass of tea on the coffee table and went to look in the room. It was packed. There was a closed-up fireplace on the far wall; Jonas figured the room was the kitchen when the house was originally built. A large wood desk, covered with typical desk implements and stacks of papers and magazines, took up the center of the room. His eyes were drawn to the wall of shelves behind the desk, which held books, binders, small boxes, and a variety of objects such as rocks, bones, turtle shells, and birds' nests. Stepping into this enticingly cluttered room, Jonas went to look more closely at the bookshelves. There were some photo albums, several field guides, what looked like a bunch of college textbooks, and a whole shelf of science fiction, which surprised him: he remembered Ms. Lizzy once told him she didn't read much science fiction. Jonas recognized some of the authors and thought he might ask her to borrow a few books he hadn't yet read. Turning back into the room, Jonas saw a smaller, neater bookcase below the front window and a tall, old dresser beside the doorway. To the right of the dresser was a narrow door that was slightly open. Jonas pushed the door a little bit and peered into to a small, dark landing. He looked for a light switch but didn't see one. Ancient air emanated from the space—earthy, cool, damp, untouched air. There must be an old cellar below. He readjusted the door to how he had found it and made his way back out of the room.

By time he crossed the office threshold, Jonas was overcome by his curiosity to see the rest of the house and headed up the stairs. To his left was obviously Ms. Lizzy's bedroom—it looked lived in, although, like the living room, it was quite neat: a bed flanked by nightstands, a couple of dressers, and an old-fashioned dressing table with a small bench-like chair covered in blue velvet. To his right was a more sparsely furnished bedroom with a bed, nightstand, winged chair, and dresser. Just beyond these doorways, along a short hallway that ended in a dormer window, were two more doors. The right door, slightly ajar, revealed a bathroom; the left door was closed. Jonas took a couple of steps and felt the slight rise in the floor where the modern addition didn't quite match up to the original farmhouse. He knew he shouldn't, but he opened the closed door.

Jonas entered a small room with soothing light green walls. A dormer window faced north, and on the near side of it was an old dresser that appeared to be in the process of being repainted white, except there was no sign of paint or brushes. The drawers, unpainted, were stacked against the wall. On the far side of the dormer was a small bookcase and nearby, in front of a curtained window on the far wall, was a rocking chair. The rest of the floor space was otherwise open except for some boxes and camping gear lining the inside wall. Three fishing poles were set in the far corner, and a big tackle box sat next to them. Once Jonas had noted the room's furnishings, he noticed there were some framed watercolors on the walls. He stepped into the room to look at them. He recognized the locations—the bluff, Narrow Passage Creek lined with spicebush in bloom, and a view of the crape myrtle in Ms. Lizzy's backyard. The last was of some birds, chickadees and titmice, on bare branches, and when he looked closely he saw a signature. Ms. Lizzy had painted these. He didn't know she drew, or painted, so well, and he marveled how she could re-create with light strokes of her hands what she saw with her eyes.

Jonas went over to the bookcase, plugged in a small lamp that had a carousel of animals as its base, and began to look over the collection of books. They were children's books—a book of classic children's tales, a book of rhymes, stories of Beatrix Potter and A. A. Milne. He picked up a collection of Kipling's *Just So Stories*, sat in the rocker, and opened the front cover. Inside was a printed label, "This Book Belongs to the Library of," and on a blank line beneath, in a child's hand, was written "Wesley Whitacre." Jonas flipped through the stories and stopped at "How the Whale Got His Throat" and began to read.

Suddenly Jonas found himself driving a car, which was exceptional in that he didn't know how to drive. But here he was, negotiating a winding road. He was distracted though: there were children in the back seat, little kids, a boy and two girls, who were making a lot of noise. They were bickering about where they should go and what they should do, who was smarter and who was taking up too much room, who was dumb and who should be quiet. Then they began to make demands of Jonas, asking for drinks, snacks, a bathroom stop. The more he asked them to be quiet, so he could concentrate on driving, so he could figure out where he was headed in this unfamiliar landscape, the louder they got. And the louder they grew, the more demands they made, the harder it was for Jonas to focus. Finally, he pulled over to the side of the road and there was the pond, Bartons Mill Pond. The children cried, "Let's go swimming!" and they all jumped in. He had never been swimming in the pond before and was amazed at how soothing its cool waters felt. He dove down below the surface, deeper and deeper, as if he were a whale and the pond was as deep as the ocean. But then he needed to come up for air, and as he surfaced, without forethought, as if he had become a whale, he swallowed the children whole. There was nothing gruesome about it, but now there was a great heaviness in his stomach, and all he wanted was to regurgitate the children. He shouldn't have swallowed them.

The book falling to the floor startled Jonas. He sat up with such a start that he nearly threw Alice, who was curled up against his stomach, to the floor. Her claws grasped him through his shirt.

"That was rude!" she exclaimed as she jumped to the floor and stood a few feet away from him.

Jonas sat there, dumbfounded, his mouth hanging open.

She narrowed her eyes at him and said, "Oh, so you're not going to apologize?"

"You're talking!"

She stretched from end to end and yawned. "So? That's no excuse for being rude."

Jonas shook his head, pinched himself. "You can't talk!"

"Really? Says who?"

"You . . . you . . . you don't talk," he reiterated.

"That's not true."

"Oh," Jonas considered over his astonishment. "Well, I've never heard you talk before."

"I've gathered that."

"What's happened?"

"You tell me."

"I don't know. Am I dreaming?" he asked, leaning down toward Alice.

"Only if you are in my dream. But I don't usually dream about you."

Still groping for lucidity, Jonas asked, "Well, what do you dream about?"

"Oh, eating, sleeping, hunting, falling, landing in water—the usual stuff."

"The usual . . ." Jonas reflected. At this point he didn't care if he was dreaming—talking to a cat was quite novel. "I have dreamt about eating, but otherwise . . . I was just dreaming I was driving a car and— you know what a car is?"

"Of course I know that horrid beast."

"Well I was driving, which I could learn to do—I'm old enough, I mean, but I haven't because I'm not really interested. Anyway, I was driving and there were some small children in the back seat arguing, and then we stopped and jumped in the pond, and it was like I was a whale or a giant fish—I swallowed them whole. . . ."

"Mm, I like fish" responded Alice, who had stretched out and was cleaning herself. "I never ate any of my babies, though. I had babies once, five of them. I was so young then. I do hope you are good to your mother." Alice looked directly at him with her eyes narrowed and then returned her attention to herself. "That was my life before I met Lizzy. Life with Lizzy has been good."

Gazing around the room again, Jonas remarked, "This room looks like it's a child's room. Why does Ms. Lizzy have a room for a child?"

Alice regarded him. "Why don't you ask Lizzy about that?'

"It's a pretty personal question."

"Exactly. So you're asking me?" She licked the pads on her right front paw but then paused and said, "It's been a while since I've been in here. I can't open the door, you know." She licked her paw once more and added, "Sometimes Happy was able to push it open, if it wasn't closed tight."

Jonas watched Alice. Besides talking, she certainly was doing her regular cat things. "Do you miss Happy?" he asked.

"Sometimes. I certainly liked talking to him more than the others." She resumed licking her paw and then paused; "sometimes I even dream about Happy."

"Ms. Lizzy thinks you've forgotten Happy. She said you don't visit his grave anymore."

"Hmm. Lizzy should know better than that. I haven't forgotten about him. I've just laid him to rest. She should do that."

"I'm sure she has."

"I'm not talking about Happy, you dunce. Look at those fishing poles. Does Lizzy fish? . . . I wish she did," Alice added wistfully.

Suddenly it occurred to Jonas. "Was Ms. Lizzy married to a man named Wesley?"

"I saw you looking around the house. His things are all over the place. You were in his den."

Jonas's parents had never mentioned this man. Perhaps they didn't know either.

"What happened to him?" Jonas asked Alice.

"He's gone," Alice said bluntly.

Jonas sat in silence. How could he ever look at Ms. Lizzy again without this new knowledge being written all over his face? Why had Ms. Lizzy kept this to herself?

"She wanted to have a baby. One baby at a time . . . doesn't make much sense," Alice commented. "After he was gone, Lizzy would sit in here for hours—in that chair you're sitting in. Happy and I sat with her. Then one day she closed the door.

"Happy and I told her not to dwell in the land of what could have been. But she never seemed to understand—she paws at it over and over again."

"Ms. Lizzy has never said a word about any of this to me," said Jonas.

"Well don't tell her that I told you."

Jonas looked at Alice, who was grooming her side. No, he wouldn't tell Ms. Lizzy that he had been talking to her cat about her husband and the baby she wanted to have. He stood up. He felt ashamed—that he had invaded Ms. Lizzy's privacy, first roaming through her house, now listening to her story. How could he apologize without telling her? How could he tell her without mentioning that Alice told him?

"I wish she didn't feel she had to keep this all to herself," Jonas said.

"She keeps her feelings to herself. Sort of like you."

Jonas looked at the floor.

"Fortunately for you," Alice said, "I have astute powers of observation."

"Yeah, I guess you do. I think most people think I don't have any feelings—or that they don't matter."

"I have the same problem." Alice got up and headed for the door. "How about something to eat?" she suggested.

"You'll get fat."

Alice turned and looked at Jonas. In the past he had interpreted this expression of hers as vacuousness. Now he realized it was one of annoyance. He followed Alice out of the room. With Alice leading the way, the two of them, both plump for their length, made their way down the stairs.

Jonas scooped a bit more food into Alice's dish and watched her eat. She then sat down and started cleaning her whiskers with her paw.

Over food, Alice seemed to have returned to her former incarnation of being a regular cat. "I never knew you had so much to say," Jonas commented. "No insult intended, but it's all sounded like meow, meow to me."

"Well, to be fair, I haven't said much to you. But then you haven't said much to me either." She finished cleaning her whiskers. "How can people know what you're thinking, how you feel, if you don't tell them?"

"That's kind of hard. I usually feel like I'm outside the conversation—that either I'm not interested in what people are talking about or they wouldn't be interested in what I'm thinking. And people can be pretty harsh, especially if you're not like them."

"Tell me about it," said Alice, as she headed toward the living room. "But they're not all that way. Sometimes you have to take a few risks, put yourself out there, like I did when I first walked up to Lizzy's door." With that she jumped up onto an armchair and closed her eyes.

Alice's last comment reminded him that he had left the door open upstairs. He returned to the room, walked across it to the rocker, sat back down, and looked across the room. Noticing the book on the floor, he picked it up and leafed through its pages until he was back to the page he had been reading, although he was fuzzy as to where he was in the story. The whale had swallowed the mariner. He finished the story, closed the book, unplugged the lamp, and stood up. When he left the room, he remembered to close the door behind him.

Jonas returned to the living room and sat down on the couch. He drank the remains of the glass of iced tea he had left on the coffee table—now mostly melted ice. He looked blankly across the room and through the sheer curtains. His mind bounced back and forth between what he had seen and what he had been told.

Alice, her eyes closed, sat in a sphinxlike position on the arm of the chair in front of the window. "Alice," Jonas said softly. One eye opened, looked at him, and closed. Clearly, she was done talking.

Jonas got up and wandered into the office to take another look at this place of Ms. Lizzy's past life. As he stood in front of the desk, he heard a creak. CB darted out from behind the narrow door that led to the cellar and ran from the room. She must have been exploring the subterranean space all along. Jonas found her in the kitchen, fetched her food, and, ready to leave, said, "See you later CB." But she had her head in the bowl and ignored him.

Jonas emerged into sunlight and hot air. He felt groggy, as if he had just climbed out of the car after sleeping on a long road trip. He looked back toward the house and saw it looked as it always did. He gradually became more aware of his surroundings—he heard the droning of cicadas and, in the distance, a deep rumbling. The leaves of the crape myrtle were rattling in the breeze—a thunderstorm was on its way. He didn't notice that Timmy, straddling his bike, was watching him from the end of the driveway.

"What are you doing?" called Timmy.

Jonas turned toward him. "Feeding Ms. Lizzy's pets," he replied slowly. What else could he say? He wasn't sure himself. "She won't be home until late." Then, as an afterthought, Jonas asked, "What about you?" He headed up the driveway.

"Oh, just riding around. I was up at the pond, taking some pictures just in case, you know, it changes. I tried to take a picture of some turtles stacked up on a log the way they do, but I don't think it will turn out very well—they slid off just as I shot the picture, so they probably will be a blur."

Jonas and Timmy headed toward Prickett Farm Road together, along Sam's field, the large garden now high in corn. Timmy waved the gnats away from his face. "Have you seen the orange flags all over Mr. Roper's property?" he asked Jonas. Another deep rumble suggested the sky was about to undergo a transformation.

"No," said Jonas, unsettled by the news.

"I guess they're already planning out roads and all."

Jonas let out a sigh, and they continued their walk in silence. When they turned onto their shared road, Timmy said, "Hey, do you want to see my pictures?"

"Uhm, sure," said Jonas, feeling he still needed something to wake himself up, to ground him in the world.

Even though they were neighbors, Jonas had never been to Timmy's house. Timmy's mother may have thought it a bit strange when Jonas came in with Timmy—they appeared such an odd pair: three Timmys might make one Jonas.

Leading Jonas to the room he shared with his brother, Timmy fetched a composition notebook from the top of his dresser. They sat down on the edge of his bed, and Timmy opened the notebook in which he had taped his photographs. Jonas studied each picture. Timmy had an eye for composition; his shots were considered carefully. His greatest limitation appeared to be his cheap camera.

"These are good," Jonas told Timmy. He pointed to the photograph of a familiar roadside wildflower. "This viper's bugloss is really beautiful."

"Wait, let me get a pen so I can write down its name."

Timmy asked Jonas to spell out the name and then went to the next photo and asked Jonas to name the flowers in it. Timmy had obviously lain on his stomach to photograph the demure flowers of sorrel and toadflax, which filled the photo up to a thin strip of blue horizon.

"You really work at getting good pictures."

"I just try to show the gifts we've been given."

A flash of light soon followed by a sharp crack of thunder got their attention. Within seconds they heard a heavy rain falling. They flipped back to the beginning of the notebook and started over again, labeling Timmy's photos. Jonas knew almost everything that Timmy had photographed.

"Is there anything you don't know?" Timmy asked incredulously when they were three-fourths through the album.

Jonas laughed.

Timmy's face lit up. It was the first time he had ever heard Jonas laugh.

"There are lots of things I don't know." Jonas paused. "I don't know how to do a lot of things—like drive or dance or use tools very well. I guess I mostly know about things—information." Jonas thought of the conversation he may just have had with Alice. "But it's all in my head. I don't know how to share it, turn it into something useful. I don't know how to convince people that even species that have no apparent use are still important. And I don't know how to protect my favorite place—the pond, the bluff, the marshy area that feeds Narrow Passage Creek. It's probably going to be changed forever, and I don't know what to do about that."

Jonas looked at Timmy, whose eyebrows were pulled together in deep concentration. Today he had talked to a cat followed by a kid five years younger than him. It was a start.

Timmy felt deep gratification that Jonas had placed this kind of trust in him. Having Jonas confess that there were many things he didn't know was flattering and also revealing. Timmy felt compelled to say something in acknowledgment of Jonas's trust. He turned toward what he knew.

"It's hard to see God's plan sometimes. My parents say that challenges can be an opportunity to do the right thing."

Jonas looked at his young friend. He didn't know about God's plan, but the advice was sound. "Well, perhaps He wants us to make the right thing happen."

• • •

Jonas's mother came down the stairs when she heard him come in.

"Are you soaked?" Sylvia asked as she entered the kitchen. When she saw he wasn't she said, "You've been gone for a while—I've been home at least an hour. Was everything okay at Ms. Lizzy's?"

"Yes, it was. I sort of fell asleep there," he told her, "and then I stopped at Timmy Donohue's."

Sylvia's eyebrows went up. "You fell asleep at Ms. Lizzy's?"

"Yeah, I didn't mean to. I was just sitting in, uhm, her house, and it was a bit warm, and I was reading a book, and I fell asleep. But then Alice . . ." He heard Alice's voice clearly just then: I hope you are good to your mother.

"What?"

"Oh, Alice woke me up. Then on my way home I met Timmy. He's been wanting me to look at his photos. He takes a lot of pictures—of plants, animals, scenery. He actually has some pretty good pictures. I helped him label them."

"That was nice of you, Jonas" said Sylvia, her expression still questioning but softening. "It probably meant a lot to him that you were interested enough to do that."

Jonas felt his body, out of habit, beginning to move away, but he stopped himself. "We're both interested in nature." He picked up an orange and began to peel it. "But from different perspectives," he added.

"What do you mean?" Sylvia asked as she picked up the mail from the counter and casually sorted through it, although she had done so when she first arrived home.

"Timmy sees nature as God's creation; I think he wants to document it with his photographs." Jonas pulled apart the sections of orange and laid them on the counter.

"And what is your perspective?" Sylvia asked hesitantly.

"I think I'm just trying to understand how the world works."

He offered a section of orange to his mother, who took it, her lips parted as if to speak. But she just looked at him.

"Would you like me to set the table?" he asked.

• •

In the morning, Jonas walked over to Ms. Lizzy's to make sure she was home and her housemates had been tended. Her car was in the driveway, but she wasn't home. Jonas continued walking to the creek and then toward the pond.

Lizzy had wandered toward the pond herself that morning after a restless night. Her mind had been full of the day's trip, which overall had been predictable and therefore frustrating. She took her usual route through the woods to the bluff. A bird called relentlessly—she recognized its song, but she couldn't remember its name, even though Wes had told her so many times. She had never tried very hard to remember because its name was not important to her. She didn't need to name the bird to be reassured by its call, to be reassured by knowing it was there and living the life it was supposed to live, to be reassured there was a world much bigger than herself. It was in knowing there was a world bigger than her own life that she typically found comfort, but this morning she was experiencing the other side: that she was too small to affect the course of events unfolding in her own backyard.

As Lizzy approached the bluff, she saw the sourwoods were in flower—racemes of dainty white urns were calling in the honeybees. She walked to the edge of the bluff and looked over the hemlocks standing firm on their perilous slope.

Even if she hadn't known the hemlocks were relics of another era, the bluff had always seemed an ancient place, a magical place, hidden from the modern world. An earthy scent emanated from the ground— humus and moss overlain with the sweet aromatic sheath of shed hemlock needles and branchlets. She loved the hemlocks—their form, their scent, their flat, dark green leaves. She was grateful they had remained here, a reminder of a long history before her, of history before humankind. She was comforted by this continuity, this sense of something greater than the here and now, something that lived on without her but gave her grounding in her time. There was nothing more primal or more transcendent than these seemingly fleeting moments of connection.

In some sense, weren't most species relicts of an earlier time? Didn't they all carry pieces of the past in their DNA—millions of years of history and change? Then, during the course of one day, the creek is no longer a creek and everything that lived there is gone—unless it could outrun a bulldozer. Saved for a day. But where to go? Once gone, a history was just that—history in a museum, in a painting, in a memory.

Lizzy walked along the edge of the bluff, toward its high eastern edge below which Mill Pond Creek continued its southern path. She glanced in the direction of the cemetery; she couldn't see it through the leaves. The dead abide in the memory, their lives history. Our walk is so brief, thought Lizzy, our footprint so transitory. But hell, there are so many of us now, our footprints amount to a stampede, a permanent scar.

Walking quietly toward Lizzy was Jonas. He was so adept at walking quietly through the woods that he realized he might scare her. He called out hello from a distance.

Lizzy turned toward him. "Hey Jonas. Thanks for taking care of the crew yesterday. Did they give you any trouble?"

"No, but . . ." Jonas hesitated. He didn't know what he had meant to say, what he could say. Ms. Lizzy was looking at him, waiting for him to finish his sentence. "Uhm, I think I fell asleep at your house."

Lizzy let out a short laugh. "I hope you found it comfortable."

"Oh, yeah, sorry," he replied awkwardly. "How did things go yesterday?" he asked with earnest curiosity but also wanting to change the subject.

"It went reasonably well, I guess. We met with Daniels, our representative, first. He was full of doublespeak—yes, he shares our concern and will do all he can to involve the appropriate state agencies. He will certainly pass on our inventory. Then he went on to say that he can operate only within the law, and the law grants private citizens the right to develop their land as they see fit as long as the use isn't a nuisance and follows local ordinances. And he claimed he didn't know anything about any backroom agreements among local governments and Roper. It wasn't much different with Earl, our senator, just briefer. I guess in the end it will come down to preserving the strip of forest along the shore of the pond, but the rest of the farm will be planted in houses. I came here to fill up on how it all looks now. See the orange through the trees, though—it's flagging. So much for the plat not being available yet."

Jonas nodded. "Well, maybe our side of the creek will stay intact—if everyone leaves things as they are. And the cemetery will be left alone. I walked over there the other day. There is a ton of wild blackberries along the back of it—I've been thinking of going back to pick some."

"I used to pick blackberries there, but I haven't since ..." Lizzy turned back in the direction of the cemetery, so Jonas couldn't see her face, "not since I buried my husband there. It was before you moved here." She collected herself and turned back toward Jonas. "I guess I've never told you about Wes. He was a game warden—worked for the state game commission. He dealt with emergencies and dangerous situations all the time. And then, one day, in a heavy fog, he came up on an accident and pulled over to help. A woman had hit a large deer. He was trying to help her get her car off the road when another car came along—too fast in the fog. The driver just didn't see them ... swerved at the last second to avoid the dead deer and hit Wes."

"I'm so sorry, Ms. Lizzy," Jonas said.

"Sam was so kind. He arranged to have Wes buried on Tutwiler ground, so he wouldn't be too far away."

Jonas didn't know what to say to her, but he wanted so to say something, the right thing.

Why am I burdening this boy with such talk, thought Lizzy. "Wes loved it here," she said, forcing a smile, "fishing, bird watching, walking. I guess I rather come here than go to the cemetery." She tapped her thighs with her fingertips. "I better get going. I work this afternoon. And it's getting hot already, isn't it? I bet the bees are even going home."

"Yes, it is," Jonas agreed. "I'll walk back with you." He accompanied her in silence.

Lizzy was thinking about the first time she had ever seen Wes. He was wearing some god-awful plaid polyester pants and a broad sky-blue tie, but he moved across the dance floor so smoothly that she had eventually asked him to dance. He was wide shouldered and long torsoed, making his center of gravity low. His hair was matted down with hair products that night, and the next time she saw him she didn't recognize him because his head was full of soft, light brown curls that gave him a somewhat cherubic appearance. She was walking down Main in Centreville when he stopped her, gently clasping her arm as he said, "You don't remember me? Halloween party at Lou's?" Then she recognized him—those indeterminate colored eyes and that impish grin that lent him an air of perpetual youthfulness. She felt somewhat embarrassed as he held her arm, so palpable was the unspoken communication between them.

He invited her for coffee, and they spent the next three hours talking in a dark restaurant booth below a faded photograph of a sphinx in front of a pyramid. Their relationship was intense from the beginning; they were inseparable immediately. She felt he was the first guy she had met who saw her the way she saw herself and had no qualms about who she was. It wasn't just that he laughed at her jokes or saw the sensitive interior of a somewhat sharp-tongued exterior. He didn't mind her strong opinions and liked her rough-edged femininity. He understood she could be brash but wasn't deterred by it; understood she had insecurities and didn't belittle them; understood she was fallible yet didn't fault her for her mistakes. In other words, he loved her for who she was. And, perhaps most importantly, there was a strong mutual attraction.

Wes also held strong convictions, and although in his genteel country manner he negotiated a broad spectrum of people, his view of the world could be quite severe. He didn't share the hopeful idealism that she brought with her at the time, but he shared his love and knowledge of nature with her. They were unapologetically honest with one another from the start, and Lizzy had thought they would wear each other out quickly, but within a year they had rented the old farmhouse together, and three years later, married, they bought it from Dolan and Ethel Tutwiler.

"A few weeks after Wes and I moved out here," Lizzy told Jonas as they neared her house, "we were having breakfast on the front porch. We heard a high-pitch whining from the hedge and discovered Happy. He was too scared to come out, but he was starved, so we coaxed him with pancakes and sausage. He was so cute as a pup. Saying goodbye to him was hard. Now it's just me and Alice who were part of that family."

When they reached Lizzy's house, Jonas stopped in to get a drink before walking the rest of the way home. As they entered the kitchen, Alice immediately appeared and looked straight at Jonas. "Meow!' she said insistently.

"Why look at that," said Lizzy. "Apparently she thinks she'll have better luck talking to you."

•   •   •

Gazing through a wall of windows onto downtown North Fork, George Roper sat at his desk. He didn't contemplate his options long; he didn't need to.

"Sally," he called his secretary, "get me Turnbull on the phone."

Moments later his phone rang.

"John, just got a call from Frank Daniels. He had a visit the other day from a group of his constituents complaining about the Bartons Mill project. He said they represented some sort of environmental group from Centreville. They had a lawyer with them, a woman named Hager. Do you know her?"

"No, but I'll look into her. You're not worried about them, are you?"

"No, but you know politicians and their constituents. It made him a little antsy about pushing for the Stumptown Road extension."

"Well Daniels knows where his bread is buttered best."

"Yes, he does," Roper responded, his mind already elsewhere. "Let's plan another little luncheon. Somewhere nice here in North Fork. Ask Jackson to set up a glossy presentation. Having the engineering company do it will give the whole affair some distance from me. Have him invite the county commissioners—but make sure to foul up the invitation to that Ayers woman. Endicott tells me she's a pain in the ass. I won't attend, but I want you to be there. Stress the financial advantages to the county."

"Will do."

"Another thing. Let's buy Agatha Prickett's five acres or whatever it is on the south side of the pond—we'll be able to add her acreage to our touted amenities. Offer her forty—it's high for unbuildable land, but she's Endicott's sister-in-law, and she's from one of those old Stumptown families that see themselves as some sort of aristocracy."

"What about House, though?" Turnbull asked. "I'm sure he will hear how much we're paying her for it. He'll try to push us upward."

"House should understand why we are willing to go high on Prickett's bite-size piece. We should push him on the contract, though, before we get further along on the first phase of the Bartons Mill development. Once he sees that start, he's bound to want more."

"How about that little corner parcel, the one that still belongs to the Bartons? Should I contact her?"

"No, it's not directly accessible from my property. Anyway, it's not worth getting the local history buffs incensed too. They won't let it be developed, so leaving it as is will just extend our 'park' for free. So, where are we on Centreville's extension?"

"We're in good shape. The PR firm we hired has gotten largely positive feedback, so the city is ready to post public notice. Enough of the county folk look forward to an extension of city services, and the businesses certainly do."

"Good. We should be able to turn the Thaller property quickly then. It's prime commercial real estate and will free up some capital."

"This extension won't be hard, and I'm sure annexation will follow, but after this one I suspect we are going to meet more resistance."

"Perhaps. But the prospect of making money often leads people to see things in a new light."

Serendipity

Timmy wiped his forehead on the sleeve of his t-shirt. He reserved the bottom edge for his nose, the center portion for his mouth, and the upper portion for his eyes. It had been a hot and humid afternoon, and he risked getting chiggers, ticks, and poison ivy as he made his way toward Mr. House's pond.

Matt was just ahead of him. They had spent the last hour or so digging earthworms. Matt's theory was the fish weren't biting because they were stuffed with the mayflies and crane flies that had been emerging from the pond, so only worms would tempt them now. This seemed reasonable, but Timmy suspected the fish in Mr. House's pond also were getting pretty tired of being caught, and then released, by him and Matt. Over the summer they had tried to alternate where they fished, but they had only so many choices: Mr. House's pond, Bartons Mill Pond, or Mill Pond Creek from the old mill site. One weekend Matt's dad had taken them out on the South Fork, and he promised he would again before summer was out.

They had walked miles of Narrow Passage and Mill Pond creeks, hunting for hellgrammites and generally exploring. Since his conversation with Jonas about insects in the stream, Timmy had been on the lookout for them. He pointed them out to Matt, but Matt didn't seem interested unless they found something dramatic, like a big dragonfly larva. Those could be pretty wicked looking. Crayfish were a good find too. Sometimes he and Matt would collect a few crayfish, build a little rock arena in the stream, and then set the crayfish inside it for a gladiator-style match. The matches never quite worked—the crayfish just hid under rocks and avoided each other. The boys watched darters grazing algae, snuck up on sliders and stinkpots and tried to catch them, chased frogs and salamanders whenever they spotted them, and kept a sharp lookout for snakes. Matt definitely seemed to prefer hunting for animals with bones.

Once in a while Mr. House would hire them for yard work, and this past week he had hired them a couple of times in preparation for a big family reunion. The Houses' home was a sprawling, one-story, red brick house with a built-in double garage and walled brick porches outside every door. There were even built-in brick planters on the front porch. Timmy's house was newer, but there was a luxury to the Houses' home that set it apart from its neighbors. Once Timmy had asked Matt about this, and Matt told him that Mrs. House's family had owned a big brick factory and she had inherited a lot of money and land—and a lot of bricks.

Matt's family was invited to the reunion, and earlier that morning while Timmy and Matt were working, Mr. House had told Timmy that he could come along too. Over the past week Matt and Timmy had picked up fallen branches and mowed and raked the yard, swept and hosed off all the porches, and cleaned all the lawn furniture, including some chairs that had been stored in an old shed and were covered with spider webs and egg sacs. Today Mr. House had had them carry some large coolers and folding tables up from the basement, clean them, and set them out in the yard to dry. They also had rolled out an enormous grill from the garage and hosed it down. When they were done with the chores, they had dug up worms in Matt's backyard and now were on their way to fish with two rods from his house.

It was still a bit too early in the afternoon to be fishing, but it was the only time Timmy had. His mother had told him to be home in time to play with Chris while she made dinner, and he knew he better not be late as he was a few days ago. He and Matt could always put the worms in the refrigerator for another trip.

They stopped at the rim of grasses, thistles, and mallows that encircled the pond and without any communication readied their poles. Matt dug through the small box of dirt and pulled out a fat earthworm. He closed the box and placed it down in the shade of the weeds. Meanwhile Timmy pulled out his pocketknife. Matt laid the worm on the ground, and Timmy cut it in half. They both baited their hooks and spread apart a few yards. They were careful not to cast their shadows on the water as they cast their lines into the pond.

Timmy felt the unmistakable pull of a bluegill nibbling at his worm. They didn't bite the bait; they just nibbled it away. He slowly reeled in his line and tried casting farther out. After the second cast he already needed a new worm. He had unsuccessfully cast half a dozen times when he heard Matt's drag. From Matt's grip on his rod, it looked like he had hooked a good-size fish. Matt was letting the fish pull out some line but was keeping his line taut. He reeled in a little bit, then let the fish pull out a little bit more. Timmy had stopped fishing and was just watching, waiting to see what Matt reeled in.

Matt called to him. "It's big. It's a bass."

Timmy set his pole down and hurried over to Matt. When the fish broke the surface, they both emitted a "wow!" It was a largemouth bass—bigger than either of them had caught all summer. Timmy grabbed the line above the fish as Matt maneuvered it to shore.

"Damn, look at the size of that thing!" said Matt.

"I wish I had my camera with me," said Timmy. "He must weigh five pounds."

Matt bobbed the fish up and down on his line a few times. "More like five and a half," he said. "He's got to be a pound more than that one from Bartons Mill."

"You don't have your De-Liar, do you?" asked Timmy, knowing that Matt didn't but hoping he somehow did. They had just grabbed some hooks. Matt's tackle box, with the small scale, was sitting on his porch. "He's got to be at least twenty inches," said Timmy, spanning the fish's length with his hands.

"I'm taking him home," Matt declared.

Timmy winced. "You are?"

"I've got to weigh and measure him."

"Well, let's go then," said Timmy. "No reason to keep him hanging on a stringer." Truth was Timmy knew he wouldn't catch a bigger fish, and even though they weren't having a competition, at least not an acknowledged one, he didn't feel like catching piddling bluegills now. It was hot, he itched all over, and he still had to ride home.

Timmy picked up his rod and the box of worms, and they headed across the field toward the road.

"Kind of a shame," said Timmy, "letting him die." The fish wouldn't be eaten; too much fertilizer and pesticide drained into the pond during a good rain.

"Yeah, I know. But he's probably my record for the summer. And I have to get a picture of him to show the guys at school. They're always saying they caught some big fish, but I'll actually have proof. You know what they say—seeing is believing."

"Yeah," Timmy agreed distractedly. Is that why he took so many pictures?

When they reached Matt's house, Matt fetched a camera, and Timmy took several shots of Matt and his fish. Then Timmy rode home, stopping occasionally to scratch the bites he now knew were chiggers. It wasn't like Matt was gloating or anything, but Timmy was disappointed that he hadn't caught any fish nearly as big as Matt's two largest. Matt kept saying it was just good luck, but they both knew fishing involved skill too. Maybe Matt was right though, because Matt certainly didn't do anything differently from him.

What is good luck anyway, thought Timmy as he pedaled home. Although he used the word often enough, what did it mean? There was God's grace, but He certainly didn't get involved in things like fishing trips. You didn't pray to God to catch a big fish, at least that wasn't the sort of thing you were supposed to pray for. To pray for good fortune didn't mean praying to win lots of money or to inherit a big house from some uncle everyone seemed to have forgotten about, like happened in books and movies. Although God was known to work in mysterious ways. But, in general, God didn't reward you with actual things; He rewarded you with grace, with salvation.

● ● ●

Timmy rode to Matt's house dressed nicely for the family reunion. He had received permission to go on this condition—and that he start home no later than seven that evening. Matt was on the porch, bouncing a ball hard against the concrete to get it to hit the underside of the porch roof. Just the day before Timmy had heard Matt's mother yell at him for doing this, so he figured Matt's parents weren't home.

"I've been waiting for you," Matt called from the porch as Timmy rode up the driveway. "My parents left already."

"Am I late?" asked Timmy.

"Nah. There's no hurry. The pig might not be done yet anyway. And the picnic is probably gonna be pretty boring."

As they rode up the Houses' driveway, Timmy's eyes landed on Mrs. Prickett. She was standing with her sister and brother-in-law, Mr. and Mrs. Endicott. Timmy had met them more than once at Mrs. Prickett's house when collecting for the paper. He reached out and grabbed Matt's arm. "You're related to Mrs. Prickett?"

"I guess," he replied as they parked their bikes in the shade of a large oak along the driveway; "she and her sister are always at these things."

Timmy knew he had to say hello to Mrs. Prickett or else she would chastise him right in front of Matt, or worse, in front of Mr. House. He decided to get it over and done with.

"Well, if it isn't my paper boy," said Mrs. Prickett as he approached her group. Mrs. Endicott had hair as white and eyes as pale blue as Mrs. Pickett's, but she was noticeably a bit younger, a bit shorter, and a bit plumper than her sister. "Are we related, Mr. Timmy Donohue?"

"No, ma'am. Mr. House invited me to come with Matt Boyce. We've been working for Mr. House this summer."

"A second job! Well I am glad to hear you are so industrious. Idleness breeds mischief in a young man," she told him, leaning toward him to emphasize her point. Then, first giving her sister a knowing look, she added, "Unfortunately, your young neighbor doesn't seem to appreciate the value of honest work."

She was talking about Jonas, and Timmy felt compelled to defend him. "Jonas has a job. He works at the library."

"Oh?" said Mrs. Prickett, her mouth turning downward as if disappointed. "Well, I am glad to hear he has a job. He's certainly old enough, and it's important for young people to learn about responsibility."

"Agatha," said Mrs. Endicott, taking her by the elbow, "the food is out. Let's go fix ourselves plates."

Timmy stood obeisantly until they turned away. He was relieved she was gone. Why was she so mean? She probably never even spoke to Jonas. Timmy went in search of Matt and found him sitting on the front porch steps, a plate piled high with food in his lap—pulled pork, coleslaw, potato salad, green beans, and a roll. Timmy sat down next to him, waiting for the crowd of people at the grill and serving table to clear. He didn't want to bump into Mrs. Prickett again.

Once he saw Mrs. Prickett's group carrying their full plates, Timmy walked the long way—clear around the back of the house—to reach the serving table and returned the same way with a full plate and a tall glass of lemonade. He had just filled his mouth with potato salad when he heard the unmistakable voice of Mrs. Prickett. Of all the places to sit, she was a few yards away at a picnic table, along with Mr. and Mrs. House and Mr. and Mrs. Endicott. At least her back was to him.

"Horace and Lillian, it is so kind and generous of you to get the whole family together like this every summer," she was saying.

"Well, you know, Agatha, family comes first," said Mr. House.

"Church, country, family—whoever is knocking on the door that morning," said Mrs. House. They all laughed in agreement.

Timmy leaned toward Matt, whispering even though he didn't need to. "Are Mrs. Prickett and her sister related to Mr. House?"

"I'm not sure. Some of these people are related to Mr. Horace and some to Ms. Lillian. Some are related to both."

Timmy nodded, knowing there were some complex family ties out here.

"So, I hear we're going to be getting some new neighbors, Agatha," said Mr. House.

"George Roper's place? I bet Stan can tell us all about that," she invited him in her saccharine tone.

"From what I've seen of the plans, it will be a beautiful development, particularly for young families," said Mr. Endicott. "Nice homes with nice-size yards, sidewalks, a playground and swimming pool, a park along the pond. It will be done right. There should be two hundred homes or more if Roper can get the wastewater issues worked out the way he wants."

"How's that?" asked Mr. House.

"Well, George is working on a deal to extend sewer lines along Due West Road to hook up to the city's municipal system. If the sewer line deal doesn't work out, he'll have to build a small treatment facility—so fewer houses."

"What do the commissioners prefer?" Mrs. House asked.

"Oh, you know I'm not supposed to talk about that," Mr. Endicott said and let out an airy laugh. "In the near term the sewer line would be good for the county—more developers, including Roper, could tap into it, and we would increase county revenues without increasing tax rates—fix some roads and culverts, add some fire houses. But the city will continue to extend its limits along that sewer line, and we'll eventually lose the revenue. Still, most of us favor the sewer line—the development is going to happen. Might as well let people along Due West make money off their land. Houses are a good cash crop, and they will bring more retail development too."

"That they are," agreed Mr. House, contentedly nodding as he forked a large piece of pork.

"Have the commissioners been hearing a lot of fuss over this?" asked Mrs. Prickett. "I received a flyer from some environmental kooks just before Christmas and again this spring."

"I've noticed a few new faces at our monthly meetings. And Suzanna Phelps has shown up a couple of times. You know she's always trying to preserve the local heritage, so I guess it's no surprise she'd be fussing about a development near Bartons Mill Pond. And she's related by marriage to Claudia Ayers, who tries to vote down every large plat that comes before the board.

"Those environmental types are a lot like summertime gnats though," Mr. Endicott said, waving his hand before his slim face, "mostly annoying, but few do bite." He chuckled and resumed eating.

"So you don't think those people will cause any real problems?" Mrs. Prickett asked. "I think one of my neighbors is involved with them."

"Who's that?" Mr. House asked.

"Lizzy Whitacre. She owns the old Tutwiler home plus a few acres. Every time I bring up George's plans, she changes the subject. And every so often she has several visitors—cars I don't recognize. I suspect she's having meetings at her house." Mrs. Prickett shook her head disapprovingly. "I've been very gracious to her over the years, allowing her to walk on my property whenever she wants, but maybe I shouldn't be, if she's a troublemaker."

"Roper will follow the letter of the law," said Mr. Endicott. "He shouldn't have any problems. Some people just think about themselves—you know, 'not in my backyard.' And then there are those who think they know what's better for everyone else."

"Oh, there's always some of those," Mrs. House chorused.

"I doubt if any of them, besides Lizzy, even live out our way," said Mrs. Prickett with annoyance.

"Actually, the Reals have been showing up at some of the commissioners' meetings," said Mr. Endicott. "You know them? They live a bit east of you, on Mail Route Road. A little bit bohemian, if you know what I mean."

"That Roper is a shrewd businessman," Mr. House said admiringly. "He owns land all over this county—he bought out a lot of farms round here starting in the early sixties. So many folks wanted off the farm, and land sold for cheap. He got most of the remaining Barton land and a good part of the Tutwilers'. Must have had some bankroll to start, and he's certainly made a lot of money since. I've met him a few times—we've had some conversations. He doesn't live locally though."

Agatha nodded knowingly. "He's from Stumptown—not as far back as our family," she glanced at Mrs. House, "but he was raised there."

"He lives just west of North Fork now," Mr. Endicott informed them. "Has a pretty nice spread."

Mrs. Endicott beamed. "We've been invited to Christmas parties there."

"So, Agatha, thinking of selling some of your land?" Mr. House asked.

"No, no, no. I will leave that decision to my boys. It is their father's family's legacy; I would not take that away from them. God has certainly blessed our family with good fortune, and He has certainly blessed my boys with ambition. But I doubt either of them will care to assume the responsibilities of a farm. They seem to have turned into city boys . . . but that's where the money is now, isn't it?"

"Yes, it is, and you certainly are blessed," affirmed Mrs. House.

"Well, there's no hurry to sell," said Mr. House. "Land is only going to get more and more valuable in these parts."

"God rewards those who wait," quipped Mrs. Endicott. "Now, I'm going to go look at those desserts," she said, working herself up from the picnic bench. "Who else is coming?"

●　　　　●　　　　●

Timmy rode his bike toward home on a stomach full of pulled pork, potato salad, dinner rolls, strawberry shortcake, custard crème pie, and homemade peach ice cream. He was feeling rather full and slightly sick. Matt had ridden with him part way but then had turned around and gone home.

Now he knew why Matt was so keen on his going to the reunion. All-in-all it had been pretty boring—the other kids were either much older, and not kids anymore, or much younger and annoying. All there was to do was eat and wander around the yard in circles.

Timmy didn't mind being alone now—somehow being bored was tiring business. But it was more than that. The talk about Ms. Lizzy and the housing development had made him uncomfortable. And as much talk as there was about God, Timmy didn't recognize Him as his own.

●　　　　●　　　　●

Agatha had suggested to Mr. Turnbull that he arrive early in the morning, to avoid the heat of the day. More so, she wanted him to arrive at a time when it would be quite appropriate to offer him only coffee. She didn't know him, and she didn't want to be put in the position of an extended visit if she didn't take to him. In fact, she already felt slighted by his visit—that George Roper was sending someone to see her on a business matter. If Mr. Roper wanted to discuss business, he should come himself.

Although she saw the black sports car pull into her driveway, she waited until after the doorbell rang to make her way slowly to the front door.

"Mr. Turnbull, I presume."

"How do you do Mrs. Prickett? May I come in?"

"Yes, certainly," Agatha replied. An impatient man, she thought, no time for polite pleasantries.

Once he was inside, she extended her arm toward the drawing room, where she had set out her coffee service.

"Would you like some coffee?" she offered.

"Oh no, had my caffeine for the day. Thank you."

"Well, I hope you don't mind if I have some," she said as she poured coffee into one of her grandmother's bone china cups. As she was adding sugar, Mr. Turnbull started talking. Truly impatient, she thought.

"I'm sure you are familiar by now with Mr. Roper's plans to develop the property just across the road from you."

Agatha nodded as she sat down.

"Well, given that your small piece of land that is adjacent to his can't be of much use to you, he thought he would offer to buy it from you. You can be assured he won't be putting any houses there, so it will remain just as it is today and provide a buffer between you and the new development. Mr. Roper just thought it would be a neighborly gesture to buy it—since his development will come right up to your property line."

Agatha regarded the well-dressed, handsome man who was trying to sell her what a less-refined person would call a line of bull. How insulting—not even showing her the courtesy of being honest.

"Oh, I think I can live with his development. You can tell Mr. Roper that I am not interested in selling."

"His offer is very generous. . . ."

"I intend for my children to inherit the full extent of their father's family's farm. Perhaps Mr. Roper does not appreciate that."

"Forty thousand . . ."

"His offer is declined. Now, if our business is concluded here, I do have some errands to attend to in town."

●　　　　　●

"Timmy! Timmy! Jonas is here to see you," Helen called.

Timmy bolted out of his room and raced down the stairs.

"Hey Jonas," Timmy said as he reached the last few steps.

"Hi Timmy. Are you busy?"

Timmy shot his mother, who was standing beside Jonas, a questioning look. Her face was noncommittal.

"I have some chores to do today. Why?"

"The blackberries at the cemetery are ripe. I thought you might like to go pick some." He turned toward Timmy's mother, "If that would be okay."

Mrs. Donohue gave a hesitant nod. "I guess it will. Let me get Timmy a bucket."

"I already have one for each of us," Jonas told her. She looked pleasantly surprised.

The cemetery was close to a two-mile walk from Prickett Farm Road, but it was still early in the day, and although the air wasn't cool, it wasn't hot. They walked in the road because the roadside had grown high in grass, Queen Anne's lace, coneflower, and bee balm. They both took note of the fancy black sports car in Mrs. Prickett's driveway.

When they reached the cemetery, Timmy followed Jonas through the wrought iron gate. Timmy had never been in the cemetery before. It was an old cemetery; a car entrance and loop road had been added at the far end, closer to Due West Road. The gate they entered opened to a path that led to the old brick chapel. It was a small building with a metal roof and a set of double doors, painted white, in front. They walked up the path to the chapel and then went around its side to look through one of the white-sashed, sagging windows. The interior was barely larger than Timmy's living room. There were five rows of pews on each side of a center aisle, and in front a simple pulpit was raised two steps from the floor—much simpler than Timmy's church.

"The blackberries are along the back fence," Jonas told Timmy.

As they walked toward the back of the chapel, Timmy saw that there were stones lying flat on the ground. From the road the thin gravestones had always appeared to be arranged a bit haphazardly. He slowed his steps and started to read the gravestones; Jonas slowed down too. The stones were heavily stained by lichens and mold, and from years of weathering the inscriptions were barely visible, the surfaces so eroded. Timmy couldn't believe how old the stones were—early 1800s, 1788, 1760. Before the Revolutionary War! The name was Barton, but the rest of the writing was barely discernable. "Look at this one," he called to Jonas.

"Wow," said Jonas, as he studied the tombstone with Timmy. "There are more Bartons right over here. Look."

Jonas showed Timmy two small tombstones of infants named Barton, and then they looked at stones of another male Barton, two apparent spouses, and one female Barton and her spouse. Leaving their buckets, they roamed among the stones. Some stones held just names, some had dates of death, and some even had birth dates; some stones related parentage, marriage, or military service; and some stones quoted Bible verse or poetry. Another family name, which they did not recognize, appeared and reappeared. Then, on a tombstone from 1827, they came across a familiar name: one of the female Bartons had married a Tutwiler, and now the name of Tutwiler began to appear along with the Bartons. More names were added as they looked at more stones, but many were hard to read. Jonas surmised from irregular gaps that some gravestones were missing. In 1881 another familiar name appeared: Prickett. The stones became easier to read as they moved away from the chapel toward Due West Road. Timmy caught the entrance of a House in the early 1900s married to a Prickett, and he eventually came across Woodrow Prickett, Mrs. Prickett's husband, which sort of creeped him out. That was a little too close—the long-dead people weren't quite so real to him but rather like names from a history book.

He looked up to see Jonas squatted down a row away. He joined him and looked at the stone. It marked the grave of a Lawrence Barton born in 1924.

"He died kind of young, huh?" Timmy observed.

"World war two. Help me look along the rest of this row. I want to see if there are any other Bartons after these."

They had stopped to read another headstone when a stern, high-pitched voice demanded, "What are you two doing here?"

They turned to see Mrs. Prickett. She looked angry and pleased at the same time.

"We're just looking at the tombstones, ma'am" said Timmy.

"We're learning a little local history," added Jonas flatly.

"I found where someone in your family married someone in the Barton family in the 1800s," said Timmy, trying to appease her.

"That would be my husband's family. My maiden name is Hodges," Mrs. Prickett told them. "You're not disturbing any of the graves, are you? This is a sanctified burial ground."

Jonas answered with a plain no, whereas Timmy added a "ma'am."

"All right," said Mrs. Prickett, looking severe. "But if I notice anything amiss, I will be having a talk with your parents."

"Do you know if Lawrence Barton had any siblings?" Jonas asked, not intimidated by her threats.

"Well, there was Edward. He left as a young man, after the war, and came back only for visits. I believe he had a daughter—her name was Adrianne. I'm sure there are other Bartons, but Lawrence and Edward's father, Wendell, was the last one of his generation to remain locally. I believe my husband's family's land was once Barton land. Most of the land around here was at one time." Suddenly Mrs. Prickett came out of her reminiscence and her icy blue eyes burned suspicion. "Why are you so interested in the Bartons?"

"I heard the Bartons still own the old mill site. I was just wondering if any are still around."

"Oh? Well, I haven't seen any Bartons in years," said Mrs. Prickett. "But I have not heard anything about the mill site being sold."

They stood there in silence for a moment. It was obvious Mrs. Prickett would not leave while they were still there.

"Well, we better get our buckets, Timmy," said Jonas as he started toward where they had left their buckets behind the chapel.

Timmy nodded at Mrs. Prickett and then hurried after Jonas. He admired Jonas's fearlessness but couldn't manage it himself.

Almost an hour had passed in the cemetery, and yet their buckets were empty. The sun was climbing in the sky as they left through the gate.

"Why are you so interested in the Bartons?"

"Cause one of them probably still owns this land we're walking past, and I'd like to figure out who that is."

"Man is it hot. I need a drink. I wish we had picked some berries."

"Yeah. Me too. I hope your mother doesn't get mad—that we didn't pick any berries. We can get a drink at Ms. Lizzy's. We can drink from the hose if she's not home."

Once their minds became set on getting a drink the rest of their walk became a march. They stopped talking and focused on their destination. With a constant background of summer buzzing accompanying them, the boys kept up a steady pace. When Mrs. Prickett's house came into full view, they both thought of their encounter with her. Timmy wondered if she had seen them from the road or just happened to stop there. He seemed to be running into her an awful lot this week. He sure hoped she didn't come driving by as they walked home.

When they reached Ms. Lizzy's house, they saw her car was in the driveway, so they went to the kitchen door. Timmy knocked, and soon Pete and Clem were at the door announcing their arrival. Lizzy showed up soon after and opened the door.

"You two are looking a little hot. Come on in and cool off. Want some tea? Water?"

They both answered yes. Lizzy filled two glasses with ice, fetched the tea from the refrigerator, and let them fill their own glasses.

"Thank you,' they said before gulping down the tea.

"Where have you two been?" Lizzy asked as she refilled the glasses for them.

"We went to pick blackberries," said Jonas, "but we got a bit distracted. Do you know who actually owns the land between Mrs. Prickett and the cemetery?"

"Well, I've always been told the Bartons still own the land. But that family was long gone before I arrived, so I never met any of them."

"Is there a way to find out who owns it?"

"Well, it has to be on the county tax roll—the bill is sent to someone, no doubt. You're thinking of tracking them down?"

"Well it may be worthwhile—having another landowner on our side."

"Our side of what?" asked Timmy, who had slid off his stool and was at the table looking through a sketch pad lying there. He was studying a picture of a curtained window in a dark room. Only the bit of moonlight that shone through the curtain lit the scene.

"Our side of saving Bartons Mill Pond," Jonas said. "Ms. Lizzy has been working to keep Mr. Roper from building all those houses there."

"Jonas has been helping too," said Lizzy, watching Timmy look through her dark period.

"They were talking about that at the picnic I went to the other day," said Timmy, turning his full attention to them.

"Who is 'they'?" asked Lizzy.

"Mrs. Prickett, and the Houses, and the Endicotts."

"As in the county commissioner?" asked Lizzy.

Timmy shrugged. "I guess so. They did mention the commissioners a couple of times."

"What were they saying?" asked Jonas.

Suddenly Timmy didn't want to say because he remembered what Mrs. Prickett had said and her sort of calling Ms. Lizzy a kook.

"Well, Mr. Endicott was saying that the development would be really nice, and he was hoping there would be a sewer line along Due West Road so people could sell their land for a lot of money. Then Mrs. Prickett asked him whether there were any people fussing about it all, and he said yes, but they were like gnats." Timmy blushed, although it was hard to tell through his still-red cheeks. He hadn't meant to repeat any of the things he had heard about Ms. Lizzy.

"Did they say anything else?" asked Jonas.

"Sure, they said all sorts of stuff. Mrs. Prickett said that she wasn't going to sell her land, that she'd leave it to her sons."

"Well that's a relief, at least for now," said Lizzy. "Gnats, eh?"

"I'm sorry," said Timmy.

"Oh, don't worry. That's nothing. I could probably come up with much worse names for people like Endicott and Roper."

"So, are all those houses really going to be built on the other side of the pond?" Timmy asked. Even though he had seen the orange flagging, he had hoped it wouldn't really happen.

"It's very likely," said Lizzy. "We gnats can pester Roper, but that's probably about all."

"At the picnic they said that Mr. Roper doesn't live around here. It doesn't seem fair that he can build all those houses here when he doesn't even live here."

Lizzy shrugged her shoulders. "It's not about fair, Timmy. According to the law, Roper has the right to do with his land as he sees fit. From his perspective, he's providing houses to people who want them."

"Do you really think he cares about that?" remarked Jonas.

"How about some water?" Lizzy asked as she watched Timmy drain his second glass of iced tea. Timmy went to the sink to fill his glass and returned to his stool.

Lizzy looked at Jonas and Timmy, two sweaty boys she had "collected" along with the stray cats and dogs who found their way to her for shelter. They had their own families, of course, but she was happy for her role in their lives—a safe adult without the strings of expectations. To an outsider her relationship with them may have seemed to be that of a childless woman filling some maternal need, and she could accept there was some truth there. But over these last months these two seemingly mismatched boys had given her something she felt she had lost: some hope for the future. As much as she saw the future dim, the world being swallowed up by an insatiable humanity, she also saw in these boys the potential to carry humanity forward.

"I'll be right back," Lizzy said. She headed up the stairs, took the few steps past her bedroom door, and hesitated for a moment with her hand on the doorknob. She then pushed open the door to the small bedroom and stepped inside for the first time in many, many months. She rummaged through a box against the wall until she found what she was looking for and then grabbed the lightest fishing pole from the corner. She left the door open behind her.

"Here, Timmy," she said as she walked into the kitchen and handed him the fishing pole and reel. "I thought you might like to have this."

"Wow. Thank you, ma'am, I mean, Ms. Lizzy." Timmy took the rod and reel from her and began admiring them. They were far nicer than what he owned. While he was examining the reel, Lizzy disappeared again. When she returned, she handed a black case to Jonas.

"Here, Jonas. This is for you."

Jonas took the case from Lizzy and slowly unsnapped it. He gently removed the larger pair of binoculars he had seen hanging from the hall tree the other day and looked up at her. "These are incredibly nice. Are you sure you want to give them to me?"

"Of course I'm sure or I wouldn't have. You'll make good use of them. I have that smaller pair, and I rarely use them. To be honest, I don't like looking up in trees for birds. It hurts my neck."

• • •

Helen's eyes narrowed when she saw Timmy had arrived home without any berries but with a new fishing pole.

"What have you been up to?" she demanded.

"We got distracted at the cemetery. We got to looking at the tombstones instead of picking blackberries . . . and then it got too hot."

"Hmm," was his mother's reply. She looked at Timmy skeptically and then turned her gaze to Jonas. Her eyes narrowed in suspicion for a moment but only met Jonas's guileless face. She turned back to Timmy. "And the fishing pole?"

"Oh, Ms. Lizzy gave it to me. I'm going to catch the big one with this pole."

Completing the cycle, the body becomes skeletonized. This stage may last up to one year. A resurgence of vegetation should occur.

Perseverance

As the early morning light spread, a deep red flamed along the border of the forest. The sumacs were turning from red to scarlet; the season for these meager trees to shine had arrived, albeit the color marked the leaves' senescence.

Traffic at the bird feeder had picked up. Early migrants, small warblers with their subtle to distinctive markings, stopped at the feeder for a day or two, joining the regular visitors. Lizzy placed her coffee cup in the sink and rubbed some cream over her roughened hands. She then grabbed her things from the table and left for work.

A late hay crop remained to be cut in the field on the far side of Agatha Prickett's house; a large assemblage of bales from an earlier cutting, their color pale with age, were lined up along the dirt road that led to the barn. The sun didn't seem quite ready to light up the sky, and as Lizzy crossed Mill Pond Creek, a light fog condensed on her windshield.

Lizzy drove past the cemetery. The leaves of autumn were beginning to collect at the base of the fence; yellow-leaved wild grape vines wrapped around the black pickets, each picket capped with a fleur-de-lis framed in a semicircle. The aged red brick of the old chapel seemed to be at home in the season's color palette of reds, oranges, yellows, and browns. Soon all the trees would be bare, except for the pines. Particularly on the overcast days of fall, the spectrum of tombstone grays added to the beauty of this place of rest.

Lizzy turned east on Due West Road and headed toward town. She was tired; she had had a restless night. Again a dream had disturbed her sleep. It was a simple dream. Wes had taken Happy for a walk, first stopping at Happy's gravesite. They had been gone a long time, and she was waiting for them, anxiously wandering in and out of the house, up and down the stairs. Over and over again she would arrive at the kitchen faucet, the water dripping. She'd get a drink of water, try to tighten the faucet, and then she would start looking for them all over again.

When she walked into the lab, Carolyn immediately greeted her with the news that several people were out sick with some sort of stomach virus. "I've called everyone on the afternoon shift, and a few can make it in early, but I have to put you on blood collection. Everyone in phlebotomy is out."

"All day?" Lizzy asked, hoping not.

"I'm juggling people wherever I can. If I can get Vince, I'll switch you out. But he's off today, and I haven't been able to reach him. For now, though, orders are already stacking up, and rounds are just getting started."

Lizzy checked the collection cart thoroughly. Everything was stocked. No more room for procrastination. "I'm off," she said to Kristen as she rolled past the reception desk.

Her first stop was the pediatric corridor. She negotiated her cart around the large buggy full of breakfasts to be delivered and stopped at the nurses' station.

"Hello Phyllis," Lizzy greeted the bent-over head of curly gray hair.

"Well Ms. Lizzy," said Phyllis with a big smile as she looked up. "It has been a long time since I've seen you doing the rounds."

"You know I hate drawing blood."

"You should have thought of that before you became a blood tech." Lizzy had been Phyllis' tag-along aide many years ago, and Phyllis had tried to talk Lizzy into nursing school.

"It's only the collection part I don't like. Let me see, I have to draw Ryan Phillips—and there are also orders for a urine sample."

"I've already taken care of the urine—there's a repeat order every few hours. What a strange one," Phyllis said, leaning in to whisper. "He was admitted yesterday. The boy's bowels were totally impacted, and he was dangerously dehydrated. Apparently he had quit drinking so he wouldn't have to pee. He was on some sort of strange mission to purify himself. Seems to me he was going about it the wrong way. It has not been pretty."

"Great."

"Well, the ugliest part is over. Put on a happy face, you don't want to scare him to death. Right there—room 407." Phyllis extended a wiggling finger to point down the hall to her right.

Lizzy wheeled her cart into the room and saw a woman she presumed to be the boy's mother sitting next to the bed, holding the boy's hand and stroking it while she talked to him quietly. Lizzy knew well that hospital stays didn't show one in one's best light; this fleshy-cheeked boy looked drawn and distressed. He had obviously been crying—his eyes were red and puffy.

"Good morning, Ryan," Lizzy said as cheerily as she could muster. "I need to get a blood sample."

"Another one?" whined Ryan, his eyes filling with tears.

"Yes. I'm sorry. We need to make sure you're on the mend." Lizzy smiled at his mother, who looked exhausted. She handed the boy a ball to squeeze, tied a band around his arm, and as she was stroking the inside of his arm to find a good vein, she tried to distract him.

"So where do you go to school, Ryan?"

"St. Xavier's."

"Oh. I know some children who go there. What grade are you in?"

"I just started sixth."

"Oh, then you must know my neighbor. His name is Timmy Donohue. Whoa! Try to relax your grip on the ball."

•   •   •

After work Lizzy ran some errands until it was time to meet Nancy; they had planned an after-work get together. She arrived early at the restaurant, the one they had discovered many years ago on their first trip to Centreville. The restaurant wasn't fancy. It had wood booths around the perimeter and some tables in the center space. Much of the lighting came from the windowed front, and the deeper one ventured into the restaurant, the darker it became. Over each booth was a well-aged photograph of a scene from a foreign land, a theme that carried over to the menu. What had kept them returning to the restaurant over the years was the menu of simple, inexpensive dishes from around the world. It certainly wasn't the décor, which looked old when they had first visited and hadn't changed since.

Lizzy asked for a glass of water and gazed out the window to the street. She had ended up collecting blood all day and felt spent. She had to take blood from the sad boy Ryan twice, but at least he was to be released by evening. Blood itself did not disturb her, but the anxiety that drawing it often elicited from patients made the task stressful.

"How are you?" asked Lizzy as Nancy slipped into the booth.

"Fine. Busy day though. Started first thing in the morning. Hannah remembered last minute that she needed to bring poster board to school, so we had a morning crisis of hunting some down while Abigail droned, 'We're gonna be late, we're gonna be late.' Then I had to run over to the store during my lunch break because Lou's help was out sick—some stomach virus—and Lou needed time to finish up a lock job. Then back to puking dogs, scratching cats—the usual combo."

"You should have called—we could have gotten together some other time."

"No, no, no. This is good. I need a break from the daily routine. I get lost in it."

The waitress arrived to take their order.

"I'll start with a big glass of your house red," said Nancy.

"I'll have the same," said Lizzy. After the waitress left, she said, "We could have waited until Friday."

"No, Friday is hard. The girls always want to have or go to sleepovers—I'm on the phone or in the car most the afternoon."

"Abigail and Hannah are great."

"Yeah, I know. So, how are you?"

"Compared with you? Just fine. But several people were out—that stomach virus is going around the labs big time. I had to collect blood all day. You know how I hate doing that."

Their wine arrived, and they ordered their favorite dish to share—a Mediterranean appetizer plate.

Lizzy continued. "And I was tired to start with. I had a dream that woke me up early, and then I kept waking up thinking I'd forgotten something."

"I've had that feeling. Was it a bad dream?"

"No, not really. There wasn't much to it. It was about Wes. He was walking Happy, and I was worried because they were taking so long to come back. And the kitchen faucet was dripping. I kept trying to get it to stop dripping."

"Did you have to pee?"

Lizzy scowled at her.

The waitress returned with their order. When she left, Nancy said, "Lizzy, you sure have forgotten something—you're alive. I don't want to sound trite or insensitive, but you need a new life plan."

"I know." She tapped her fingernails on her glass and then picked it up. "Wes wouldn't want me to be unhappy. And I'm not. I like the life I have now."

"Perhaps. But Lizzy, what do you think your dream is about? You're wandering in an empty house waiting for someone to return who won't."

"I just can't do it."

"What? Let yourself be happy? Are you punishing yourself for something?"

"I just don't want to forget, to let him fade. It would be like letting him die twice." Lizzy looked down at the table to regain her composure. She hadn't realized how close to the surface this eruption had made its way. She wanted to remember Wes as he was, as they were, and not fall into her own grief. Yet it didn't seem there would ever be an end to the well of grief she kept boarded up.

Nancy reached across the table and put her hand on Lizzy's. "Babe, I would never suggest you forget Wes, and I'm certainly not saying another relationship would be a panacea. I'm just saying I want to see some modulation again—you've been somewhat of a flatliner."

Lizzy laughed. "I thought that was maturity."

•   •   •

The wind had picked up, and a light rain started falling as Lizzy drove out of town. The battle of the fronts had begun a few weeks ago—cold fronts pushing in from the north, warm fronts pushing back from the south. Sometimes the battles were skirmishes, and rains would fall as the moisture-laden warm air was wedged upward and cooled; other times the fronts met in great battles of wind, thunder, and lightening, although these dramatic clashes were more characteristic of the spring. There was no permanent victor in these battles of the great air masses—as the seasons changed so did their relative strength.

By the time Lizzy reached Narrow Passage Road, the rain had passed, but a persistent southerly breeze remained. Lizzy dropped her things on the table and then hurried back out to get Pete and Clem from their pen. Although the rain had been light, she wanted to limit collateral damage by getting them in before they got absolutely muddy. She grabbed the kitchen towel, wiped their paws, and then carried the muddy towel to the pantry. By the time she returned to the kitchen, Alice, CB, Pete, and Clem were all lined up, waiting for dinner. In fact, it was uncanny how calmly they were waiting and how they did appear to be arranged in a neat row. Maybe they knew something—Lizzy had read something about animals predicting the weather. Then Alice spoke, "Meow!"

"All right," said Lizzy, "I'm getting to it." She fed the cats first out of habit, and the dogs knew well enough to stay away from the cats' food. As she fed Pete and Clem she heard the wind picking up. Looking out the kitchen window, she saw red and golden leaves being carried aloft on a strong breeze. Then she heard some sharp thumps coming from the front of the house. Was it hail? She hurried across the living room, opened the front door, and stepped onto the porch. The wind was shaking loose the bounty of acorns from the white oak.

A moisture-laden breeze was coming from the southeast. These winds always reminded Lizzy of being at the ocean, even though it was hours away. To her east, a full moon was rising, its illumination amplified by the thin veil of soft clouds that slid past it. To the west the sun was setting amid wisps of white, pink, and an intense aquamarine blue.

The acorn rain was now an occasional ping on the roof. Late-season crickets were beginning to call. Day was yielding to night. Lizzy looked at a star that seemed to have appeared instantaneously in the sky above her head and wondered what she would wish for at this juncture in her life. However, the ringing phone interrupted this thought before she had her answer. It was Donna.

"The county commissioners have Roper's subdivision plat on schedule for Thursday. The meeting starts at four. Do you think you can make it?"

"Yes, I can. I'm scheduled for the morning shift this week. I want to see how this unfolds."

"Me too! I'm glad you can go. It will be good for as many of us to attend as possible. Hager will be there, Seymour plans to speak, and Dr. Dave said he would—do you want to speak?"

"I think they'll cover everything."

"See you there, then," said Donna.

Lizzy put down the phone and considered a moment before picking it up again and dialing the Meyers. Jonas answered.

"Roper's subdivision plans will be reviewed by the county commissioners on Thursday," she told him. "The meeting starts at four. If you'd like to go perhaps you could ask Russ, Mr. Henderson, if he's going—he could give you a ride from school."

"Yeah, I would like to go. I'll ask him tomorrow. Uhm, thanks."

No sooner had she put down the receiver than her phone rang again.

"Hello Lizzy, this is Agatha Prickett. It has been so long since I've bumped into you that I thought I'd call and see how you are doing."

Bumped into me, thought Lizzy, I thought it was stalking.

"I'm doing just fine, Agatha. How have you been?"

"Oh, glad that it is finally slowing down a bit from that busy time of year when the crops are coming in. Even though I lease my fields, there's a lot to do during the season. And we were blessed with a good summer, I must say. The Lord sent us just the right amount of rain—not too much, not too little. How did you do with your little garden?"

"Very well. I'm still harvesting beans and a few late stragglers—tomatoes and the like."

"It keeps one busy, doesn't it? It seems like you've been awfully busy lately—are you putting in a lot of overtime? Some days you're gone from dawn to dark."

Ah, this was a fishing expedition. Was it just a coincidence that she was calling now, days before Roper's plans came up for review?

"Just trying to spend more time with friends."

"Well I'm glad to hear that, Lizzy. Anyone special?"

"No, just old friends from college days."

"Friends are blessings. I am very thankful for my church friends, all very good people. And not just all old people like me," Agatha added and laughed appropriately.

Lizzy didn't know what to say. Her hesitation unfortunately invited Agatha to continue.

"You really should come to one of our church socials. It would give you an opportunity to meet some new people . . . perhaps even a nice young man."

"I think I'm getting a bit old for a young man," Lizzy said, trying to dismiss Agatha's invitation without directly declining.

"Speaking of young men, I heard that Meyers boy had a job over the summer. I was glad to hear that—idleness breeds mischief."

"Yes, Jonas worked at the library." Although she knew she should ignore Agatha's remark, to circumvent further conversation, Lizzy had had enough of Agatha's insinuations about Jonas. "And Jonas is actually a thoughtful young man. I'm very fond of him."

"Oh! I am sorry, I meant no offense. He just has a strange manner about him."

"He can be a bit awkward, but I find him to be very genuine, sincere."

"Well I am glad to hear that he's honest. It is a virtue."

"That it is," Lizzy said, noting the irony of their pretenses here. "Speaking of which," she said, grinning at being able to use this favorite device of Agatha's, "I really have to get some dinner in me, Agatha. I just got home from a long day at work a bit ago. Thank you for calling."

"Oh, sorry if I kept you. Let's chat again soon. Have a good evening. Goodbye now."

After hanging up the phone, Lizzy started to reheat a vegetable soup she had made the night before and listened to another gentle wave of rain that had begun to fall. I better get those beans tomorrow, she thought, before we get a cold snap and I lose them.

· · ·

Right after work the next day Lizzy dug a colander out of the cabinet and with it in hand headed for the garden. She had planted another two rows of green beans late in the summer, and now the broad-leaved bushy plants dangled their tender fruit. She had relocated her grandmother's recipe for dilly beans, and she needed young, tender beans to make it. Systematically working down the first row, she pulled the beans from the stems gently so that she wouldn't pull the entire plant from the damp soil. Beans were still coming on, and she might be able to harvest more if the weather held another week or so.

The ground had largely soaked up the rain from the previous night, but the garden was a bit muddy. Toward the end of the second row, she stretched her arm to reach under the last bean plant and scraped her finger against something sharp—a thorn. She looked at her finger; a thin line of blood marked the cut.

Lizzy examined her hands—they were full of scrapes. She had dug in the earth this past spring so that she could again witness green emerging from seed, food coming forth from the earth, life continuing as it had for a time she could not fathom even if she could ascribe a number. Her hands held the scars of returning to gardening; they were scars of living. None of them—her hands, the vegetation, the earth's surface—passed through life without scars. Bean leaves grew with the trenches of leaf miners embedded, oak leaves with the galls of wasps. These leaves persevered, mostly; they were scarred but still able to perform their miraculous photosynthesis.

She looked at the cut again. It stung. She had better go clean it.

After washing her hands at the sink, Lizzy filled a glass with water. She took a sip, dumped the remainder, let the water run some more, and refilled her glass. She then went to the bathroom and tended her cut.

Back outside Lizzy saw CB scampering up the trunk of the crape myrtle.

"What are you doing, you silly girl?" she asked CB, whose eyes grew wider before she bolted farther up the tree. Shaking her head, Lizzy looked over to the pansies; they had undergone a resurgence following their midsummer wilt; the mushrooms that had sprouted were gone except for a few that were shriveled and barely perceptible.

Lizzy continued on to the garden with gloves and pruners. She intended to remove the culprit that had cut her finger. When she examined the bush growing at the edge of the garden, she saw it was much larger than she had surmised; its base was at least half an inch in diameter. She wondered how she could have missed seeing it before. It must have been growing for months. She decided to try to dig it out—she probably could even transplant it.

She began to dig around the thorny base with her gloved hands— first an inch, then two, and still no roots. She continued to dig. Her hole became deeper and wider, and the stalk, thicker and thornless below the soil surface, just kept going down. For a moment she thought she heard water flowing—more likely, she surmised, she was hearing her pulse. Wiping the perspiration from her forehead, she sat back up on her haunches and was dizzied by her own quick movement. She pressed her hands to the ground for a few moments to steady herself and considered cutting the stem. But she had become obsessed with finding its roots, its origin. One hand on the edge of the hole, she leaned into it and continued digging. Suddenly the earth around the plant gave way. Lizzy reflexively grabbed the stalk as she started to fall. But rather than falling, she slid down the smooth stem and was able to right herself before hitting bottom.

She landed on her feet, hard—in cold water, on rock. She held her breath until her body forced her to open her mouth to inhale. Her heart was racing, and it was a full minute before she heard anything other than her own heartbeat. It was then she heard the steady trickling of water. She consciously worked to control her breathing and assess her situation. She wasn't hurt.

The hole she had dug was three to four feet above her head and let in enough light that she could see she was in an underground cavern. Would anyone hear her if she called? The dogs. Would they fall in too? Or would they cause the roof of the cavern to collapse on top of her? Nausea overwhelmed her. How could this be? How did this happen? Would she die here?

Lizzy began crying, deep, choking sobs. The binding had ripped open, and there was a gaping hole. All that she had held inside could no longer be contained. Her heart opened to the grief of the world, every sorrow, every loss, every pain. The hollowness she had felt those first few days returned to her—not that it had ever truly left. The seam continued to tear. She cried for the last five years of her life, living with a weight she wouldn't set down. She didn't want to let their life together dissipate into nothingness, so she had attempted to live in stasis, longing deeply for a life that was past. The Wes she knew would be buried with her. She cried for all the things she had been denied in his death. She cried for her own loneliness.

Gradually she became angry. Angry at what? At whom? At the world? At Wes? At herself? She couldn't blame anyone else. These last years were her own doing. She had let so much time pass, going through the motions of life without allowing herself to find any real warmth. She didn't think anyone would love her the way he had. She hadn't let anyone. She had kept her own family closed out, she had pushed Russ away. She continued to cry in a steady stream—for all she had left undone and might never get to do. She cried for the baby that they had wanted but never had. Tears fell from her face and joined the small stream of water that flowed at her feet beneath the surface of the earth.

Lizzy's crying gradually subsided, and she was spent. Her anger was washed away. She felt cold and empty now, almost numb. Damn, she thought, wiping her face on her sleeve, I'm going to drown myself. She looked around. She had ended up in a sink hole in her own backyard, under her garden—her first positive undertaking in all these years. She looked at the stalk that had brought her here. It appeared to be rooted in solid rock, growing from the bowels of the earth itself. Its base was almost five inches in diameter. How had it sprouted in this underground spring? How did it grow without light? How in the hell was she going to get out of this hole?

Lizzy shook the stalk. It was more substantial than it looked. She reached up the stalk as far as she could, gripped her hands tightly around it and, in one jerky motion, pulled up her knees and clasped the stalk tightly with her legs. It swayed but remained erect. After a few seconds, she dug her feet into the stalk and pushed up quickly, extending her legs until they were almost straight. She had gained at least half a foot above the ground. She then loosened her right hand and slid it upward followed by her left hand. Once she had extended her grip upward, she clasped the stalk tightly with her hands and quickly drew up her knees. She immediately began to slide back down the stem but quickly stopped her descent by tightly re-clasping the stalk with her legs. She rested a few seconds, although there was nothing restful about her position, and then forcefully straightened her legs. Again she extended one hand at a time and repeated the maneuver of pulling up her knees and straightening out her legs. She repeated it, over and over again, slipping down a little each time but slowly creeping upward, biting her lower lip to turn her attention away from her growing fatigue and the constant fear she would slide all the way back down. She didn't know how long she could continue, but she had to—she had to save herself. As the stalk tapered, it swayed precariously with each move she made. She was afraid it wouldn't hold her weight much longer; she was afraid she couldn't hold on much longer.

Finally, the top of her head was in the opening she had dug; she was looking at a thick layer of clay and soil. Without moving her hands, she pulled her knees into their bent position. She slowly slid her left hand up the slim stem and then her right. She paused, knowing her next move could undo all her progress, but she had to make it. She could not just continue to cling where she was. She quickly threw her right arm from the stem and pressed her forearm hard to the ground. Without hesitating, her feet clasped tightly to the stalk, she pushed upward as hard as she could. Her shoulders just cleared the hole, and she flung her left arm from the stalk to the ground in front of her, digging her fingers into the soil. Every bit of her body was trembling. With her legs already fully extended she had to use whatever strength she had left in her arms to pull her torso out of the hole. She pressed down hard on her forearms and elbows, and pulling with her upper arms and pushing against the stalk with her feet, she managed to get her waist above the hole. She flopped her upper torso on the ground and lay there panting. Then she slowly slid her arms in front of her and wiggled forward using the muscles of her trunk as if she were an earthworm. Once enough of her legs were clear of the hole, she rolled away from it. Breathing hard, she lay on her back, limbs splayed, exhausted. She closed her eyes. Her mind went blank.

Lizzy felt a touch as light as a newborn's fingers on her cheek. She opened her eyes and through moist eyelashes saw Alice staring at her. "Go Alice, tell Timmy that Ms. Lizzy fell into the well." Alice just sat there, unimpressed. Lizzy slowly sat up and looked at the rose bush, with its solitary bud, rising above her row of beans.

Alliances

Jonas couldn't imagine a finer day. The morning sun was shining brilliantly in crisp, cleansed air. The night before a bolus of warm air from the south had tried to slide in, but the northern front had pressed back, wringing the moisture from the warmer air mass. The morning dew revealed glistening silk strands of spider webs in the tall roadside vegetation. Feathery white seeds of milkweed wafting through the air were caught in these silken traps.

It had been cooling off gradually for several weeks now. Jonas enjoyed these early days of cool weather. He would miss much of the day's glory, though, for he would be getting on the school bus in a minute. He could hear the bus as it turned onto a quiet Narrow Passage Road. He didn't mind school as much this year, now that he saw it as a path toward doing what he wanted. And this morning he needed to talk to Mr. Henderson about going to the commissioners' meeting.

Jonas entered the cafeteria without the discomfort he had felt every day for the previous two years. Perhaps it was because his classmates had matured. Perhaps it was because they had become accustomed to him. Perhaps it had nothing to do with how anyone treated him but had more to do with how he felt about himself.

He made his way straight for Mr. Henderson's room, hoping to catch him before classes started. Jonas knocked gently on the classroom door, then opened it and stuck in his head. Russ was sitting at his desk, absorbed in a book.

"Mr. Henderson?"

Russ looked up and then stood up. "Jonas. Come in. You know, you can call me Russ when we're not with other students. But that may be weird for you—whatever is comfortable. What's up?"

"I was wondering whether I could get a ride with you to the commissioners' meeting after school tomorrow. Ms. Lizzy thought you might be going."

"Yes, I am, but my planning period is at the end of the day, so I was going to leave a bit early to get there on time. Hmm . . . what do you have last period?"

"History."

"With whom?

"Boyer."

"How about I write Mr. Boyer a note that you've been working with me on an extracurricular project and we need to make a field trip in relation to it."

"Well, that's actually true, isn't it?"

Russ smiled. "Yes, it is. Just come here by 3:30, and we'll take off. But please make sure it's okay with your parents. Here, let me write a quick note that you can give to Boyer today." Russ returned to his desk.

•   •   •

Jonas handed his note to Mr. Boyer at the start of the class. Mr. Boyer read it, flashed a look of mild annoyance at Jonas, and then grudgingly muttered, "Okay. Make sure you've read the next chapter by Friday." Mr. Boyer was perpetually grumpy, but Jonas wasn't bothered by his demeanor: at least he was universally and consistently grumpy, which didn't require any modification of behavior on Jonas's part. As was usually the case in history, Jonas enjoyed the text, which seemed to prepare him adequately for homework and tests. The class was currently studying early European colonization of North America.

Jonas's school habits had not changed much from previous years. Although he was making a conscious effort to listen more to the teacher and other students, he still had a tendency to lose track of the discussion around him. He was focused on a map of the distribution of various immigrant groups in colonial America when he either remembered to listen or something being said caught his ear. Kevin, someone he had "known" since middle school but had never talked to, said, "I think the European attitude that the land be used and 'not wasted' is still in force today—we continue to exploit whatever bounty we have."

"The Native Americans didn't try to dominate the land, they revered it," added Anna, another student Jonas had known without knowing for years.

"They revered it because they believed it was full of spirits," Robert condescended. "I don't think our modern economy can be built on some spiritual Native American relationship with the earth. And whatever romantic notions you may have about the Native Americans, there are far too many people today to live the way they did."

"Exactly. Human population size is detrimental to the environment," said Jonas.

Jonas's classmates were so unaccustomed to his voice that they all turned to look at him.

"If our resources were distributed more equally," said Josh, "the earth is capable of supporting a human population perhaps five times what it is today."

"Why would we want to live on an earth where the human population has reached its maximum density?" said Jonas.

"Amen," called Kevin.

"That's enough," said Mr. Boyer. "We're getting off topic here."

As Jonas bent over to slip his book into his backpack at the end of class, he felt someone standing over him and looked up. "Hey man," said Kevin, "you should speak up more often."

And from her desk, Anna nodded in agreement.

•   •   •

The sourwood leaves were scarlet. Jonas stopped and held a raceme of the small woody seed capsules between his fingers. He couldn't resist squeezing one and dropping the tiny seeds into the palm of his hand. As the fall progressed the capsules would dehisce, and the seeds would be released. Autumn held the fruition of summer's efforts. Thousands of seeds, but only a few would become established. He scattered the seeds in an arc.

Jonas sat on the ground near one of the hemlocks that seemed to defy the very precipice of the bluff. He suspected its life had not always been so precarious, that its position had been acquired through erosion. He closed his eyes and listened. It was quiet except for two squirrels barking at one another in the distance.

Jonas had wandered to the pond out of an unfamiliar restlessness. When he got home from school, he felt an overwhelming need to do something so had headed out of his house and, as usual, had ended up here, the heart of his world. Looking toward the still surface of the pond, he saw a few late-season damselflies skimming just above the water. Clouds floating overhead reflected on the pond, and Jonas looked skyward. Puffy cumulus clouds rode the cool, high-pressure system. He thought of how as a young child he liked to imagine he could walk on these cottony masses. He wondered if Timmy imagined heaven as an actual place among the clouds, as it was often depicted in paintings. He couldn't fault anyone for looking upward and wanting to see a pristine place, a righteous universe.

Jonas returned his gaze to the pond, and his eyes ran over the logs along the northern bank. Some sliders were out sunning themselves; a few were stacked in a pile. Within a month's time they would be deep in the pond, waiting out the cold weather. How they must savor every bit of sun now, thought Jonas. Over one-hundred-thousand years ago, humans had begun wearing clothing; even earlier they began using fire. Humans had learned to modify their environment, which allowed them advancement and expansion seemingly without bounds. Modifying our environment is considered progress, Jonas reflected. The cost, though, is that people are becoming more and more disconnected from the world around them.

A loud splash in the pond caught Jonas's attention. The sun had shifted, and a line of turtles on the westernmost log had slid from their now sunless spot. Jonas realized that as much as he wished more people would share his concern, his connection to the natural world, he had allowed himself to be disconnected from people. He had to be connected to both. He had taken a step today, and he was restless to move forward.

•　　•　　•

When Lizzy opened the door, she was intending to slip into a seat in the back row. But Donna was watching the door and motioned to Lizzy to take the empty seat beside her; Doug sat on Donna's other side. Lizzy was surprised to see so many of the group's members there on a weekday afternoon.

"You look so nice," whispered Donna as Lizzy sat down.

"For what it's worth," said Lizzy.

"It's worth a lot still," replied Donna. "Look at those suits," she motioned toward a group of four men across the aisle and up two rows. "That's Roper, the one with the coifed gray hair; I gather the rest are his 'team.'"

"I wish strength in numbers had some clout here."

"Ms. Hager, Seymour, and Dave have signed up to speak. Mike wanted to too, but we convinced him all bases were covered and we shouldn't keep repeating the same message."

Lizzy looked at the dais at the front of the chamber. Four commissioners were already seated, reviewing papers and conferring with one another. One chair was still empty. Suzanna's cousin-in-law, Claudia Ayers, was easy enough to pick out. Lizzy also recognized Stan Endicott. She had met him years ago when she and Wes first had moved to Narrow Passage Road. He had aged well. He was a tall, lean man, scrubbed well and dressed neatly. His face lifted into an easy smile in response to the commissioner sitting next to him, but in repose his taut lips effected a stern countenance. In the center sat a large man who looked to be approaching his sixties despite his still-dark hair. He was the chairman, a man named Bosch. Another commissioner, Charles Yates according to his name plate, sat to the right of Stan Endicott. He was the youngest of those seated.

When Harold Schwab, a heavy set, balding man, entered the room, ascended the dais, and took the seat next to Claudia Ayers, the chairman announced, "This meeting of the Board of County Commissioners is called to order." To the right of the dais and perpendicular to it was a table at which two women were seated. The older of the two, who had been waiting for Bosch's signal, stood and said, "Would all please rise for the pledge of allegiance."

Lizzy felt as if she were back in school; it had been awhile since she had been to any function at which she had said the pledge. After the pledge, the older woman donned her reading glasses and led the commissioners through the agenda while the younger woman assisted her with papers and recorded the proceedings. Donna had a copy of the agenda, which she had picked up when she had entered, and Lizzy read along with her. The meeting started with recognition of two county employees for their numerous years of service upon retirement. Bosch said a few perfunctory words of appreciation. The woman then called a man seated in the first row, a Mr. Krueger, who presented a brief report, the impetus of which was to get approval for some transfer of funds within the county budget.

Lizzy watched the commissioners, most of whom seemed to be reading the rest of their agenda through these opening items. The proceedings moved on—acceptance of the dedication of a right-of-way and acceptance of a letter of credit as a road improvement surety. Then they authorized the purchasing director to request bids for several individually named road surfacing projects. Lizzy found it difficult to keep her mind from wandering; she wondered whether the commissioners were listening—they were probably well practiced at pretending to pay attention. Or perhaps they truly were invested, making sure their constituents' concerns were being met.

Finally George Roper's "request for approval of the plat of subdivision of parcels 6A, 6B, and 7 of the Barton Tract" came up on the agenda. Mr. Turnbull was invited to speak. A well-proportioned man with closely trimmed blond hair approached the lectern that stood between the two aisles. Even from a brief glimpse of his profile, Lizzy knew his chin was smooth and he smelled slightly sweet. His dark indigo suit was tailored for him, and she couldn't imagine him in a different skin.

"Chairman Bosch, Commissioners, thank you for this opportunity to present our proposal." He had a pleasant drawl—not too deep, just enough to lull one into thinking he was truly the salt of the earth, although Lizzy presumed he was a viper. "I am here today as Mr. Roper's legal counsel. You have before you a summary of the development plans for Mr. Roper's approximately one hundred and sixty acres that are accessed primarily from Due West Road." Turnbull paused as the younger woman got up from the table and distributed glossy folders to the commissioners. He then continued. "Mr. Roper's firm, New Horizons Corporation, has employed the prestigious company, Aaron Butler Engineering, to design a modern, family-centered community. The development will offer single-family homes on half-acre lots and include sidewalks, two playgrounds, a swimming pool, and access to a beautiful natural area that will be maintained as a park with a walking trail."

Turnbull paused again as the commissioners rifled through their folders, reviewing the schematics. "As you may already know, New Horizons, A.B.E., Mr. Reid, the County Engineer, and Mr. Hunt, his counterpart for Centreville, have been working closely to resolve the issue of wastewater from this development. You have before you now a letter of credit as surety for the construction of a sewer line to Centreville's extraterritorial jurisdictional boundary. You also have before you a copy of the city's commitment to extend its sewer lines to this boundary. We are requesting that the Board of County Commissioners approve and execute a utility easement agreement between the county and New Horizons Corporation for the purpose of installing this sewer line. And, of course, we ask for approval of the plat as it has been submitted to you."

The chairman then asked his fellow commissioners whether they had any questions or comments. The first to speak was Stan Endicott.

"I have reviewed this proposal closely and am impressed with both the quality of the planned subdivision and the attention given to issues such as wastewater. I also feel that New Horizons is performing a service to the entire county by investing its own capital to make this portion of the county amenable to residential and commercial development. Our county revenues and businesses will be positively impacted."

Looking at Claudia Ayers' heart-shaped face surrounded by wisps of soft blond hair, Lizzy didn't expect the firmness with which she spoke. "I must say my interpretation is almost the exact opposite, Mr. Endicott. Our county revenues may be positively affected, but it will be a short while before the city starts extending its boundary farther along Due West Road, so those revenues won't be ours for long. Furthermore," she continued, "I think it is highly questionable that landowners along Due West Road want to accelerate development. I don't think we can assume that they do, and I don't believe this board should approve these requests without greater examination of their implications."

"Respectfully, Ms. Ayers," Harold Schwab said, looking toward the ceiling, "we have this sort of discussion on every sizeable plat we receive. Mr. Chairman, I move we vote."

The woman who was leading the board through the proceedings quickly stood and said, "Commissioners, I need to inform you that we have members of the public who have requested to speak to this plat approval request."

Bosch looked down to his agenda, then looked up, clasped his hands before his chin, and said, "Thank you, Mrs. Fulcrum. We will proceed with public comment at this time."

"Would Ms. Hager please come to the lectern," Mrs. Fulcrum said.

Ms. Hager was suited just as were Roper and his team, but the overall effect was not quite the same. With curly black hair that defied taming and being barely over five feet, she could not afford Turnbull's relaxed posture for risk of not being taken seriously. Still, when she spoke, her tone was calm and confident.

"Thank you for the opportunity to speak, although the first point I would like to make is that a development of this size and with its implications warrants a public hearing. This is not a simple request for approval of a plat of subdivision—this development will change the nature of the community in which it is situated, which is still rural; it will impact the nature of development several miles to its east and will likely encourage development to its west; and it potentially will cause damage to a unique natural area on its southern edge—the very natural area it touts as an amenity.

"I am here as a representative of a citizens group, the Greenspace Alliance of Ware County, of which several members are here today." Hager turned toward the attendees and gestured with her arm toward members of the group. "We request that this review process include a request to the State Board of Environmental Quality by the Board of County Commissioners to conduct an environmental assessment of the aforementioned natural area followed by a public hearing upon completion of that report."

Turnbull jumped up. "That is a totally transparent attempt to forestall this project with unfounded demands. There will be a fifty-foot margin along the pond, much of it forested. But more importantly, there are no grounds upon which the commissioners are required to call a public hearing for a development on private property. It is Mr. Roper's right to develop his property, and he and New Horizons Corporation are providing a service by providing affordable homes in a country setting."

Lizzy kept waiting for the chairman to admonish Turnbull for interrupting, but he didn't. She looked at Ms. Hager, whose focus had not strayed from the board during the interruption.

Hager calmly continued, "In a moment a biologist will speak to whether or not there is potential harm to Bartons Mill Pond and its associated wetland from the development. Requesting the commissioners to approve a utility easement to New Horizons Corporation extends the request beyond Mr. Roper's own property and puts the approval request squarely in the realm of a public hearing."

Turnbull, who hadn't returned to his seat, broke in again. "You will see in your packet that A.B.E. has designed an alternative to the sewer lines. We can forego about twenty-five home sites on the eastern edge of the property, right behind Trinity Cemetery, and construct a small-scale sewage treatment facility. The effluent from the plant would be piped into Mill Pond Creek. A.B.E. has run the numbers to ensure that this facility will meet state standards—it is New

Horizons's second choice, but it is an option." Turnbull turned slightly to indicate the man who sat on the other side of Roper, "Mr. Jackson from A.B.E. would be happy to give you a full explanation of how this system would work."

"To turn Mill Pond Creek into a sewage chute definitely would require public input," said Hager.

"Mr. Chairman," interjected Stan Endicott, "I believe there are others who have signed up to speak, and I believe there are time restrictions in place."

"Yes, you are right. Thank you, Ms. Hager. Next speaker, please."

Lizzy and Donna looked at each other in disbelief. Murmurs rose around them. "Can you believe that?!" Donna whispered. "Roper's guy used half of her time." Lizzy shook her head and grimaced in response.

"Quiet, please," Bosch called firmly.

"Mr. Real," called Mrs. Fulcrum.

Seymour, wearing what Lizzy assumed was one of his few suits, made his way to the lectern. "Thank you, commissioners, for this opportunity to address you. I am speaking as a nearby property owner to Mr. Roper's proposed development. My wife and I have lived on Mail Route Road for almost forty years, longer than Mr. Roper has owned his property. I feel I am a long-time member of the community, although my roots do not compare with those of some of the other property owners around Bartons Mill Pond. Ours is still a rural community, and the people I've talked to want to see it remain that way." Seymour placed his hands on the corners of the lectern and leaned forward. "You can say it's Mr. Roper's right to do with his land what he chooses to do, but the fact is that what he does with his land affects all of us around him. If he builds this development, it is those of us who actually live out there who will feel the impact of more traffic, more noise, more night light, and less wildlife. And we will no longer be a rural community. We will be a suburban community, and soon there will be a convenience store and soon thereafter another business will follow. Mr. Roper has his rights, but his neighbors should have some rights in this matter too."

"You all just want to turn back the clock," muttered someone in Roper's group, perhaps louder than he had intended.

"It's not about turning back the clock. It's about looking to the future," came a voice from a few rows behind Lizzy.

Lizzy swung around, but she knew who had spoken. Russ, seated next to Jonas, looked as surprised as she was.

All of Roper's team, except Roper, turned to look at Jonas.

"It's about a future with open spaces, with habitat for wildlife," Jonas continued. "It's about not squandering our natural resources."

Roper's team wore smirks on their faces.

A sharp crack got everyone's attention. Bosch had brought down his gavel hard. He looked at Seymour and asked, "Anything else?"

"No," said Seymour, "except to thank the young man for his comments. It's his future we have to protect." He turned and gave Jonas a smile and slight bow and then took his seat.

"Are there any other speakers?" Bosch asked Mrs. Fulcrum.

"One," she replied, "Dr. David Clayton."

"Oh yes. Dr. Clayton," said the chairman, "would you please limit your comments to five minutes. And I request that all other members of the audience remain silent."

Dr. Dave, looking uncomfortable, was dressed up for the occasion. He had donned a sports jacket and nice trousers. He introduced himself and his field of expertise. He then gave the board a quick introduction to Bartons Mill Pond, not unlike the one he gave to the group months before, albeit shorter. He focused on the uniqueness of the pond and its immediate surroundings and mentioned that members of the citizens' group and his colleagues had made an extensive inventory of the site.

"So can you say as a biologist that any particular plant or animal will become extinct because of the proposed development?" asked Yates.

"As a species, no," said Dave, "but as far as occurring at this locale, yes, it is likely that we may see some species become extirpated—that is, they may no longer occur in or around the pond."

"But you're not talking about the pond becoming too polluted for the fish and what not," stated Schwab waving his hand, a trace of impatience obvious in his tone.

"No, not if basic precautions are taken. The greatest threat is a loss of species diversity, that is, the number, the variety, of species that occur there. And over time we may see infiltration by more generalist or invasive species—nonnative species or native species that essentially grow everywhere."

"Heartier species, in other words?" said Schwab.

"When you simplify an ecosystem to fewer species, the whole ecosystem becomes more vulnerable," Dave said, trying to teach an ecology lesson in a few sentences. "In the long run, what you call heartier species don't necessarily leave us with a healthier environment."

Wanting to push the vote forward, Bosch terminated the discussion. "Thank you, Dr. Clayton. Mr. Roper, would you like to say a few words or have someone respond to these comments on your behalf."

Turnbull was moving to stand when Roper's hand rested on his arm. They exchanged a few words, and then Roper stood up and adjusted his light gray suit jacket. The color highlighted his hair well. From behind there was nothing distinguishing about him—average height, neither heavy nor thin. He did not move toward the lectern but spoke from where he stood. And when he spoke, his voice was smooth and genial.

"I see a group of neighbors—and I suspect very few of those gathered here are actually neighbors to my property—who want to protect their idyllic country life. He turned to look at them briefly, "I have no problem with that."

Lizzy saw Roper had a pleasant but indistinct countenance.

Turning back toward the commissioners, Roper continued. "However, to keep their views unobstructed, their days quiet, their walks private, their drives through the country peaceful, they want to deny the reality of an increasing desire for homes with the same country amenities. They want to deny others what they have to preserve those amenities for themselves."

He proceeded as evenly as he had started. "I see a need, and I am putting my land, and my resources, to good use by providing families affordable homes in a safe, healthy environment."

Right, thought Lizzy, you are doing this out of compassion for your fellow man.

"I want to remind you," Roper said, "that New Horizons has followed the letter of the law as regards all our filings and requests. I have, in good faith, followed the appropriate requirements." He paused a moment, and when he resumed, his volume and pitch had dropped slightly. "Although I don't want to, if necessary, I will take any requisite legal action to ensure my rights—not just for myself, but for other landowners who may find themselves in the same position. I know the commissioners will fulfill their obligations."

When Roper sat back down, Howard Schwab said loudly, "I move we approve plat number 85-074 submitted by New Horizons Corporation."

"I second the motion," said Stan Endicott

"Aye's?" asked Bosch. Four hands went up. Claudia Ayers sat with her hands folded before her, her lips pulled tightly in frustration. "The ayes have it," said the chairman. "I need a motion on the matter of the utility easement agreement between Ware County and New Horizons Corporation."

Claudia Ayers was about to voice an objection when Mrs. Fulcrum jumped up.

"Mr. Chairman, the county attorney is still reviewing those documents. There are some issues of maintenance and liability to be resolved. I suggest the easement agreement be tabled until the next board meeting."

"Thank you, Mrs. Fulcrum," said Bosch. "Being that there is no other business on the agenda, this meeting is adjourned."

Lizzy filed out into the lobby with the rest of the group. They were all glum.

"I've never wanted to run for public office," Seymour said, "but I'm thinking about it now."

"It's obvious we were closed out from the beginning," said Doug. "The county attorney is already working on resolving easement issues with Roper. So much for good faith and the letter of the law."

"I need to talk to Claudia," said Suzanna. "I don't know if she even knew about that."

"Is there anything we can do?" Donna asked Ms. Hager.

"It doesn't look good. No endangered species, no public water supply, no sentiment to manage growth. I was hoping we could pressure them into a public hearing regarding the easement, but they did not bite."

"We're not giving up?" asked Mike.

"No," said Ms. Hager. "We can come back and challenge the easement agreement, but we have to consider whether an on-site treatment facility is preferable. Let's all think about where we can go from here and talk soon."

"We really have no leverage unless we can get more of the affected landowners actively involved," said Seymour. "Maybe we can all work on that angle."

"Anyone ready to go find solace in a bottle?" asked Doug.

Lizzy was disheartened. It was as she had thought: they hadn't had a chance from the beginning. Roper had too much influence over the board. She listened as Hager and Seymour tried to divine a thread of optimism, but she saw the decision as final, the fight lost. She made her way over to Jonas as the group began to disperse.

"Jonas, thank you for speaking up."

"Didn't matter much, though, did it?" said Jonas. "Roper and his minions were amused, not moved."

"You stated your case, and that's what's important," said Russ, joining them. "I don't know if anyone up there, besides Ms. Ayers, was even willing to listen."

"Ready to head home?" Lizzy asked Jonas.

"How about the three of us go to dinner?" said Russ. "My treat. We can give your parents a call, Jonas."

●   ●   ●

Jonas looked up at the faded photograph of a sphinx in front of a pyramid. They had been rehashing the meeting, but the waitress's arrival to take their order had put their conversation on hold. When she left, the conversation resumed.

"Did you really expect we'd be able to stop him?" Lizzy asked Russ.

"I guess 'hope' would be a better word. One has to keep trying," Russ smiled at her. "Eventually one will find an inroad."

Lizzy narrowed her eyes at Russ. "Jonas," she redirected her attention, "did you know that Russ wanted to be a lawyer when I met him in college?"

"And you were going to be an illustrator, I recall," Russ rejoined.

"That was a long time ago."

"We're not that old, Lizzy." Russ said, looking into her eyes.

Lizzy could not turn away. There was such candor in his expression. Maybe Wes wasn't the only one who saw her clearly.

"So you decided to be a high school science teacher instead?" Jonas asked Russ, breaking the momentary silence.

"Not at first, but yes, essentially. The summer before my senior year I arranged an internship with a law firm. I was already interested in environmental protection and had taken several relevant courses, although I must admit there was a whole lot about the environment, about biology, I didn't know. Perhaps that's what motivated me to switch." Russ shrugged. "Anyway, I spent the summer reading various court cases as well as laws and regulations that pertained to them, and I realized an adversarial approach wasn't for me." His eyes darted to Lizzy's, who met his gaze. "Not that there isn't a big role for the legal system and law enforcement in environmental protection. I just decided I rather advocate for the environment through education than by battling corporations or legislators. So, I changed my major and spent an extra year in school."

"I'm not sure what I want to do exactly," said Jonas, "but I do want to study biology—maybe botany, or something else."

"It's not important that you don't know exactly what you want to do at this point, Jonas. What is important is that you know what interests you and you want to explore it. Are you going to sign up for my advanced bio class next year?"

Jonas nodded. "Yes, I'm planning to. But I would like to be doing something now. I really enjoyed doing the inventory—I learned a lot."

"Well, that doesn't have to stop," Russ said, turning his palms up. "Why don't we see if we can get you involved in a project with 'Dr. Dave' or the botanist you worked with, Michael? I might be able to facilitate something through the school so that you can even earn some credit for it—like an independent study."

"I would like that."

Russ then leaned in toward Jonas and said in a conspiratorial tone, "But in the meantime, we need to uncover the truth about Ms. Lizzy here. We need to determine if there is any veracity to the rumor that most blood bank employees are actually vampires."

•　　•　　•

"You must be worn out," Lizzy said to Jonas as they drove out of town. They had parted with Russ after dinner. She had enjoyed visiting with Russ, watching him interact with Jonas. He had grown into the profession he had chosen. There was a nurturing quality about him; she realized she had seen it before, in the various groups they'd been in, but she hadn't recognized how fundamental to his character it was. Regardless, over the course of the evening she had let her guard down, and it felt good to be relaxed around him.

"I hope you don't have too much homework," she said when Jonas didn't answer.

"No, I don't. And I'm not tired, not at all. I feel funny using the word, but I feel exhilarated."

"Oh?" said Lizzy.

"The idea of continuing to work with Dr. Dave or Michael. And at lunch today I met with a couple of students at my school. We're going to start a club. I need to ask Mr. Henderson to be our sponsor; I should have asked him tonight. We're going to call it SOS."

"And what does that stand for?" asked Lizzy, the corner of her mouth raising into her lopsided smile.

"Students for open spaces. We need to recruit some more students first, but we talked about where we're going to start. All the parks in town are playgrounds or ball fields. There aren't any parks where you can walk through the woods or sit quietly by a creek—like I can do whenever I want. We're going to start a petition, write the paper—things like that—to push for a new kind of park. We're thinking one along Phelps Mill Run, with a trail, would be a good start."

"You've become a regular social activist," said Lizzy, laughing. It was as if some switch in Jonas had been turned to "on."

•　　　•　　　•

When Jonas arrived home, his parents were full of questions. Since the first meeting he had attended with Ms. Lizzy, his mother had not mentioned going with him, as if she understood she needed to leave this endeavor to Jonas alone. He sat down and actually told Sylvia and Phil all about the commissioners' meeting—all except the part when he spoke.

"It was obvious that most of the commissioners wanted to approve the development plan and didn't care about what anyone said against it," Jonas surmised.

"There's a lot of money in real estate development—developers hold a lot of sway with local officials," Phil said, "even with state ones."

"If Mr. Real does run for county commissioner like he said he might, I'm going to work for him," Jonas told his parents.

"Oh, I almost forgot," Sylvia said. "There is a letter for you. It's from someone named Adrianne Holt. I left it on the kitchen counter."

As Jonas hurried toward the kitchen, his parents smiled at each other and shook their heads.

On his way to the kitchen, Jonas caught sight of himself in the long mirror in the foyer. He backed up a step to look at himself. Having reached six feet over the summer, he didn't look quite as round, his face quite as undefined; he was firming up some.

Jonas found the letter and opened it. It was written in a neat, small cursive.

> *Dear Jonas,*
> *Yes, I am the Barton descendant who owns property at*
> *the junction of Bartons Mill and Narrow Passage roads.*
> *Thank you so much for tracking me down. It's been a number*
> *of years since I've been in Centreville—my grandfather used*

*to take me out to the old homestead at Bartons Mill Pond
whenever I visited as a young girl. When my father inherited
the land he sold most of it—I believe to the man you
mentioned, George Roper. My father had no intention of
returning to the Centreville area to live, so selling the
property seemed a good idea at the time. I have always been
happy to know, though, that my father kept the mill site and
the five or so acres around it. Knowing that that small piece
of ground was still in the family has always lent me a sense
of belonging to a place, to a history. I inherited the parcel from
my father a few years ago. I'm always so busy with my own
life that it has been easy to forget that life goes on in places
that remain unchanged in my memory. Since I have received
your letter I have been wondering what to do. I've decided to
make a trip with my family to Centreville soon. I will talk to
county officials about donating the land in perpetuity for a
park or historic site named after the Barton family. Funny
how a family so connected with a locale can completely
disappear from it.*

*Thank you for writing. I look forward to meeting you
when I visit.*

Sincerely,

Adrianne C. Barton Holt

Windfall

"Monday will be the feast day of Saint Francis of Assisi, the patron saint of nature. Saint Francis founded the Franciscan Order and pledged himself to a life of poverty and repentance. In his early twenties he was praying in a neglected chapel when the crucifix spoke to him and said, 'Francis, go and repair my house which, as you can see, is falling to ruins.' Francis immediately went to work to repair the chapel in which he had been praying."

Timmy heard the story of Saint Francis almost every year. He always loved the stories about Saint Francis—not so much the parts about him always giving away his clothes and living like a beggar, but the parts about him preaching to the birds and making peace between the ferocious wolf and the townspeople. He listened to Miss Florence's flutelike voice. Whereas Sister Gertrude had focused on the saint's marriage to Lady Poverty, Miss Florence, like Timmy, seemed to prefer the stories about the saint's love of nature. She told them that Saint Francis believed that it was the duty of Mankind to protect and enjoy nature as stewards of God's creation; that all of nature showed the beauty and goodness of the Creator.

Timmy was looking out the window at the manicured lawn that ran to the sidewalk along Main Street. There was a huge white oak between the window and the street, a tree so perfectly formed.

From just above his head Miss Florence asked, "Mr. Donohue, would you like to rejoin us?"

It was warmer than it had been for a few weeks, and although Timmy had grown tired of the heat in August, this return of gentle warmth was welcome. He knew from past years the warm spell would not last more than a day or two. It was the perfect weather for fishing—the bass would be biting on a warm day like today. But after he finished collecting for the paper, he was supposed to go straight home to clean his and Chris's room.

Timmy rode up Ms. Lizzy's driveway and noticed that Alice was sitting where Ms. Lizzy had buried Happy. She was looking into the dense arched stems of the crape myrtle. Among the remaining orange and yellow leaves and browning flower clusters, CB was climbing upward. Timmy laid down his bike and walked up to the tree. "What are you doing?" he asked CB, and she looked down at him with her crazed yellow eyes in their mismatched patches. He leaned over and petted Alice, who was sitting on the bed of browned flowers Ms. Lizzy had planted there. "She's pretty silly, isn't she?" Then he went and knocked on Ms. Lizzy's storm door. Clem and Pete arrived promptly to greet him.

"Hi Timmy. Warm, isn't it?" Lizzy said as she grabbed Clem's collar so he wouldn't push Timmy aside. Pete, on the other hand, allowed him to enter unaccosted. "How about a glass of lemonade? I was inspired to make some yesterday."

"Oh yes, please, I love lemonade," he said as he entered the kitchen. He sat on a stool while Lizzy fetched it. On the counter were a few jars of green beans—particularly thin beans.

"You've been putting up beans?" asked Timmy.

"These are special beans," said Lizzy as she put down a plate with some pretzels, "they're dilly beans."

"Dilly beans?"

"I pickled them. Here," she said, pushing a jar toward Timmy, "take one home with you."

"Thank you. My mom really enjoyed all the vegetables you gave us from your garden this summer. She said maybe next spring we'll put in a garden, if all of us will help."

"Gardens are wonderful, but they take some real work too." She saw that Timmy had already drained his glass, so she fetched the lemonade to refill it.

"That hasn't changed much, has it?"

"What?" Lizzy asked as she filled his glass.

"Ms. Lizzy, why, if God knows everything, would He give us something wonderful and then take it away? So we would always wish for something we lost?"

"I don't know, Timmy. Perhaps some good comes from envisioning a perfect time or place. And perhaps," Lizzy turned to look out the window over the sink, "remembering what has been lost can guide us toward finding something like it again.

"But when you have a garden you realize that there is some reward in toiling for your food. And the cycle of seed to plant to fruit to seed is miraculous in itself, no matter how it came to be."

•   •   •

Deep in thought, Timmy pedaled his bike toward home. What if the story meant something else? What if it wasn't so much that Adam and Eve sinned but that, with time, they began to see things differently, began to ask questions? What if God didn't actually throw them out of the Garden, but rather they couldn't see the Garden the same way once they began to question the world around them? Sort of like losing one's faith.

Timmy didn't even see Matt, also on bike, coming straight toward him. He was taken by surprise when Matt rode up beside him.

"Been fishing?" asked Matt.

"No. I've been collecting on my paper route."

"I went this morning and caught a largemouth out of Mr. Horace's pond that must have weighed almost five pounds."

"Nice," said Timmy with a trace on envy. "That's almost as big as your record."

"I know. This weather won't last much longer. Until tomorrow night they say, then a cold front is supposed to move through."

"I didn't figure it would last very long."

"You want to come over and go fishing this afternoon?"

"Can't. My parents invited a family from my dad's office over for dinner. I've got to go home now and help clean up."

"Well they should be biting in the morning, how bout then?" asked Matt.

"Have to go to church."

"Aw man, you always say that."

"I know."

"Can't you skip it once in a while? I mean, what would happen if you did?"

Timmy shook his head. "Nah, my parents would never let me."

"Well, I'm going this evening and in the morning. It probably will be the last good fishing weather till spring. See you later."

"Yeah, later."

•

Timmy hadn't thought it out beforehand, but when his mother came to wake him for church, he rolled away from her groaning.

"What's wrong, Timmy?"

"I don't know, mom. My stomach hurts. My head hurts. I don't feel like moving, but I'm getting up." He rose up onto one elbow.

"I was wondering why you weren't up yet. You stay in bed," she said, feeling his forehead. "I'm going to go tell your father you're sick. He can take your sisters and brother to church, and we'll stay home."

"Oh mom, I don't want you to miss church. I'll get up."

"No, you're sick. You may have a light fever—you feel a bit warm to me."

"Yeah, but I don't want you to miss church." He counted to five slowly. "Why don't you go? I'll be okay. I'll just stay here, in bed."

"I don't think so, Timmy. I don't want to leave you alone while you're sick. You might begin to feel worse while we're gone."

"Really, mom, I'll be okay. Maybe some aspirin will make this headache go away, and then my stomach will feel better too."

Helen gathered up Chris' church clothes and left to check on Timmy's sisters. Timmy lay in bed, vacillating between getting ready for church and confessing his sin today versus pursuing his hoax and waiting until next week to confess it—would waiting really make a difference in the end? Maybe he did feel kind of sick. And who knew how much longer he would be able to fish at Bartons Mill Pond. By spring it might be ringed with houses. There could be lots of other kids there trying to catch the trophy bass, mucking up the water. He could, he would, pray while he fished. He would ask for forgiveness for lying, and for missing church. Next week he would confess. If only his mother would agree to leave him home alone.

Helen came back with aspirin. Timmy told her he was feeling a bit better already, he just wanted to go back to sleep. He insisted he would be fine, he would just rest in bed, and he would call the Meyers or Ms. Lizzy if he felt worse. He insisted he was old enough to stay home for the few hours they would be away. Helen finally relented and left some phone numbers next to the phone in her bedroom.

Timmy listened to the car start and waited to make sure his family had really left. Often, someone would leave something behind, and his father would turn around if they hadn't reached Due West Road. After a few minutes, he jumped from bed, hurriedly dressed, grabbed the pole Ms. Lizzy had given him, and ran downstairs. He flew down the road and took the short cut through Mrs. Prickett's property, figuring she had already left for church. A sudden southern gale seemed to push him toward the pond.

Timmy cast eastward along the southern bank, with each cast throwing his line out a bit farther. Soon he was knee high in water—cold, crystal clear water. He looked down at the water weed, which hid his feet. For a long time nothing bit. Finally, barely beyond the edge of the water weeds, where the trunk of a long-fallen hemlock lay below the surface, just as his lure hit, he saw a ripple on the surface, a big ripple. The fish hit the lure, and Timmy flicked up the tip of his rod in a smooth motion to hook the fish. He started to reel it in, slow and steady, rod tip up. The fish pulled hard, and Timmy let out some line. Then Timmy reeled in again, slow and steady, then let out some line. After repeating this maneuver several times, the fish finally came into view. It looked much smaller than Timmy had imagined given its wake, and he was disappointed. He pulled the rod tip all the way to his left to force the fish to swim laterally in front of him. Its scales flashed a brilliant greenish silver through the water. As Timmy continued to reel in the fish, the strength of its pull belied its size. Then, only a few yards in front of him, the fish turned laterally of its own volition, and Timmy could not believe his eyes. It was an immense fish! It was an enormous fish! It was the size of a small car!

Momentarily stunned, Timmy's grip loosened, and immediately the fish began to swim away, pulling Timmy's rod and reel out of his hands. Reacting a second too late, Timmy lurched forward, trying to grab his pole. He couldn't let the fish get away. He had to show it to Matt. He had to catch it to show everyone!

Timmy began to chase his fishing pole, which was headed toward the eastern edge of the pond where the waters were deep behind the old dam at the top of Mill Pond Creek. He had to get to the fish before it reached the outflow. He tried to run, but with each step the water pushed back in equal measure, and the thick vegetation ensnared his feet. Despite the water's chill, he threw himself into the pond, swimming in the deepening water, trying to catch up to the escaping pole. The handle of the rod was just an arm's length ahead. Timmy thrust his feet hard against the bottom of the pond and sprung out of the water like a coil. He landed with his hands on the rod, but as he grabbed it, the fish snapped the line and hurled itself out of the water and up into the air—not a few inches or a few feet but into the air, flying as if Timmy's landing had catapulted it. The fish rose in a spray of water and blocked out the sky momentarily; it arched upward and eastward, toward the cemetery. Timmy couldn't see the fish land, but he heard a thunderous roar.

Timmy climbed out of the pond and onto the bank as quickly as he could. He immediately was extremely cold—a fierce wind was blowing and the entire sky had darkened. He began to shiver uncontrollably, but he had to find his fish. No one would believe him.

He couldn't cross Mill Pond Creek at the pond — the juncture of the old dam and bluff was a dangerous spot — so he dropped his pole on the narrow bank and rushed through the woods toward Narrow Passage Road, snapping leafless branches and being raked by greenbrier thorns all the way. He finally spilled onto the road. He didn't care if Mrs. Prickett was home and saw him. He had to find his fish. He had to have it to show everyone. He was shaking violently as he ran down the road, freezing and burning simultaneously.

And then it appeared amid swirling leaves and branches — his parents' car. It screeched to a stop, and his father and mother jumped out, yelling. But Timmy couldn't hear what they were saying above the wind and his own voice crying, "My fish, my fish, I have to get it." When his father grabbed him, Timmy tried to pull away, but he had no strength; he was exhausted.

"He's burning up with fever!" Tim shouted to Helen. "What is he doing out here?"

"Quick," said Helen, "Get him to the car. We have to get him home and out of those wet clothes."

Tim picked him up, and they hurried toward the car.

"What was I thinking, leaving him alone?" Helen cried. "Oh God, please let him be all right."

Tim put Timmy in the front seat, and for the short ride home Timmy struggled with Helen, reaching for the door handle. "The fish, the fish, I have to get it. Then you'll see."

Timmy's parents got him to bed. At first he struggled, but suddenly, completely spent, he fell into a restless sleep.

He was burning. He felt as if the outer layer of his skin had been peeled off and every nerve cell in his body was exposed. It was dark except for glimmers of red, and a pungent odor seared his nostrils. A mechanical drone went on and on relentlessly, metal against metal in an uneven rotation. Timmy knew he was in hell. As his eyes adjusted to the darkness he could just make out movement around him — bowed-head, rounded-back figures moaning softly and pacing slowly, without destination. He began to cry to Jesus, over and over, "I am sorry. Please forgive me. I lied to my parents. Please forgive me. I tried to catch the fish. Please forgive me. I didn't believe." And still he burned. All he wanted was a little drink of water. "Please Jesus, save me."

Gradually the burning lessened, and his skin no longer felt as if it were being raked. Water touched his lips. The noise and odor faded, and darkness graded to the deep of night with a few distant stars. He was filled with hope that he was in purgatory, that he was being cleansed, that he would not be punished for eternity. He tried to pray, "Hail Mary, full of grace," but he couldn't focus and kept losing his place. So he just pleaded, "Forgive me, forgive me," over and over.

Suddenly all discomfort was gone, and he was surrounded by white light, as if in a cloud. Before him were two enormous doors. They were intricately carved gold, picturing fruit trees and flowers and birds. He knew they were the gate to the Garden of Eden. He pushed with all his might to open the doors. They were so heavy they resisted all movement. He pushed and pushed, desperate to get in, and finally the door yielded enough for him to slip through into daylight. The sky was a vivid, clear blue—a blue richer than any he had ever seen. The air was spring-like—warm but with a faint breeze that cooled the skin of any heat but carried no chill. And it smelled of sweet blossoms but not too sweet. He heard birds singing—first one flute-like call, then another—some songs he recognized, others were unfamiliar. The ground was covered with wildflowers—those he had photographed and exquisite ones he had never seen before. The leaves on the trees were the vibrant green of early spring.

Timmy knew where he was. He was ready to see angels, he was ready to see Jesus, he was ready to see God. He held still and waited. Nothing happened, so he figured perhaps he was supposed to walk somewhere, to the right place. Just beyond that tree, standing on that rock, revealing Himself in the sky, He would appear. Timmy continued to walk and pause through the landscape, taking in divine scenes of flowering bushes covered with extravagant butterflies, squirrels eating pine cones in sky-high evergreens, swans gliding along the surface of perfect ponds, big-antlered deer walking through meadows. Timmy kept expecting that Jesus would appear to him at any moment. He walked from day into the night and into the day again, never tiring, never becoming hungry, although he was a bit thirsty. He traversed from field to forest to mountain to ocean and back to forest and then field again.

On a small rise in the middle of a meadow stood an enormous tree with broad, shiny leaves, somewhat akin to a white oak. Its branches formed a huge crown that was perfectly symmetrical. Timmy then noticed a man beneath the tree, leaning against its trunk. As Timmy approached, he could see the man was older, with silver hair. The man, dressed in a fine light gray suit, was peeling a piece of fruit, an apple perhaps, with a pocket knife. Somehow Timmy knew this was Mr. Roper, even though he had never met him.

"Hey," Mr. Roper called in an inviting tone, "Are you the boy who caught the big one out of my pond?"

Timmy wasn't sure how to answer. He didn't want to think of the pond as belonging to Mr. Roper, but he couldn't say no either. That would seem a lie, and he didn't want to lie, certainly not here in front of God.

"I almost caught a big fish out of Bartons Mill Pond."

The man's laugh sounded like puffs of air being squeezed out of his lungs. "Don't you know you're never supposed to catch the biggest fish? You're supposed to leave the biggest. There always has to be something bigger and better to go after."

"Yes, sir," Timmy said reflexively.

"What's your name?"

"Timothy."

"Do you want to make some money, Timothy?"

Money? In God's garden?

"It's eaaaaasy money," Mr. Roper encouraged. "Just make sure each one of your neighbors gets one of these." He dropped the apple to the ground, and it rolled toward Timmy. Mr. Roper leaned over and cut the cord on a stack of large white envelopes that were at his feet. He picked up the top envelope, opened it, pulled out a glossy brochure, and held it up for Timmy to see. There were pictures of fancy new houses on perfectly manicured lawns. Then the man pulled from the envelope what looked like an oversized check. "I'm making a generous offer to all the folks around here—I just need someone to deliver it. Why, you can drop these off while you're delivering the paper." Mr. Roper offered the oversized check to Timmy.

Timmy backed away from the check being extended toward him. "I'm sorry," he said hurriedly, "but I'm late getting home." With that he turned and ran.

Mr. Roper called after him like a barker at a carnival, "Come on back here, boy. Come on now. I'll pay you well."

Timmy ran into the woods and quickly realized he was approaching Bartons Mill Pond. He saw large leaves floating on the surface, but as he approached the pond's edge he saw the leaves were fish—dead fish. Then he noticed an old man, older than any man he had ever seen but still seemingly strong of body. He wore strange, worn, old-fashioned clothes—clothes like Timmy had seen in a history book. The man was casting a net into the water and pulling the dead fish to shore. Timmy approached him. "What happened?" Timmy asked.

The man seemed not to hear or see Timmy, but then he began to speak. "My pond is falling to ruins." He continued to cast his net and pull in fish, still oblivious to Timmy's presence.

Standing there Timmy gradually realized he was hearing the sound of running water. It had been constant in the background for a while, the melody of water flowing over rocks in a stream. It dawned on him that he was listening to Narrow Passage Creek. He followed the creek to where he could cut across Ms. Lizzy's yard. As he passed Happy's grave, instead of seeing the violet-blossomed crape myrtle, he saw the white flowers of a dogwood tree in bloom. He continued on his way home, the sound of the stream never leaving his ears. Then suddenly he saw the ceiling of his room, the blades of the fan softly creaking as they slowly rotated. He sat up in bed. He had to go to the bathroom.

As he made his way to the bathroom he began to realize he had been dreaming, although the dream had been so vivid, so real, it didn't feel like a dream at all. Walking down the hall he felt as if his insides had been completely drained from him, stirred up in a bowl, and then poured back in. Everything around him was completely different from how it had seemed just that morning. In the bathroom he took a big drink of water.

Timmy heard his parents in the kitchen and went downstairs. They looked at him with worried expressions when he entered the room. They were drinking coffee. His father was dressed for work. It was already Monday.

"The papers . . ."

"Don't worry—Eileen and I delivered them yesterday. How are you feeling?"

"I'm fine," Timmy said. "I feel better." He didn't know how to explain to them how he felt different. "Have I been asleep since yesterday?"

"A restless sleep, yes," said his mother. "You don't remember me waking you at all, do you? You were half asleep."

"I'll go get ready for school."

"I'm not sure you should go, even though your fever broke last evening," she said. "Maybe you should stay home."

"I'm okay."

"If you're sure," said his father. "But this evening we need to talk about yesterday. You don't know how lucky you were, young man."

•   •   •

Ryan had returned to school after a long absence. Miss Florence had told the class that Ryan was very sick, in the hospital, in fact, and they had been praying daily for his speedy and complete recovery. He was already in the classroom when the rest of the class arrived, seated at his desk. He was pale and seemed a bit thinner. Still, his eyes flashed with hostility when Timmy passed him.

Timmy approached Ryan at recess, and Ryan reflexively stepped back away from him.

"Listen," Timmy said, "I just want you to know that I'm not in any sort of contest with you. I don't care if your compositions are picked. I don't want to be Pope. I wouldn't even want to be president."

"Why not?" asked Ryan, his voice and face full of distrust.

Timmy wasn't ready to tell Ryan or anyone else what he was thinking; he wasn't completely sure himself. What he did know was that he had walked through the Garden of Eden only to discover he had been there all along.

"I guess I want to follow Saint Francis; I want to tend the Garden."

•   •   •

When Timmy got home from school, he grabbed his bike and went to the end of the driveway where the bundle of papers had been left for him. He pulled out his pocket knife and squatted to cut the string when a headline gave him pause: "Tornado Rains Fish."

He hurriedly cut the string and freed the top paper.

At approximately 11 a.m. Sunday morning, a tornado touched down briefly on Due West Road just west of its junction with Bartons Mill Road. Formation of the storm cell was rapid as a strong, fast-moving cold front passed through the area earlier than had been predicted. In what meteorologists say was an unusual but not unheard-of event, small fish appeared to rain from the sky as the tornado passed, indicating the tornado had likely touched down over a body of water. What is unusual are the fish themselves, which are almost one inch in length, completely white, and eyeless. Biologists called upon to identify the fish suspect they represent a previously undiscovered species that apparently dwells in an underground cave or aquifer. State authorities have been called in to determine the origin of the fish, suspected to be an unexplored aquifer underlying Bartons Mill Pond.

Timmy sat on the ground by the pile of papers, stunned. As the news sunk in, he jumped up. He had to tell Jonas. And Ms. Lizzy. He ran to the Meyers's door and rang the bell. Then he realized Jonas wouldn't be home for perhaps another hour, so he folded the paper with the article showing and wedged it between the door knob and door jam. He grabbed his paper satchel, hopped on his bike, and rode straight to Ms. Lizzy's. He was delighted to see she was home. He dropped his bike, ran to the door, banged on it twice, and before she appeared, he rushed inside calling to her. Pete and Clem jumped up on him to share in the excitement.

"Ms. Lizzy, Ms. Lizzy, you have to see the paper!"

Lizzy came from the hallway, and the smile on her face was not lopsided. "I just heard. Russ, a friend, called. It's wonderful news. Roper can't do anything for now—not until this fish is studied, until the aquifer is mapped. It may be that everyone's well around here taps into that aquifer. It may be everyone's drinking water supply for miles. They just don't know yet."

Timmy's smile was pure radiance. He hadn't realized how relieved he was, how worried he had been. He knew that Bartons Mill Pond and the land around it was only a small place, but it was their treasure, their oasis, and rescuing it seemed to be like saving the world.

Lizzy looked at Timmy's beaming face and realized how much they shared this happiness, this relief. And it wasn't just her and Timmy—it was Russ and would be Jonas and the Tutwilers and Donna and Doug—all of them as they heard the news.

"Do you believe in miracles, Ms. Lizzy?" asked Timmy.

Lizzy smiled and shook her head. "I believe the tornado was a wonderful act of Mother Nature. And fortuitous too. But it doesn't matter what we call it—the outcome is good."

"Yes ma'am," Timmy smiled, "it doesn't matter what we call it."

It had been years since Lizzy had something in her life she felt like celebrating. "You know what?" she said to Timmy. "I think I'm going to have a party—now that you could probably call a miracle. I'm going to invite a whole bunch of people who have been trying to save the pond to come out here to celebrate. You're invited too—your entire family."

"I better start working on that," replied Timmy. "I may be in just a little bit of trouble with my parents."

•   •   •

Timmy and Jonas went to Lizzy's late Saturday morning to help her get ready for the party. Even though the evening promised to get a bit nippy, Lizzy had pulled out all her lawn furniture and had borrowed some from the Tutwilers. Early that morning she had raked up the browned pansies over Happy's grave and had planted some chrysanthemums.

Timmy was wiping off the chairs and arranging them. Lizzy had Jonas help her string some holiday lights from tree to house to tree around the yard. Inside she had put out cups and plates on the counter, and she had all sorts of snacks on the table and ready to be taken out of the fridge. CB, Pete, and Clem were thrilled—they weren't accustomed to so much excitement. In fact, Pete and Clem were getting so excited that Lizzy asked Jonas to put them in the fenced yard. Alice, on the other hand, was trying to ignore the hubbub. She sat at the edge of the vegetable garden, staring intently inward, as if she were too occupied to be disturbed. On Jonas's way back from the dog enclosure, he stopped to pet her and looked over the garden too.

"It's looking pretty shaggy, isn't it?" Lizzy said, joining him. "But it's good to leave the dead plants there until spring; they'll fertilize the soil." In truth, she had been avoiding the garden ever since she had collected that last batch of green beans.

"I was just looking at that rose at the far end of the garden. It's blooming pretty late, isn't it?" said Jonas.

The sun was already on its afternoon descent when the first guests, Seymour and Leslie, arrived. Sam and Leona arrived next, and each gave Lizzy a warm hug. "It's about time you had a yard party," said Sam.

The rest of the Donohues came across the road, Donna and Doug drove up, and then Lizzy lost track as everyone else seemed to arrive in rapid succession. For a moment, between accepting dishes and finding serving implements, Lizzy thought of Agatha Prickett. She had considered inviting her, thinking that not unlike herself Agatha had been lonely since losing Woodrow. But then Lizzy decided she didn't feel that magnanimous. She suspected Agatha was looking through her curtains right now, agitated that unfamiliar cars were parked along the road, perhaps crossing that crucial boundary line. In that Lizzy felt she had brightened Agatha's day.

Russ had arrived with the crowd and had disappeared with Jonas in tow. Suddenly Lizzy heard music in the yard, and Russ and Jonas came out of the kitchen grinning. Russ was carrying two glasses of wine.

"Now you're set. Jonas told me most of your neighbors are here, which is good. We can be as loud as we want." He handed her a glass.

Kids were running through the yard—all the Donohues, Nancy and Lou's kids, and Dave's young sons. Jonas was introducing his parents to some of the graduate students he had met while helping with the inventory. The Reals were catching up with the Tutwilers, the Donohues were chatting with Nancy and Lou.

There had not been this much life around Lizzy in a long time, not since the days when she and Wes would invite everyone for potlucks. Not since Wes's funeral. Thank goodness for raining fish, thought Lizzy.

"Where are you?" asked Russ.

"Well, as they say, we've won the battle, but we haven't won the war."

"Let us rest from the battle today and savor our victory," said Russ. He took her glass of wine and set it on a table. He grabbed her hand, pulled her toward him, put his other arm around her waist, and twirled with her. And after two seconds of feigning resistance, Lizzy slipped her arm around Russ's waist and held him as tight as he held her.

•   •   •

Jonas headed over to Ms. Lizzy's. He had offered to help her take down the lights in her yard, and she had called him to ask if they could do it that afternoon because tomorrow she would be working the evening shift. Tomorrow he returned to school. Tomorrow everything would be back to normal, but not really. Jonas felt his whole life had changed in little over a week. But he knew it wasn't one week—it had been over the past year.

Jonas climbed the stepladder and untied the strings of lights from where they had draped them a day earlier. Alice watched as if worried Jonas might fall, whereas CB tried to eat the unwound portion of the light strand. When Jonas and Lizzy finished, they went inside with Alice, CB, Pete, and Clem following them.

"Anything to drink?" Lizzy asked Jonas.

"Sure—water would be fine. You know," Jonas said, petting Pete, "Pete has sure grown into his own." He took his glass from Lizzy.

"Yes he has. Clem's a bit disappointed about that. You know, I still dream about Happy," she told Jonas as she got herself a glass of water. "Usually we're just walking down the road together, visiting. He doesn't stop to mark the trees anymore, though."

"Soon it will be a year since you buried him."

"A very full year." She looked out her storm door. A gentle wind was blowing the tall brown stalks of grass outside. The grass reminded her of sea oats at the coast, and she realized it had been a long time since she had been to the ocean. She should go to the coast soon. Maybe she would ask Russ if he wanted to go. She imagined being there, standing at the water's edge, looking out over the waves.

Lizzy looked down at her glass. The water in it, she now knew, came from a different kind of ocean. The pond was only a small, visible part of a larger body of water. The state already had started mapping the aquifer. Her well tapped into some arm of it—from what she had already learned from the paper she suspected that arm stretched across her backyard, under the garden, below Happy's grave, toward the shed and the well, and continued on below the Tutwilers' field. She looked at her glass more intently. It suddenly became clear.

"Jonas, the water . . . the aquifer . . . Happy's grave—I think I buried Happy too close to the well."

Jonas regarded his glass. "Well," he said, looking up. "I guess we've all survived drinking Happy."

Acknowledgments

This novel has been simmering for many years, and because of that, I may forget to thank someone whom I should. Likewise, I have lost the page of notes, with the attribution, on decomposition. For these lapses, I apologize.

I want to thank Joan McKinney Ott for taking me on a tour of the hospital lab where she worked. For reading the manuscript and sharing their thoughts, I thank Betty Abolafia-Rosensweig, Beth Alderman, Taina Litwak, Linda Mussehl, Jim Ott, Amy Scheck, Jil Swearingen, Mary Wilson, and Debby, Mort, and Pearl Silverfine. For her insightful comments on the manuscript, I thank Sara Kocek of Yellow Bird Editors. For his help and advice on writing synopses and queries and negotiating the writer's life, I thank Michael P. King. And I thank the team at Black Rose Writing for bringing this book to fruition.

Finally, I must thank Elizabeth Hager, who many years ago told me she thought she had buried her basset hound, Happy, too close to her well. And perhaps I borrowed the farmhouse she lived in then . . . and a bit of her acerbic tongue.

And always, my deep appreciation to Jim Ott, who has encouraged me along the way and has kept me laughing.

About the Author

From living above her parents' hardware store in Brooklyn to living a mile down a gravel road in semi-rural Texas with her husband, two sons, and the local wildlife, Eva Silverfine has explored a variety of urban to rural landscapes. On that journey, she earned two degrees in the environmental sciences, worked in a research lab, and eventually retooled as a copyeditor. She freelances for several academic presses and writes personal narrative and fiction in the in-between spaces. Her short fiction has appeared in a variety of journals, and she has published a collection of essays, *Elastic Walls*.

Note from the Author

Word-of-mouth is crucial for any author to succeed. If you enjoyed *How to Bury Your Dog*, please leave a review online—anywhere you are able. Even if it's just a sentence or two. It would make all the difference and would be very much appreciated.

Thanks!
Eva Silverfine

Thank you so much for reading one of our
Small Town Fiction novels.
If you enjoyed our book, please check out our recommendation
for your next great read!

What the Valley Knows by Heather Christie

"A taut, compelling family tale."
—Kirkus Reviews

National Indie Excellence Awards- Young Adult Winner
Readers' Favorite Gold Medal Young Adult - Coming of Age
Maxy Awards Young Adult Winner